About the Author

Kim L. Hubbard has been an actor, director, and writer for over fifty years and has appeared in numerous films, television series, and commercials. Currently, he is the editor of his town's local newspaper, *The Homer News*. He is also a published playwright whose works have appeared in theaters across the country. He resides in upstate New York with his wife Beth and has the joy of having his children and grandchildren living close by. *Black Moon: The Legend of Jake Benteen* is his first novel.

Black Moon:
The Legend of Jake Benteen

Kim L. Hubbard

Black Moon:
The Legend of Jake Benteen

Olympia Publishers
London

www.olympiapublishers.com
OLYMPIA PAPERBACK EDITION

A CIP catalog record for this title is
available from the British Library.

ISBN: 978-1-80439-645-2

This is a work of fiction.
Names, characters, places and incidents originate from the writer's
imagination. Any resemblance to actual persons, living or dead, is
purely coincidental.

First Published in 2024

Olympia Publishers
Tallis House
2 Tallis Street
London
EC4Y 0AB

Printed in Great Britain

Dedication

To my wife, Beth. You have put up with a lot of my nonsense, but after more than fifty years together, you have never lost faith in me. It was you who told me to get off my duff and write... something. Anything. So, during COVID, I wrote this story.

And to my daughters, Amanda and Mariah. You have both given me so much more than I deserve. A father could not be prouder of what you have brought to the world.

And finally, to my many friends who encouraged me to keep plugging away. Family and friends are what make it all worthwhile. Thank you all.

Acknowledgments

To my big brother, Mike. My main "*spudd.*" He has been the driving force in getting me to believe that what I have written on these pages has value and to send it out to publishers because… you never know. He is also the man I call to get my facts straight about guns and horses. So, if I got something wrong… yell at him.

Chapter One

The shooting had finally stopped. One horse lay dying, kicking and twitching horribly, as it tried to free itself from the tangled reins of the singletree it was harnessed to. The second horse in the team was unhurt and strangely calm, only dragging its right hoof across the blood-soaked ground in a steady rhythm. The blood being pounded into mud came not only from the wounded animal fighting a losing battle for life but also from the driver of the wagon it was pulling. His lifeless body was propped up against the right front wheel but had rolled on its left side. A twenty-year-old .36 caliber Navy Colt, with one ball left in the chamber and the hammer cocked, filled his right hand.

In the back of the wagon was a young woman of perhaps sixteen years. She was alive and physically unhurt, thanks mainly to the seed bags and boxes of provisions stacked in the bed of the wagon. They provided just enough shelter from the haze of bullets that shattered everything around her. The words, "Oh God" and "No" were mixed with the tears of a pitiful and barely audible cry that spoke of fear, anguish, and confusion. As she lifted her head from behind a box of dried fruit and bags of flour, the sight of a century-old cottonwood tree caught her eye. Nothing moved. Only the smell of sulfur from the countless explosions of gunpowder hung in the air.

Slowly, the young woman sat fully up in the back of the wagon. As she scanned the terrain from side to side, she called out a name. "Ben?"

There was no reply. Only a snort from the dying draft horse broke the silence. She called again.

"Ben… where are you?" Only silence. "Ben… please answer me."

It was a plea, made in a whisper. Still no answer. She grabbed the back of the wagon seat and pulled herself up on her knees. Her body shook from the chilling cold of terror that had settled into her bones. Once more, she called out to her companion. This time, however, the tone in her voice suggested she did not really expect a reply. Instinct made her call out just the same.

"Ben?"

"I'm over here, little darlin'," came a mocking voice from behind a clump of cottonwood trees about twenty yards to the right of the wagon. "Bring yer pretty little self over here soze yer daddy kin give ya a great big hug." A childlike giggle followed.

The young woman released a cry at the sound of the unfamiliar voice and dropped back down behind the supplies in the wagon. "Oh, God no," came the refrain. "No… no."

A riotous laugh erupted from the other side of the wagon. It came from a ditch about twenty yards to the left of the road. Its contents were mostly covered with tall prairie grass. Only a large, mud-colored shape could be seen shifting position. The terrified young woman began shaking and sobbing uncontrollably. Her mind and body were in a tug-of-war of indecision as to whether to stand and surrender or try and make a run for it back to town, a distance of more than ten miles. Neither choice seemed sensible, let alone feasible. If only she knew what happened to Ben, she thought. Because of her body position, she was unable to see the fate of her companion, a family friend and all-round handyman in her town. She used to ride with him across the border for supplies that her family couldn't get in town. It was always a long, hot trip but Ben was like a father figure, maybe more of an uncle, who was fun to be with because he told wonderful stories of faraway places he had traveled as a younger man. Inside her high-buttoned blouse was a silver cross on a thin, gold chain. She reached between the buttons with her left hand and pulled out the cross and pressed it in her clenched fist, holding it against her chest. Her lips moved as she began a silent prayer.

"Orin? I can't see the old coot," asked the man from the ditch. "The wagon's in the way. Did I git 'im?"

A scoffing laugh came first. "No, you didn't git 'im, ya idjit," came the terse reply from behind the cottonwood tree. "*I* got 'im! You can't hit nothin'! Never could."

A tall, thin man stepped out from behind the shelter of the tree and advanced toward the wagon. His clothes were worn and tattered and looked as if they had become a part of his body. His hat was a tattered slab of felt that barely managed to stay on his head.

"That ain't true and you knows it, Orin!" shouted the other man as he pulled himself out of the ditch and took off running around the front of the wagon. He was equal to the other man in size and shape but appeared several years younger. His clothes were covered in a layer of dirt and mud that made it hard to distinguish anything specific. "I'm just as good a shot as you and you knows it! Daddy always said so!"

The two men ultimately met on the right side of the wagon and settled over the body of the man in question, Ben. Their attention was momentarily diverted from the young girl who was still in the back of the wagon, hiding behind its contents and clutching her cross, whispering prayers of salvation.

"Don't git yerself all in a pile, Buck!" said Orin as he lowered the barrel of his Sharps and poked it at the lifeless body of Ben. "I'm just tellin' facts. It's clear as daylight the hole in this feller's head come from my rifle, not yorn!"

Buck stepped forward, placing himself between his brother and the dead man. "Now jest how in hell kin you tell that, Orin. We both got Sharps." He pulled Ben's lifeless body into a sitting position and gave the fatal wound a brief examination. "It could jest as well be my bullet in his head as yorn." Buck stepped back, satisfied he had successfully made his case.

"Can't be nothin' of the kind, Buck!" snapped Orin. "I was shootin' from behind that cottonwood yonder and I was aimin' at his head, which I done hit right there! You was shootin' from the other side a the wagon. See, you went and shot one a the horses." Orin pointed an accusing finger at the tortured, dying animal and laughed. "I ain't dumb enough to shoot a horse. That's just plum wasteful!"

Buck began stomping his feet and pounding the butt of his rifle on the ground. His behavior was reminiscent of a three-year-old child throwing a temper tantrum. "It ain't true, Orin!" cried Buck. "You ain't takin another one away from me. It jest ain't fair!"

Orin was hunched over, holding his belly and howling with laughter at his little brother's fit. Buck kicked at the dirt with his boot heel and flailed his arms about wildly. As both men stood occupied with their own family squabble, a high-pitched scream that seemed to echo for miles erupted from the lips of the forgotten victim now standing up in the back of the wagon. The brothers immediately forgot about their dispute over whose marksmanship was the better and became transfixed on the vision of the young girl screaming at them.

14

"Stop it, damn you! Stop it!" she cried, still clutching the cross in her left hand and pounding the side of her head with the other. Both men gasped a shock of air that caught them by surprise, then exchanged looks of disbelief mixed with amusement. The young girl's scream was horrific in its evident level of pain but left Orin and Buck completely unmoved emotionally.

"Well did ya hear that, Orin?" remarked Buck, with a snide giggle attached at the end. "She liked to broke my ears screamin' like that!"

The young woman's primal scream awakened something in Orin to rival the bloodlust he had just tasted when he killed Ben. Seeing her frail body shaking in seizure-like sobs pulled him in a trance toward his prey. Although he heard his brother's remark, his reply was more to himself and one of self-intent.

"Yeah, I shore did," he said as he let his rifle slowly slip from his hand and drop to the ground by the dead man's body. Orin wiped both hands across his face as if to clear his eyes, then combed his lice-ridden hair with his fingers. His miserable excuse for a hat fell, unnoticed in the dust. As he staggered toward the wagon, he began to grope himself unconsciously while he mumbled his desires.

"I ain't had me a piece of young meat like this in a long, long time." Orin reached for the side of the wagon with both hands and threw one leg up over the side like he was jumping a high fence. He stood face-to-face with the girl now, she still clutching her cross and he still groping his privates in anticipation of his perverted sexual feast. As Orin surveyed his prize, Buck ran around to the back of the wagon to get a better look at his brother's impending performance. By his actions, it was obvious Buck was always in the position of feeding on the scraps his

15

brother left him. It was also obvious by his words that Buck resented his role as the beggar.

"Come on now, Orin. Don't use her up afore I gets a chance at her." Buck started hopping from one foot to the other like he had been holding his urine too long. He pounded his fists on the flatbed of the wagon as he screamed his plea again. "Damn it, Orin! Let me have a chance at her!"

Orin didn't hear his brother's cries. His ears were closed to all sound and his eyes were wide open and transfixed on the woman's body shivering before him. Her bosom was full and heaving in heavy breaths brought on by mental shock. The ribbon that had held her hair in a piled bun at the back of her head had come untied, leaving her long blond hair to tumble down across her face. Orin reached out with uncharacteristic gentleness and lifted her hair like a wedding veil until it fell back down over her shoulders. Although she was looking directly into Orin's vile, bloodshot eyes, her own green eyes were unfocused and even appeared clouded. But Orin's eyes were crystal-clear and locked on her breasts. His hands melted the fabric of her dress with a vicious tear that propelled her body the length of the wagon. An involuntary expulsion of air was the only sound she made as her frail body tumbled over the wagon's contents and off the back until she lay sprawled, bare-breasted on the ground.

Buck, who had been whining like a tortured puppy, took this sudden physical overture as a sign that Orin had tossed her to him. He grabbed at what was left of her dress and tore the remains as if they were wet paper. Buck then pulled her to her feet and flipped her over the flatbed of the wagon onto her stomach so that her legs hung down, dangling a few inches from the ground. Although the chain had snapped when Orin tore her dress to the waist, the silver cross remained firmly clutched in her left hand.

16

Still, she made no sound. No pleas for mercy. She was beyond that.

As Buck feverishly tore at his own clothing in an effort to expose his member, Orin let out a growl that spoke of a lion defending its kill. With two large lumbering steps, he covered the distance from the front to the back of the wagon. His right foot swung out high and hard, catching Buck, square under the chin. The blow lifted him off the ground and dropped him flat on his back. Orin then leaped into the air, bringing his body crashing down on top of Buck. Although the boot to his jaw stunned Buck, he still managed to drive a knee into Orin's ribs as he came down, pushing him back under one of the wheels of the wagon. Both men gained their feet quickly and held their positions. Orin was trying to catch his breath when he noticed movement coming down the road behind his brother. In the desert haze and dust, it was hard to make out just what it was. Buck didn't notice, as he was reaching for the waistband of his pants, which had fallen around his ankles.

"Damn you, Orin," Buck screamed, as he pulled his pants back up. "What'd ya go and do that for?" He rubbed his hand across the fresh bruise on his jaw and grimaced in pain. "I think ya done broke one of my chewin' teeth."

Buck then noticed his brother's attention was not on him, but rather on that strange *something* moving behind him and over his left shoulder. Still holding his pants in one hand and his jaw with the other, Buck turned around to see what Orin was so obviously concerned with. As both men squinted through the kicked-up dust, a tall, dark rider on a blood-red mare came into view. The horse's pace was slow and deliberate. The rider had wrapped the horse's reins around the saddle horn. In his left hand, with the butt of the rifle resting on his left thigh, he carried a Winchester,

17

model '86. His hand was positioned inside a large brass loop that modified the lever action. His right hand hung loosely down at his side, hovering over a nickel-plated Colt .45 with a black pearl handle. The leather loop that wraps the hammer was already slipped free, as was the tie-down strap for his leg, allowing the Colt to hang straight down. Inlaid on the black pearl handles, in gold, were the initials J.B. The same initials were also hand-tooled into the black leather holster, which had bullet loops for twenty-eight cartridges. All loops were filled. When he reached a measured distance of about thirty yards from the wagon, the horse stopped, though no signal was given by the rider. The butt end of the Winchester was moved over to the man's right hand, where he slipped his hand into the brass loop. With a seemingly effortless flick of his wrist, the rider spun the Winchester around once, loading a .45-90 shell into the chamber. After that motion was complete, the rider remained stone still. Orin and Buck stood mesmerized by the specter before them. Orin was the first to speak.

"This ain't no business a yorn, stranger." Orin's voice showed obvious signs of fear which he tried to mask with an absurd show of bravado. "If you know what's good for ya, ya best move on! Ya hear!"

Horse and rider remained still. A slight breeze had kicked up, sending dust and the smell of death into the air. Buck began walking backward toward his brother. He had every intention of retrieving his discarded rifle that lay in the dirt by the back of the wagon, but Orin took a few steps forward, pushing his brother aside.

"I ain't gonna tell you again, mister. You go on about your business and leave us to ours." Orin was whistling in the dark.

Buck panicked and dove for his Sharps. He knew there was

18

still a bullet in the chamber and pulled it to his side as he scrambled to his feet. His mouth was open wide as if he was about to speak when the rider snapped his Winchester to his shoulder and fired. It all appeared to be done in one smooth motion, fast and efficient.

Orin jumped, looking first to the rider, then quickly to his brother, then back to the rider. An instant after the single shot had hit its mark and before the smoke even cleared, the rider spun his Winchester as before, resetting another cartridge in the chamber. He then resumed his previous pose, Winchester resting on his left thigh, horse and rider remaining stone still. It was so fast that Orin debated with his own sanity whether the man had moved at all. He swallowed hard and rubbed his eyes with both hands to clear the dust. Then, Orin looked over at his brother.

Buck was still standing, swaying slightly from front to back. At first, he thought the rider had missed, or maybe just fired a warning shot. Buck's mouth hung open and his eyes darted from side to side without purpose. Then, Orin noticed what appeared to be light coming from inside Buck's gaping mouth. It was such an odd sight because there was no logic to it. Suddenly, with legs locked in death, Buck toppled over on his face like a statue broken from its pedestal, the Sharps locked with a death-grip in his hands. When he hit the dirt, Orin soon realized where the strange light was coming from. The rider had not missed or fired a warning shot at all. The bullet found its mark by entering directly through Buck's open mouth and exploded out the back of his head, leaving a hole the size of a large man's fist. The searing smell of cooked flesh and brain soon filled the air.

"Buck?" Orin took a few cautious steps toward his fallen brother and called out his name again, oblivious to the realities before him. "Buck?" He grabbed his head, pulling at his hair,

19

then turned back to the lone rider. "You killed my brother, you bastard scum sucker!" Orin turned back to his brother's remains and walked a circle around him soaking in the carnage of the single gunshot. "You blowed the back of his whole damn head off!" Pointing an accusing finger at his brother's killer, Orin declared his intentions, however unrealistic they were. "I'm gonna tear your Goddamn heart out and stomp it into the ground! Ya, hear me? You're a dead man!"

The lone rider made a clicking sound that singled his horse to walk slowly forward. The Winchester remained in his left hand, the butt of the rifle still on his left thigh. With his right hand, he slipped around the handle of his Colt, pulling it out of the holster about halfway, then let it slide back into place. It was a strategic move to make sure the Colt was free.

Orin's eyes grew wide with terror at the sight of the rider advancing toward him. He took two involuntary steps backward toward the forgotten young woman who was still lying on her stomach draped over the flatbed of the wagon. His eyes shot a desperate look at her as he reached behind his back and pulled out a skinning knife. With his left hand, he grabbed the young woman's hair and pulled her naked body upright, using it to shield his own. The only clear target he offered of himself was his right shoulder. His head did a peek-a-boo behind hers. He then snapped her head back by the hair, exposing her delicate throat, which issued no sounds.

As he placed his knife against the skin of her throat, he screamed out his defiance. "Come on, bushwhacker! Keep comin'! I'll be drinkin' the little bitch's blood if you keep comin'!"

The rider clicked orders to his horse again, which walked on pace and then stopped less than ten yards from Orin and his pathetic hostage. Orin could see the rider's face now. He had a prominent mustache that drooped low on the sides. Just under his bottom lip was a curl of hair that grew wider as it spread down and under his chin. His eyes were cold blue and never blinked, despite the swirl of dust in the air.

"You drop that Winchester now or I swear I'll slit her throat!" Orin's voice was shaking and squeaked his threat in a high-pitched scream.

"I don't think so."

Orin was confused. These were the first words the rider had spoken and he wasn't sure what "I don't think so" meant. Was he telling him he didn't think he would drop his rifle, or that he didn't think Orin would actually slit the girl's throat? It was a perplexing problem and one he was not mentally equipped to deal with.

"What's that you say?" Orin shuffled nervously behind the wall of shivering flesh.

"The only reason you're alive is because she is," said the man with the cold, dead eyes. "As soon as she drops, so do you. Think about it."

Orin paused to consider his options, which were extremely limited. There was undeniable logic in what the man said. "Well... how do I know you won't just up and shoot me anyways?" he asked, pressing the knife tighter against the girl's throat until it broke the skin, releasing a tiny bead of blood.

"You don't," came the reply. "That's the chance you'll have to take."

Orin almost balked but regained his pathetic excuse for courage and decided to press his case further. "I don't think so, gunfighter," he barked. "I got nothin' to lose, so that means I got the upper hand here, not you! She's dead fer sure if you don't do

21

what I say."

Orin then slipped his skinning knife under the right breast of his hostage and dragged it across her chest. The cut wasn't deep but was still enough to draw rivulets of blood down her stomach. Still, the girl made no sound. It was obvious her mind had shut down, so she was nothing more than a life-sized rag doll now. Her eyes were blank, even though they were aimed straight ahead, and her breathing was so shallow it was impossible to hear or even feel the intake and release of the dry desert air.

"Now I am serious mean," howled Orin, "I will peel the skin off her inch by inch if you don't drop that Winchester... and I mean now!"

The rider slipped his thumb down to the hammer of his '86 and slowly released it to safety. He then passed the butt end over to his right hand again and rolled it upside down, letting his hand spin inside the brass ring until he gave it a last snap that buried the rifle inside the rifle boot hanging down the left side of the saddle. The action was too fast for Orin to react, but the end result made him scream with rage.

"I said to drop that rifle, gunfighter!" He raised his knife up high, placing the tip against the woman's breastbone. "Don't press me no further!"

The rider offered no reply but pulled his left boot from the stirrup and turned his foot around so that the boot heel came back inside the stirrup. Orin saw but did not comprehend the movement. The rider then stood up in the saddle, resting most of his weight on his left heel, newly planted backward in the stirrup. He also raised both hands just below shoulder height, in a move that seemed to be indicating surrender.

Orin tasted victory. "Smart move, gunfighter, 'cuz I'd a sliced her up, fer sure," he said. His voice was almost gleeful.

"Now step down off that horse… nice and easy like."

With his left foot still facing forward and with the heel seated firmly in the stirrup, the gunfighter slowly lifted his right leg over his horse's head. His horse remained so still that he was able to step down gracefully, still facing forward without even turning his back. The dismount was so unorthodox that Orin's jaw dropped open in amazement. He also let his knife hand hang loose for a brief moment, dropping it away from the girl's chest.

Seizing the opportunity, the rider pulled his Colt and fired a single shot. The movement was so smooth and fast that it was completed before his foot touched the ground. The bullet struck Orin directly in the ball of his right shoulder, which twisted him wildly to his right, releasing the skinning knife from his grip and sending it flying harmlessly through the air until it landed in a chukka plant. The girl dropped to her knees, then fell to her side where she curled herself into a fetal position. Orin stayed on his feet, screaming in pain and shouting curses and useless threats at the man who had bested him without even breaking a sweat.

Orin was now leaning against the back of the wagon. It was the only thing holding him up. His right arm was useless, as he clutched the shoulder with his left hand, blood spurted through his fingers. "You're gonna die hard, you bastard son of a bitch!"

The gunfighter's expression changed for the first time, showing the slightest signs of a smile. "You, first."

Five more shots rang out from the silver Colt with planned precision. The first bullet of the barrage struck Orin in his left shoulder, equal to the one on the other side. Both his arms now hung uselessly at his sides. Two more shots followed in quick succession that blew apart his right and left kneecaps, dropping him forward at first, then forcing Orin to flop over on his back like a fish snapped out of the water by a hook on a string. Orin was beyond experiencing pain that was comprehendible. He grunted and sputtered words and sounds that could not be understood. The man stepped forward until he stood directly over Orin's outstretched body. With the two remaining shots, he completed the mutilation and blew apart the would-be rapist's crotch.

Orin screamed and rolled his body from side to side as if searching for words to express the pain he was experiencing. He puffed and sputtered blood as he looked up at his executioner with pleading eyes that begged for release. Finally, coughing through a mouth full of blood he said, "Finish me." He gasped for air and added, "If you're a Christian man, you'll finish me."

The man looked up to the sky and tipped his low-brimmed Stetson back on his head and caught sight of two buzzards already circling above the devastation, waiting for the carnage to stop. The sight brought a wry smile to his lips as he appreciated the irony. He flipped open the cylinder guard on his Colt and removed the empty shell casings on the ground between Orin's legs. Pulling one shell at a time from his holster, he refilled each chamber, then snapped the guard closed and spun his Colt once, burying it in his holster. Orin just continued muttering and spitting out blood and pitiful pleas for mercy. The man then pulled his hat back down, shading his eyes.

Orin begged for mercy again, asking his perceived executioner to finish the job he started. "Please… don't leave me like this. Kill me. Please. For the love a God, finish me!"

"God's got nothing to do with it. Only me." Looking skyward again at the circling buzzards he added, "I think I'll just let nature's scavengers finish you off," replied the gunfighter, with self-assured calm. Then he walked over to his horse, pulled his bed roll from the saddle and removed the blanket. As Orin sputtered and moaned, the man leaned down and gently spread the blanket over the young girl's naked form. The sun was intense and so brutally hot that the man leaned down again to lift the edge of the blanket and pull it over the side of the girl's face to protect her pale skin.

Orin's breathing had settled into a steady rhythm of long, deep breaths, interrupted by the gurgling sound of blood in the back of his throat. The rider, this mystery man, this gunfighter, so completely ignored Orin's condition and obvious agony and stepped over him as if he were nothing more than a pile of dirt and began taking stock of the wagon and the surrounding area.

After clearing and repacking some of the provisions in the wagon, the gunfighter rolled the child up into his arms and placed her in the flatbed, making sure to shade her body from the heat of the sun as best he could. He also made sure there was enough room to put the dead man's body he found lying under the front of the wagon. He assumed the dead man was either the girl's father or other relative, maybe just a friend. It didn't matter. He wasn't going to leave him there.

In life, Ben was a man of average height, standing just under six feet, but packing a solid two hundred pounds. In death, Ben was one difficult mound of flesh to maneuver. The gunfighter gave brief thought to burying the man alongside the wagon trail and marking the spot for any family or authorities. But given the heat and the orbiting scavengers, it just didn't seem fair to have this man's body torn apart along with those of Orin, Buck and the draft horse, now dead, that was still hooked up to the wagon. The gunfighter reluctantly made the decision to pack Ben's body in the wagon, along with the young woman. Placing Ben's dead and distorted body next to the girls was not ideal, but given her condition, the gunfighter thought it wouldn't make much difference.

He then set about clearing the wagon from the dead horse so he could harness another in its place. Given the setting of the ambush, the gunfighter assumed Orin and Buck had probably staked their horses close by. He would use one of theirs in place of the dead one. If necessary, he would use his own horse, but that was something he did not want to do. His horse was special. A close bond of trust and mutual respect had been built up over several years. They operated on instinct, often reading each other's needs without the use of the spoken word. But this wagon was heavy and was going to need two horses to get it back into town. If he couldn't find at least one of the others he would have no choice but to harness his own to share the work of pulling a heavy wagon. Somehow, he knew his horse would understand.

Fortunately, he was able to find Orin and Buck's horses staked just over the hill behind the cottonwood tree. Unfortunately, they were scrawny, underfed animals that had been poorly cared for and obviously mistreated, which made the gunfighter mad enough to want to shoot Orin and Buck all over again. Seeing a mistreated horse, or animal of any kind for that matter, was sure to anger him faster than harsh words, insults or threats would ever do.

After walking the two sad-looking animals back to the wagon, the gunfighter removed both saddles and tossed them on top of the other supplies and next to Ben's corpse. They weren't worth much, maybe a few dollars at most, but the money could go to the girl's family or that of the dead man. It was something. Given the condition of the horses, he simply didn't have the heart to subject either of them to further abuse. Instead, he tied them to the back of the wagon and reluctantly chose to use his own horse to help pull the load back to town.

"Sorry to do this to you, Teacher," he said gently, as he hooked the oversized harness across his friend's back, making whatever necessary adjustments he could to the rigging. When he finished, he stroked his hand down Teacher's nose, then gave her a firm pat on the neck and said, "I'll make it up to you when we get this poor child back to her kind." His horse, his friend, Teacher, snorted her disapproval at seeing the harness but didn't resist being connected to it all.

As the gunfighter climbed aboard the wagon, he looked back at his cargo and shook his head in sadness. "I hope you've got family left back wherever you came from, child. You're going to need them." The child never answered or made any sound. Not that he expected her to. He snapped the reins and gave a muted command to the new team. "Hup! Hup! Come on now. Hup." The new team pulled away, struggling at first, but then managed to find a rhythm as they got turned around and headed back along the road to town. Orin's whispering pleas could be heard fading away in the distance.

"Finish me! Please! Finish me!"

Chapter Two

It was just after high noon and the New Mexico sun was beating down with a vengeance. The buzzards were well into their feast on Orin, Buck and the draft horse as the gunfighter was now more than an hour on the road. He was taking it slow and easy. His horse was not meant for pulling a wagon and he didn't know how far from the town where the girl and her companion were likely to have come from. Options seemed limited. This was new territory for him, so his sense of time and place was unreliable.

Before he chanced upon the events of the morning, he had just been following the road east, hoping to come across a sign or road marker pointing the way to a town, any town where the people weren't judgmental or hostile. All he wanted was a hot bath, some decent food and a drink, in no particular order. It was only by blind luck that he crossed paths with Orin and Buck when he did. An hour's difference one way or the other and he likely would have missed them altogether. And the girl and her companion would have been killed and tossed off to the side of the road or covered over with scrub brush. He didn't like to think of what would have happened to the young girl in the bed of the wagon had he not come along when he did. Such is fate.

At a T-shaped divide in the road, a signpost stood prominently, indicating three choices from which any traveler could select. One choice was a town called Tres Mesa, ten miles due south. The road appeared more beaten down, as if from a constant stream of men on horseback. The other choice was

Delgado Station, also ten miles, but due north. That road showed signs of heavy wagon traffic, with obvious ruts carved into the sun-baked New Mexico ground. The third choice was back in the direction he had just come, a road that also showed signs of wagon traffic.

Where there are wagons, there is commerce and trade, he thought, which means better food and accommodation. For the sake of his passenger, it also meant a better chance of finding a doctor. Even the sign for Delgado Station was an inviting advertisement. The name was carved neatly into a single wooden plank and even had the words, "Visitors Welcome" carved underneath. An appealing thought, for sure.

In contrast, the sign for Tres Mesa was barely legible. It was hanging vertically by a single nail and appeared to have several bullet holes in it. Whether the use of the sign as target practice was an indication of what lay ahead in that direction for any would-be visitor was a curiosity that would have to wait for another time. If ever. Given instinct, and his own history, he had always done his best to avoid anything that even smelled of danger or trouble of any sort. He already had enough of that in the back of the wagon. Putting all of the events and people into perspective, logic dictated that the wagon and its two companions came from Delgado Station rather than the other town. The road he brought the wagon back on offered no sign to indicate another town that was ten miles or less back in that direction. So, his real choice was clear. Delgado Station it was. With a tug on the reins, the gunfighter turned the wagon due north, toward what he hoped would be decent, understanding people that could help this poor young woman he was carrying.

After covering what he estimated to be about five miles, the gunfighter noticed a cloud of dust on the horizon, which indicated to him that they were riders coming straight at him at a full gallop from the direction of Delgado Station. His Winchester lay at his feet in the boot trough. He reached down and pulled it out, placing it across his lap. He gave a quick glance and feel of his Colt for assurance. It was fully reloaded now, as was his Winchester, so he knew he was ready for trouble if need be.

The flat land of the southwest can make judging distance a bit tricky. What might appear close up can take half a day's ride before realizing it will take the rest of the day to get there. Experience told the gunfighter it would take at least half an hour for the riders to cover the distance between them if he remained still. Traveling at the speed he was, he estimated about twenty minutes before contact. That suited him just fine.

As the time passed and the wagon lumbered slowly forward toward town, the gunfighter was making plans for the myriad possibilities of the reception that awaited him. It had been his experience that people were often too quick to judge before all the facts were in, especially when the circumstances were so obviously tragic.

Although he was a good deal further south than he traditionally traveled, people were spreading fast. With people comes news, however distorted or untrue. It was possible that his name and reputation preceded him. If he was recognized, it was also possible, even likely, that people might jump to the wrong conclusions. It had happened before.

Anticipation can be a dangerous thing if one hasn't got the steady nerves for it. For the young and inexperienced, or just plain foolish, it can get you killed. The gunfighter had covered a lot of ground in his thirty-six years, so having the chance to set his mind and body to the variety of possibilities before him was just what he needed. He only wished he had a nice, sweet cigar to smoke while he waited.

Finally, at a distance of roughly thirty yards, both riders pulled up fast. Their horses bucked and snorted in protest at being reined in so quickly on a dead run. The gunfighter kept the wagon moving forward. The rider to his right spoke to his companion.

"Hey, Jeff, ain't that Ben's wagon?" he said.

He was a young boy comparable in age to the girl wrapped in the blanket. The rider to his right appeared a little older, perhaps eighteen and had trouble written all over him.

"You're right, Pete. Looks like somebody done some highway robbin' and made out pretty good for himself."

"I don't know, Jeff. Maybe that ain't Ben's wagon," questioned Pete. Something about the two horses pulling the wagon didn't ring true. The gunfighter kept the wagon rolling forward. "He's got one horse that don't look right. It ain't no draft horse, that's for sure. And he's pulling two more." Jeff crossed his horse directly in the path of the wagon. Pete strayed off to the side and watched. With the road blocked, the gunfighter had no choice but to pull up.

"Whoa there. Hold up," he said. His voice was low and calm. "I'm going to need you to get out of the way, son. I've got trouble in this wagon. One needs a doctor and the other an undertaker. I expect you've got both up ahead."

"Yeah, we sure do," answered Pete, quickly. "Doc Gibbons is... "

"Shut your mouth, Pete!" Jeff shot a quick glance at Pete who lowered his head in submission. Then, he glared back at the gunfighter with a cocky smile and said, "I ain't never seen this fella before, so he ain't got no right knowing our business before we know his."

The gunfighter took a deep breath for calm and shook his

head. How many times had he seen a loud-mouthed punk like this, full of piss and vinegar just looking for a fight? Too many times, he thought. Now was not the time to play this kind of game either.

"I've already explained all I'm going to, son," he said. "I haven't got the time or the patience for your foolishness. There's a young girl back here that's been through enough. Now clear off so I can get her some help."

Pete stood up in his stirrups to get a better look at the wagon's contents. He could see a tuft of blond hair and a body wrapped in a brown blanket. "Hey, I think that's Juneann he's got back there, Jeff!" Pete's voice cracked when he mentioned the girl's name. He also spotted the body of a man rolled over on his face. He looked at the gunfighter and asked, "Is that old Ben?"

"I don't know their names, just that they need caring for," said the gunfighter. He was now doing exactly what he didn't want to do, wasting time explaining things to two young boneheads when he should be getting this wagon to town and real help. "Now I've wasted all the time I'm going to on you boys. Back off and let me through."

"Or what?" asked Jeff, with as much sass as he could muster. His eyes twinkled with the mischief of youth but lacked the clarity of someone with the brains to know when to play and when not to. He turned a little to his side and rested his left arm across his saddle horn. "You want to move on ahead, you'll have to go through me." He then shot a smile in Pete's direction, expecting some show of support for his brave stance against this stranger. Pete just let his eyes dance from boy to man, not knowing what to say or do.

"Son, if you had half the brains God gave a dog, you'd realize you're playing a fool's game." Again, the gunfighter's voice was even and slow, showing no signs of fear, just annoyance and the beginnings of a fading patience.

Jeff took the gunfighter's words as a challenge and not those of a man on the verge of backing down. Still leaning on his saddle horn, he said, "I see that fancy Winchester you got layin' across your lap there. You think you can get ahold of it before I blow your ass off that wagon?" This time, the kid didn't smile. His eyes were cold. He really was too dumb to know what he had gotten himself into.

"Son, you couldn't beat me on the best day of your life and me with one foot in the grave. Now move your horse out of the way." The gunfighter noticed the boy's eyes squint when he was told to move out of the way. That usually meant trouble. To try and ward off whatever foolishness was brewing in his hot-headed brain, the gunfighter gave him a final piece of advice. "Whatever you're thinking... don't. It's too nice a day to die."

That last statement may have been a little extreme, thought the gunfighter, but if he was a typical dumb-ass young kid, it may have the desired effect and make him think twice about his next move. Unfortunately, although he was a typical dumb-ass kid, the gunfighter's words didn't have the desired effect. Instead, it was Pete's eyes that popped open wide at the gunfighter's words. He knew his friend wasn't going to take a challenge like that lightly.

Jeff sat up straight in his saddle and placed both hands on the grips of two .45 caliber Smith & Wessons. He carried the rig high on his hips like a dude who imagined himself a gunfighter. On that score, he was everything the real gunfighter suspected and more. This boy was in a desperate race to catch the tail end of the fading West and the imagined glory of the gunfighter's life.

If Jeff had plans to draw his pistols, the decision was canceled before the signal from his brain reached his hands. The bark of a Winchester ripped two shots that tore away the holsters from the hips on either side of Jeff's gun belt. It was an impossible shot that Pete would retell for the rest of his days and no one would believe... until they heard the name of the man that did it.

Both young men's horses bucked at the gunfire, but only Pete was able to hang on. With both hands free of his reins, Jeff was bounced off his saddle and hit the ground hard, landing on his butt in the middle of the road. The impact sent shockwaves straight up his spine and into his skull, giving him an instant headache equal to the worst hangover from cheap whiskey he had ever had. It also knocked the wind out of him and made him groan in pain as he searched for air. His horse bolted down the road heading back the way it came, in the direction of town.

The sudden gunfire also awakened the girl named Juneann. She sat up quickly, letting the blanket fall. Her plaintive voice called out once more for her dead companion spread out beside her in the wagon. "Ben?"

Pete's eyes were even wider than before at the sight of the naked young girl. His mouth was also hanging open wide enough to catch birds.

"Close your mouth, Pete," scolded the gunfighter. "She's nothing to gawk at. After what she's been through, she needs help, not wild eyes."

Pete quickly turned his eyes away, embarrassed at being caught looking at the naked girl, and not showing more respect for her troubles. "Sorry... but I know her. That's Juneann. What happened to her?" he asked, with genuine concern.

"Never you mind about that right now," said the gunfighter

as he turned his attention to Juneann. "Go back to sleep, Juneann." His voice was soft and gentle. "We'll be home soon." Juneann offered no reply but obeyed his instructions by curling up in his blanket as before. She appeared to fall back to sleep instantly.

"You got a last name, Pete?" The gunfighter knew the boy had no weapon of any kind and casually laid the Winchester back across his lap. Pete was glad to see that. "Yes, sir. Pete MacDougal, sir."

"Well, Pete MacDougal, you appear to have more sense than your friend here, so I am going to rely on you to get back to town and tell that Doc Gibbons you mentioned to be ready for a patient. You got that?" His words were stern, but not laced with any malice.

Pete took his meaning for what it was and was about to jam his heels into his horse's rump when he held up. "What about Jeff?" Pete looked at his friend who was still holding his stomach and trying to get to his knees. Jeff finally found his breath and just made it back on his feet and was dusting himself off with his hat when the question of what to do with him arose.

"Jeff will be walking back to town," said the gunfighter. "Now get moving boy!"

The gunfighter's tone was decidedly different this time and unmistakable. Pete didn't need to be told a third time. He drove his boot heels in hard and took off for town.

Jeff was incredulous at the suggestion he walk back to town and shouted his disapproval. "What? You expect me to walk back to town? Why, that's prit-near five miles!"

"That will give you just enough time to calm down and reconsider your life's direction," said the gunfighter. It was clear his words were not a suggestion and the subject was not open to debate. Jeff lowered his head and kicked the dirt. "Pick up your toys and toss them up on the seat next to me," added the gunfighter.

Jeff noticed his guns lying in the dirt, still in their holsters. One was just a foot or so away from him. As he bent over to retrieve it, he paused. Something incredibly stupid was running through his head that needed to be snuffed out quickly.

"Whatever thoughts you may have, son, forget them," warned the gunfighter. "I already gave you one chance. That's one more than I give most men. Don't press your luck." Jeff huffed and puffed his displeasure as he picked up both weapons without incident and tossed them up on the seat of the wagon.

"Can't I at least ride into town with you?" Jeff's voice was pitiful and almost childlike in its plea.

"No," replied the gunfighter. "You were one step away from dying today. I want you to think on that. The walk will do you good. Now step aside." Then he settled the Winchester further back in his lap and picked up the reins. He didn't wait for Jeff to consider his options and snapped the reins of the wagon, moving the horses forward. Jeff had to jump out of the way to avoid getting trampled. "I'll leave your guns at the sheriff's office," said the gunfighter. "You can pick them up after you've cooled down."

"I ain't never gonna forget this, mister!" said Jeff, spitting through his teeth. "You made a fool outta me!"

"The foolishness was your own doing," answered the gunfighter. "And it damn-near got you killed. Think on that next time you take it in your mind to call someone out." As the wagon rolled past the kid, the gunfighter noticed he was struggling to hold back tears of embarrassment and frustration.

"We'll be meeting again, mister. You can count on it!" To

emphasize his anger, Jeff jabbed his right index finger in the direction of the gunfighter on the word, "count." He stepped off to the side of the road to begin his long walk home when he stopped suddenly. "I'm gonna blow you away, cowboy. There'll be blood in the streets of Delgado Station come mornin'." Then the boy spat into the dirt and stomped off with his head down to begin his long, hot trek back to town.

"Of that, I have no doubt," replied the gunfighter softly to himself. "Just let me have that drink and cigar first."

If Jeff had been listening, really listening, not to the words, but maybe to the emotion behind them, he would have detected a note of sadness in the man's voice. But the gunfighter let the threats end there, knowing they would likely resume later. They always did.

He clicked loudly and snapped the reins on the horse's backs. "Come on now, hup!" They had rested some during the brief confrontation with the two boys and he knew now that the remaining distance to town was relatively short. It wouldn't tax the horses too badly if he ordered them to pick up the pace. Besides, he wanted to get some distance between himself and the young hothead he was leaving in the dust. That boy wasn't the only one who needed to cool down.

Chapter Three

With the quickened pace, he was soon able to put some distance from the boy with whom he would cross paths later. Of that, he was certain. By the sun's position, the gunfighter estimated the time to be somewhere between three and four o'clock. He stopped carrying a pocket watch about ten years ago because it never seemed to make much difference what time it was anyway. If it was light out, he got up. If it was dark, and he was tired, he went to sleep. He found that the less he exposed himself to strangers and the curious, the less risk he took in finding someone foolish enough to want to challenge his reputation in an effort to embellish their own. So, time didn't really mean much to him when he wasn't working as a hired gun for others to clean up a town or to settle a dispute.

If he was on his own time, he preferred to stay out of sight and alone. He liked reading, mostly, but if there was any sort of performance in town, he often attended those. It didn't especially matter what type of entertainment it was, as long as it was distracting and took his mind off who he was and what he did for a living. A particular favorite form of entertainment were magicians, like Alexander Herrmann or the young Howard Thurston. He also loved music, opera specifically, and had seen many of the singers of his time. Jenny Lind was a particular favorite, as was Giuditta Pasta. He also enjoyed seeing Edwin Booth and Edmund Kean perform Shakespeare, as their respective styles were so very different. Mostly, however, he preferred to be left alone.

The stifling afternoon heat was still potent, but he sensed it was beginning to back off a little. What he really wanted was the feel of a cool breeze across his face as he sat on a saloon porch with a cold beer. It had been a long time between drinks, a good home-cooked meal, a hot bath and a soft bed. It had been even longer since he had a soft woman to roll with. Right now, though, he would settle for that cold beer and sweet cigar. Priorities.

A quick glance at his cargo told him Juneann was still asleep. With any luck, she would make it all the way into town that way. He didn't want to have to deal with whatever nightmares she would be reliving if she awoke before they got to town. That was something for doctors and women folk to handle. Chances are she wouldn't remember him anyway. By his recollection, her mind was already shut down and retreated into the blackness of terror when he showed up. A pang of guilt gnawed at his belly when he thought about what she must have seen and felt. He had heard the gunshots that signaled the attack on her and Ben but was too far away to understand their meaning. But as he got closer, it was her screams that made him decide to investigate. By the time he got close enough to see what was happening and evaluate what was taking place, Ben was already dead and the attack on Juneann had just begun. Now, the thought that he might have been able to spare her at least some of the pain she endured if he had arrived sooner was troubling. He tried to put such thoughts out of his mind, knowing he had already done more than most men would have dared. That should be enough, he thought. Now, all he wanted was to get this poor wretch of a child to people who would take care of her. That's all. Then, he would be free of his responsibilities. Maybe this good deed would even make up for some of the lower depths he had allowed himself to slip into at various times of weakness in the not-so-distant past. Thoughts of a hot bath, a hot meal, a cigar and a cold beer returned to his head.

Another dust cloud appeared over a rise in the road ahead. It was small and indicated only one rider moving at a pace somewhere between a gallop and a canter. The gunfighter took a deep breath, reset his Winchester over his lap and awaited the arrival of his next encounter. His first thought was that whatever excuse for a sheriff this town had was heading out to escort him in, hopefully without issue. That would be his preference, assuming he was a reasonable man. If not, then things could get ugly again. His second thought was that it might be the town doctor coming out to start treatment on the girl right away. That would be good. Then, a third alternative came to him, one that didn't sit well. It occurred to him that whoever it was heading his way likely got his information on the day's events based solely on the word of the young boy, named Pete MacDougal. That could be either good or bad, depending on how much Pete stretched the truth and to whose favor he slanted it. The gunfighter would know soon enough.

Within a matter of a few minutes and another fifty yards each way, the rider came into view. Immediately, the gunfighter knew who was riding out to greet him.

There is something about the way a man sits on a horse. It's a signature of sorts. It is possible to tell who a particular rider is, even if the face can't be seen, assuming you knew him to begin with, of course. Distance isn't entirely relevant. Style and comfort in the saddle say it all. Some men are born to it, some aren't. The man approaching the wagon was definitely in the latter of the two categories.

His body language was unmistakable and spoke of a man

who would rather be anywhere else but on the back of a horse, any horse. His hunched-over and slumping body seemed to be crying out in pain with every step his horse took. Occasionally, he would even stand in the stirrups as if to stretch his legs and back.

"Well, I'll be damned if it isn't Val Avery." The gunfighter laughed and pulled up on the reins. "Whoa, there. Hold up." When the rider reached talking distance, somewhat less formal salutations were exchanged.

"Jake Benteen, you son of a bitch!" roared the saddle-sore rider. "I thought that was you young Pete was talking about. Ain't nobody carries a Winchester like yours or shoots it like you neither."

"Just as graceful on horseback as ever, I see," chuckled Jake.

"Yeah, well you can kiss my tired, bloody ass, Jake," roared the sheriff. "If it wasn't for you, I wouldn't be out here bursting my piles on this damn roan's back."

Jake took this opportunity to make mention of the badge that hung on Val's vest. "A sheriff's job is never done. Isn't that what they say, Val?"

Val sensed a bit of scolding in Jake's voice. "It's what old gunfighters do, Jake," he said with a little defiance thrown back. "They either get killed by one or become one. I chose to become one."

"How long have you been a law dog, Val?"

"About ten years now," he said, "give or take." Sounding out the years made him sit up straight. "To tell you the truth, I didn't think I'd last this long."

"That would have been my guess." Jake extended his hand and found it greeted firmly by his old friend. "But it's still good to see you."

41

"So, you want to tell me what happened?" said the sheriff, taking on a more official tone to his voice.

Jake took a quick glance over his shoulder to see if Juneann was still asleep, then lowered his voice. "Can't this wait 'til we get to town, Val? I'm not sure how much longer this child is going to stay out. I'd like to get her to the doc while she's still asleep." Val saw the look in Jake's eyes and knew his request was more than reasonable and spoken with sincerity.

"I don't see why not. No sense conducting business out here when we could be doing it over a cold beer, right?"

Jake smiled his appreciation at Val's professional courtesy, as well as the suggestion of that cold beer he'd been dreaming of earlier. "I'd appreciate that, Val. Thanks."

"Mind if I ride along in the wagon with you, Jake?" The sheriff was clearly uncomfortable sitting in the saddle. "It would sure give my backside a rest."

Jake smiled and jerked his thumb to the back of the wagon saying, "I'd appreciate the company. Tie your horse to the back of the wagon with the others and climb aboard. Be as quiet as you can though," Jake added with a whisper. I don't want to chance waking the girl."

Once Val got his horse tied off, he took a moment to check on Juneann, who was still asleep or possibly just comatose. The sheriff had pulled his bed roll from behind his saddle to use as a cushion, tossing it up next to his friend. He then climbed up and spread it out to form a pillow. Delicately, he settled himself on to the padded buckboard seat. "Ah, that's a might better than a saddle, I'd say."

Jake chuckled, then delicately snapped the reins and started the final leg into town. As they rolled along, Jake decided he would fill Val in on the events of the day after all, keeping his

42

voice low and soft as he told him what he did and why. The fact that his old friend was now a sheriff made Jake feel obligated to explain why he shot Orin and Buck outright instead of trying to talk then into reason and possibly take them in for trial. As it turned out, just hearing the names Orin and Buck was all the sheriff needed to hear to know that Jake's actions were justified.

"You don't have to explain yourself to me on their account, Jake," said the sheriff. "Them two was as bad as they come, and that's saying a lot. As far as I'm concerned, you done the territory a big favor taking them down."

Jake was relieved to hear there would be no trouble from his old friend for taking the law into his own hands.

"I should tell you though," added Val, "I'm not the one you have to worry about. Nor anybody from Delgado Station as far as I can tell. It's some of them boys over in Tres Mesa that might not take it kindly what you done. One of 'em… in particular."

"Who's that?" asked Jake, a bit puzzled. "Like you said, they were about as low a pair of human animals as I've seen, so I can't imagine there'd be anyone too shook up at their passing."

"You'd think," replied Val, "but the boys over in Tres Mesa are a pretty tight bunch. They all ride for a real bad one, named Wolf. He's a sick one that you don't cross unless you want your hide peeled and hung out to dry. Ever hear of him?"

"Heard of him, sure. He's got a reputation as a real sick one a smart man would be wise to not turn his back to. Never met him though," Jake said. "Last I heard he was that he was down near Natchez. I didn't know he made his way out here."

"Sad but true." The sheriff shook his head as if he hated to even think of the man he was about to describe. "And you're right. Wolf is about as sick a man, sick in the head, that is, as I have ever seen or heard tell about. At first, I thought some of the

43

stories folks were tellin' were just plum bullshit. You know how people stretch the truth? Like stories you might tell children at bedtime. But the more stories I heard, the more truth there seemed to be in them. I guess that's what makes him hold his men together. Fear. As a gang, they are about as bad a bunch as you and I ever faced back in the day. But even back then, it was usually no more than one or two at a time. Six, tops. When Wolf got run out of about every other state east of here, he got it in his mind to form something of an army of his own. He's got that bunch tied pretty tight. You hurt one, you hurt 'em all. Least, that's what he preaches."

"How have you managed to stay clear of them this long, Val?"

"It's funny you ask that, Jake," answered Val, reluctantly. "Truth is, the sheriff I took over for made a deal with Wolf."

"A deal?" inquired Jake with a tone suggesting disbelief. "From what I've heard of this Wolf, he's not the kind that is known for keeping his word."

"Well, you're sure enough right on that score, Jake," answered the sheriff. "But from what I understand, it was something of a business decision."

Jake cocked his head to one side and said, "Business decision? How so?"

The sheriff laughed, expressing his own level of disbelief when he said, "There's an old Indian legend about how two tribes that kept fighting over who owned the fish in a river. One tribe lived on one side and one on the other. Finally, they decided to meet to stop the fighting and said, 'From here on, you fish on your side of the river and we'll fish on our side and nobody fish in the middle.' The fighting stopped."

"So, they formed a truce?" asked Jake. "Is that what you're

saying?"

"That's about the size of it, I'd say," replied the sheriff. "There are no warrants on them in New Mexico, so they keep a low profile down here. They stay in their town, and we stay in ours. If they need supplies, they usually send a rider and a wagon. They pay cash. We don't ask where they got the money from either, just so long as they didn't get it stealing from us."

"And if they did?" Jake's question was pointed and laced with suspicion.

The sheriff smiled. "So far, they have just been fishing on their side of the river. Their side being across the border in Mexico. As long as they do their thieving there, I have no jurisdiction. Live and let live."

"So, you have accepted this truce, then," stated Jake, bluntly.

"Exactly," answered his friend.

Both men sat silent for a few moments, engrossed in thought until Jake asked the obvious question. "So, would it be fair to say, the truce has been broken?"

The sheriff offered a wry smile and said, "Shattered, would be more like it."

Jake's shoulders slumped a little at the realization he had possibly taken on an entire town of bloodsuckers whose sense of loyalty was based on a level of honor no better than a nest of snakes. It certainly wasn't what he had bargained for when he made the decision to take down Orin and Buck and save the young woman, Juneann. He couldn't help but think to himself, "Next time, mind your own damn business and ride on." But that just wasn't his way. Seeing an innocent girl like Juneann destroyed by the likes of Orin and Buck was more than even his callused life could take. That other thought crept into his tired mind again that maybe he wasn't as bad a man as he or others thought him to be. There just might be hope for him yet. Still, the realization of what troubles he may have brought to his friend and his town gnawed at him.

"Looks like I brought a mess of trouble your way, Val. I'm sorry." Jake never looked at his friend, but only stared straight ahead.

"Nothin' to be sorry about, Jake. You did what needed doin' and thank God you did. Fact is, it looks more like it was Wolf's side that broke the truce, not ours." The sheriff patted his friend on the shoulder.

"You think Wolf will see it that way, Val?"

Val considered Jake's question before he spoke. "Well, if I were a betting man" – he paused and winked at Jake – "and I have been known to place a bet or two, I'd say Wolf will use any excuse he can to justify breaking our truce." Val slapped his friend on the back. "But don't you worry about it now, Jake. You did the right thing. Believe me! We'll find a way to deal with it. You and me."

"I appreciate that, Val, but it could get bloody." Jake cleared his throat of the trail dust and spat off to his left. "If the stories about Wolf are true, a lot of innocent people could be hurt. I sure didn't mean for that to happen." He pulled his hat off and wiped his brow with his shirt sleeve, then stuffed the hat on his right knee and gave his head a stiff rub through his scalp as if he was trying to shake some reason or logic loose to help him explain his feelings. "Times have changed, Val," Jake continued. "People have changed. There's no place for the likes of me anymore." Another thought hit him hard and sudden. "I'm tired, Val. Dead, dog tired. I've been wandering across this country, getting farther away from civilization with every step."

Val let out a knowing sigh and leaned back against the seat.

He seemed almost relieved to hear Jake's words of awareness of the changing world. Jake scanned his old friend's face and saw the look of recognition in his eyes.

"You know what I'm talking about, don't you?" asked Jake of his friend.

Val took a moment to answer, filling the space with heavy sighs and muffled laughter.

"I was surprised enough to hear those words coming outta myself 'bout ten years back," he said. "But I sure never thought I'd hear 'em from you. I always thought you were that breed of gunfighter that loved the life more than anything and would carry it to the grave. Fact is, I thought fer sure I'd hear of you being gunned down long before now. Kind of surprised I didn't."

Jake was a little surprised by Val's comments and observations but couldn't find fault with them. The surprise came more from the fact that it was from a man he never thought knew him well enough to know what was in his soul. Part of him was relieved to be able to share the secret. Another part, the cautious part of a seasoned gunfighter, was wary of showing any sign of weakness.

Gunfighters seldom made friends. It simply wasn't part of the trade. If you knew someone, another gun hand, it was more by reputation than anything else. Paths would inevitably cross from town to town, and most would acknowledge the others' existence if it came to a face-to-face encounter. But such meetings usually amounted to nothing more than a handshake or a tip of the hat. Occasionally, an exchange of drinks would take place out of professional courtesy and perhaps a little curiosity. Some even worked together on occasion, cleaning up the odd wild town and making it civilized for so-called decent folk. Then, once the job was done, being asked to leave so that a gunfighter's reputation wouldn't tarnish the town's now cleaned-up image. They love you when they need you but can't wait for you to leave when the job is done.

The image of one fast gun seeking out another to claim a notch on his pistol grip was almost purely a dime-novel fantasy. Oh, it happened from time to time, but it was almost always some young punk looking to become a legend with one shot, or a fading legend trying to recapture his lost glory. Neither succeeded with any regularity. What Jake and Val were about to face, should it come to a showdown with Wolf and his men, was more typical of a gunfighter's role.

Realizing what may lay ahead made Val curious about Jake's past and the legend he carried with him. "When did you first get branded, Jake?" asked Val. It was a question asked by a man who already knew the answer, but he wanted to hear the truth from the legend himself.

Jake looked at Val with a quizzical stare. Surely, he knew the story of how his friend became a famous gun hand – Jake Benteen: The Deadliest Man in the West! Everyone knew the story, more or less. Winchester or Colt, there was no man better. As true as that fact was, the story behind how he became that way was mostly fiction.

"You mean to tell me you never heard what happened in Alagordo Wells?" Jake asked his question with a bit of a glint in his eyes and a self-mocking tease in his voice. "Surely you've read the story of the fastest and deadliest gun this side of Kansas City?"

"Well, I've heard the bullshit version," returned Val, with a snicker. "We've all got our own bullshit versions of our legends. Now, I'd like to hear the real version. The truth. If there is one."

The *real* version, as Val requested, wasn't really all that different from the bullshit version. The facts were substantially the same. Young Jake Benteen wandered into the Bull Moose Saloon on a Tuesday night looking for nothing more than a stiff drink and a pretty young lady to twirl around the dance floor. He was nineteen and had just finished his first trail drive and had money to burn.

Circumstances he can't recall found him sitting in on a poker game that was way out of his range of experience and finance. His trail boss, Big George Kelly, was holding most of the table stakes, which didn't sit well with four of the other players in the game. They were from a rival outfit that didn't make it into town until after Jake's crew took up most of the good rooms, food and women. Always a sore spot when it came to driving a herd to market after months on the trail. The cowpunchers and trailhands that got there first got the pick of it all and often wore out the welcome the town had for any more drovers by the time they managed to drift into town.

Fatigue, bad food, and whiskey that would burn a hole in your pants helped fuel the resentment the other players had against Big George as they continually watched him rake in pot after pot. It didn't help that his booming laugh filled the bar and even hushed all other sounds as he boasted yet another winning hand.

"Well will ya look at that!" he howled. "Four beautiful ladies and one king to satisfy them all!" Big George lunged his massive arms across the table to claim his latest winnings when one of the players, Bob Creed, slammed a Bowie knife into the middle of the pot.

"I have had it with you, fat man!" Creed was on his feet glaring into Big George's face with eyes that were totally devoid of reason. "You been taking every damn pot for the last half hour.

That ain't natural. Somethin' just ain't right!"

Another sore loser, Jed Watts, echoed his own resentment and offered the too-often-heard explanation for why anyone could win so easily. "Ever since you took the deal, you been playing a winning hand. Only a cheater could be that lucky."

The third and fourth men in the game, Fred Velde and Kyle Bass, didn't add to the conversation, but just pushed their chairs back away from the table and stood, hands at the ready, resting on their pistol grips. All conversation in the room stopped as everyone's attention was immediately drawn to the drama unfolding around the poker table. The bartender wiped his hands on a towel and quickly moved to the other end of the bar where he had a scattergun tucked under the lip. Jake was still seated, but his back was to a corner post at the end of a wall that broke away into a larger room behind him.

Big George was trapped in the corner with no room to maneuver. Although he was aware of his position, he never showed any concern and just continued to pull the pot of coin and paper to his side of the table. Then, he settled back in his chair and pulled out a cigar stub from his vest pocket. He slowly placed it in his mouth, burying it deep until it was smothered in the full red beard that surrounded his large, round face. He chomped down hard on the stub and then rolled it back and forth in his mouth before he spoke.

"Why is it when boys play a man's game and lose, the first thing they cry is that somebody must be cheating?" Big George calmly folded his arms across his huge chest. He was angry but was trying to control his rage by continuing to crush the cigar butt in his teeth.

"You got a better explanation, fat man?" demanded Creed.

"Yeah," answered Big George, as he pulled the saliva-soaked butt from his mouth. "I'm a good card player and you're not!" Some nervous laughter erupted from various parts of the room that seemed to share that observation. "You've been playin' a fool's hand all night, bettin' on pure horse shit. Don't blame me 'cause I took advantage of it."

Big George then reached inside his vest for a match. The move was misinterpreted by Kyle Bass who pulled his Remington. He was standing too close to the table and the barrel caught on the edge as he was raising it into position and discharged. The bullet exploded under the table and lodged into the top of Bob Creed's foot who let out an agonized scream and started hopping around in a half-circle until he finally dropped to the floor.

As he hit the floor, Creed pulled his own hog leg and fired one shot that struck Big George under the left side of his jaw and exited out the other side of his right cheek, taking a couple of teeth with it. The bullet buzzed by Jake's face and lodged in a coat and hat-rack leaning against the wall. A mixture of tobacco juice and blood spattered across Jake's face.

All Jake could clearly remember from here on was that he was in a fight for his life that operated on pure instinct, otherwise known as self-preservation. Exactly when he pulled his own gun remains a mystery to him. Big George did manage to pull his gun right after he was hit but was struck by four more bullets almost at once. No one was ever sure exactly where these shots came from. Two slugs hit him square in the chest, a massive target that was hard to miss. Another shattered his left forearm. The last one carved a trench on the right side of his face that tore away his ear. Only one shot was fired from Big George's gun as he fell back against the wall, but it was potent. Fred Velde reeled back from a bullet that split his jaw at the chin and traveled at an upward angle until it settled in the center of his brain.

Jake remembered seeing his own gun-filled hand firing shot for shot, but just who he hit and where, he did not know for certain. It was only the image of each man's face that ran through his mind as he sent hot lead in their direction. Suddenly, his legs crumpled beneath him as he felt the impact of a bullet sink into his thigh. His body slammed against the wall and slid down to the floor. Another bullet caught him in the meat of his left shoulder, knocking the wind out of him. Jake found himself sitting on the floor now sitting almost face-to-face with Bob Creed. Between them was the dying hulk of Big George Kelly. Creed aimed his pistol at Jake and began fanning the trigger. Nothing happened. His gun was empty. Jake followed suit but was stunned to discover that his pistol was also empty. In a macabre ballet of death, both men tried to shuck their pistols of the empty shell casings and get at least one live round to fire in defense.

Jake reached for his belt, only to find it empty. He was just a poor cowboy, after all, and didn't have the money to spend on keeping his belt loops filled with fresh rounds. Creed was just pulling a bullet from his own belt loop when Jake caught sight of Big George's right hand waving feebly at him. He was trying to get Jake's attention and offer his loaded .45 for him to use against Creed. With the last of his life's energy, Big George rolled his body and tossed the gun to Jake. When Jake leaned forward to grasp the weapon, a bullet from Creed's gun sprayed splinters of wood from the wall where Jake's head had been. Jake pushed himself up and fired one shot through Creed's right eye. Creed's head snapped violently back, bringing his body upright. His one remaining eye stared directly at Jake, then rolled up into his head as his body fell back on the floor. He was dead before Big George

Kelly closed his eyes, knowing he had saved Jake's life with his dying breath.

Amid the chaos and death, other hands were drawn into the dispute, some out of a perverted sense of honor, others out of sheer panic and stupidity. In the end, seven men lay dead. One innocent bystander caught a bullet in the back as he tried to run through the bat-wing doors after the first shot was fired.

Big George was the only fatality from Jake's outfit, but it was a heavy loss. He was a man well-liked and respected. Everyone that knew him swore that the accusations of card cheating were just the typical rantings of a bunch of sore losers. Big George Kelly was a good card player who used other men's weaknesses against them, often bluffing his way to a winning hand. He didn't need to cheat.

The last five victims were from Bob Creed's bunch. It was a heavy toll for one outfit to take and one not soon forgotten. The bitterness that followed would last for years and Jake's name would forever be at its core.

Eyewitness accounts are seldom reliable in a gunfight, especially when it comes to who started what and who shot who. It often depends on which side of the fence your loyalties lay. In Jake's case, his outfit claimed victory, morally as well as in body count. Unbiased observers probably had it right when they recounted seeing each man so crazed with fear that they were shooting each other as much as they were shooting a supposed enemy. Ultimately, the truth didn't matter.

The owner of the brand Jake rode for, John Bennett Preace, even bought into the legend because it made good business sense, making it easier to get men to ride for him. He did ask Jake to leave though, once he was healed and gave him a three-hundred-dollar bonus as a going-away gift.

By the time the first printed account of the shootout hit the streets, Jake had been given the mantle of hero for defending the honor of his outfit and avenging the foul murder of his friend, a man, in truth, he hardly knew.

One artist's rendering of the incident portrayed Jake with two six-guns blazing away as he sent each man to an early grave. In the ten weeks it took for Jake to recover from his wounds, the death toll had risen to an even dozen men, all felled by Jake's hand. At first, Jake tried to dispel the false stories and set the record straight for those who would listen. Eventually, he gave up and foolishly let the legend grow.

"I have to admit, in the beginning, I liked the attention," Jake said, as he concluded his version of the story. "I was a young, foolish kid and I liked how people reacted when they saw me or found out who I was. I could walk into a saloon and the masses would part like Moses at the Red Sea. It got so I never paid for a drink. There was always somebody that wanted to say they bought Jake Benteen a shot of whiskey. I even read accounts of people buying me drinks in towns I'd never been to. Sometimes I'd get my room and board for free just because people were afraid of me, or they wanted to capitalize on my name by bragging that I slept in this room or that one. I wouldn't be surprised to hear I slept in about every hotel room this side of Kansas City. Hell, even the women were free." Jake shook his head in amused disgust.

"Do you remember the first time you had to back up that reputation?" asked Val. His voice was quiet and serious, and this question too seemed almost rhetorical.

Jake caught the tone and found it odd, but let it pass for the time being. "That's the part I wasn't ready for," he replied solemnly. "That's how naive and stupid I was. It just never

54

occurred to me that anyone would ever dare challenge me."

"You started to believe your own legend, then," answered Val with a knowing smile.

"I suppose," replied Jake, shaking his head at the memory. "At first, anyway."

"But someone did challenge you early on, right?" asked Val. "Someone tryin' to settle a score?" Jake sat up straight in the wagon. "Wasn't that Jack Parrish who called you out in Abilene, Kansas, 'bout fifteen years or so back?"

Jake thought for a brief moment. "Seventeen years, actually. He claimed he was working with Creed's outfit on that cattle drive, but I don't know that for certain. A lot of men claimed that, or claimed they were at the saloon that night." Jake laughed again at the absurdity of it all. "If everyone who claimed to have been there had actually been there, there would have been enough room to fit them all." Both men laughed and then Jake shot a surprised look at his friend. "Have you been reading up on my history, Val?"

"Don't need to, Jake. I was there. In Abilene, that is." The sheriff smiled. "That was the first time you were actually called out, right?"

Jake paused before he answered, looking off in the distance. "I guess it was, yes. Forgot his name, though… until you mentioned it."

The sheriff shook his head in dismay. "That's bad, Jake. A gunfighter doesn't forget a killing, no matter what the reason, time or place. It's when the memories fade that your soul dries up, and soon you are just a walking shell of a man waiting for death to call. A man, any man, especially a gunfighter, doesn't forget that."

"Then you know it was pure luck I walked away," said Jake,

55

a little embarrassed. "The whole gunfight is just a blur. What did you see?"

"All I know is, he beat you to the draw," replied Val. "From where I was standing, he should have knocked you outta your boots. But he dropped dead instead of you."

Jake snapped the reins on the horse's backs and called out for them to pick up the pace. Then he hunched over and rested his elbows on his knees.

"He missed, I didn't. That's really about the size of it," said Jake. "His bullet ripped just under my left armpit a second before I had even cleared the leather. My bullet caught him in the throat and broke his neck. Pure dumb luck."

Val reached an arm around Jake and patted him on the back. "Well, it may have been pure dumb luck back then, but you can't have survived this long without some real talent and skill for the trade. From what I've heard and seen, you growed into the part over the years."

Jake shook his head and shrugged his shoulders. "I guess you could say that," then looked off into the distance again, at nothing in particular, before he continued. "Since then, I have had to practice every day of my life just to stay one step ahead." Jake looked at Val for some show of recognition or understanding of what he was saying. "Any of this sound familiar to you, Val?"

Val removed his hat and fiddled with the brim for distraction. "Pretty much all of it… 'cept, I was never the gun hand you are. Not solo, anyway. That's why I got out when I did."

Val turned and looked into the back of the wagon. Everything was calm. Juneann was still sound asleep and old Ben was well past putting up a fuss. Seeing the reason for his being called out of town and remembering Jake's description of the incident made him consider his next question carefully. It was an important question and one that he had wrestled with himself some years earlier. Now, it was Jake's turn to consider where his life was going and what was driving him there.

"I need to ask you a tough question, Jake." Val paused a moment, waiting for a reply that never came. He continued. "The killing. Is it different?"

Jake knew what the question was going to be even before he heard it. Val was right. It was a question he had been asking himself a lot lately. Still, he put off giving a direct answer by asking one instead. "Different how?"

"You know what I mean, Jake. How they feel… inside." Val let the last word trail off on the wind.

"Inside?" Jake gave the word some serious thought before finishing his answer. The first killings were still a blur, even after all these years. The hype built up around them created a legend and distorted any real sense of understanding over what they meant. The many others that followed took on a status that only added to his mystique, but never caused him to consider how they affected him. Now, with the times changing fast and people growing tired of his type, he was beginning to examine his life in a different way. "I don't feel them anymore," he said finally, in a voice that was also devoid of feeling. "Now, they just leave me feeling empty. I don't even see them in my dreams anymore."

Jake's old friend sighed heavily and just shook his head slowly. "That's bad, Jake," said Val. "Real bad. Taking a life has got to mean something, even in our line of work. Once that's gone, in the end, you're little better than Orin or Buck."

"In the end, maybe I'm just as bad?" Jake said with a sad smile.

"No, no, I don't believe that, Jake," scolded Val. "That's not what I meant. If that were true, you'd of ridden on by and let those boys do their worst to young Juneann. Or maybe even joined in and taken your turn."

Jake turned his head away to his left and didn't speak. Val continued. "I don't know you well, Jake. Not like the old days. There's been a lot of years and distance in between our crossing paths. What I know about you now is mostly by reputation and the stories I get from others. The ones I trust say you're honest and give a man more than a fair chance to back down. And only a decent man would go to all the trouble of bringing in Juneann and Ben to a town that don't know him or know what to expect. That shows me you got something left inside. Something that's good."

Hearing Val's little sermon made Jake feel better. A little better. It had been bothering him how cold and unmoved he felt when he shot Buck and then left Orin to die in agony, peeled to the bone by buzzards. Not guilty, just unmoved. He wondered if it was hearing Juneann's screams that awakened something in him and started the torture of self-doubt he was bringing on himself. Whatever the reason, he was glad he had someone to talk to who knew what he was going through.

"Is that what it was like for you, Val?"

"Like I said, I didn't have as much history piled on me as you, but it was still pretty much the same, I guess. I just woke up one morning and realized I couldn't remember the name of the man I had killed the night before. I couldn't really remember much of anything about him, 'cept that he was causing trouble and the town had hired me to clean up any men that was causing it. Only then, I didn't have the law on my side. The badge. I was just a hired gun paid to kill if it came to that. That's when I decided that, if I was going to ever kill a man again, the law was where someone like me belonged."

"Why's the law so different from what we do?" Jake's question was laced with cynicism.

"There's a big difference, Jake," replied Val, stiffly. "The law may not be perfect, but at least there's reason behind it. People count on it and look up to it when it's done proper. Sometimes it's a fine line between what I do with a badge and what I did without one, I'll grant you that. But I can tell you for certain I sleep a whole lot better knowing I did something because the law and the people that back it said I could. My life means something now."

Val's voice was loud and commanding. It had something of the preacher in it. Jake feared the volume might awaken Juneann. He also wasn't sure if Val was so forceful and intense for Jake's benefit or his own. Either way, he appreciated his friend's opinion and observations and let the subject end there for now.

"Reflecting on the past isn't going to do either of us any good if what you say about Wolf and his bunch is true," cautioned Jake. "Maybe it's best I let you take this wagon in and ride on. That might spare you and your town some hard times."

Val considered Jake's offer. It was a good one, and one that made sense. It was even something he considered proposing himself, even though it bothered him to turn away an old friend and a man who had just done his town and the territory a big favor in saving young Juneann and removing the likes of Orin and Buck from the earth.

"As much as I hate to say it, Jake, that may be best. There's no tellin' when or even if Wolf and his men will get wind of what happened to Orin and Buck, but if they do, your being gone could help cool things a might."

Jake nodded his agreement. "Do you think I have enough

time to get a decent meal, a hot bath and a solid night's sleep?"

"And maybe even a few cold beers," added Val with a wink. "On me."

"I'll take it, with thanks, Val."

As the wagon rounded a sharp bend in the road, a small wooden bridge covering a wide, dried-up riverbed to control the spring runoff from the mountains came into view. Just over the bridge was the town of Delgado Station. It was a typical southwestern town in many respects. Since it was a regular stop on the stagecoach run to all parts east and west, it had a healthy economy with more than its share of successful businesses.

With its own bank and one large church, it was a town on the rise. Its population was just over five hundred, if you count the outlying farms and ranches, which all lay north of the town line. No one dared venture too far south for fear of running into any of the men from Tres Mesa. As the sheriff had described, it was something of an unwritten rule. You stay on your side, and we'll stay on ours and we'll all get along just fine. Besides, Tres Mesa was close enough to the Mexican border, which is where most of their raids took place. That meant they could slip back across into US territory where the Mexican authorities couldn't follow. Why risk making both sides angry? So, Wolf and his men knew enough to stay clear of causing any trouble. Messing with anyone from Delgado Station was just too risky and could stir up unnecessary problems. Orin and Buck forgot the rules. Now, it was an open question as to what would happen once word got back to Wolf and the men at Tres Mesa about this breach of protocol.

There was even speculation that the railroad was considering making it one of their stops. Further speculation settled around the railroad's concern over Wolf and the gang at Tres Mesa. The prevailing theory was that the powers that be were waiting for something to be done about the gang before they committed to expanding a rail line in their direction.

On this day, however, as Jake pulled the wagon down the town's main street, only one man stood waiting his arrival. That lone citizen was Doc Gibbons. As far as Jake could see, the rest of the town was deserted. At least, for now.

Chapter Four

Doc Gibbons was a portly man of just over fifty years of age. He stood about five feet and change and always wore a Mexican sombrero to block out the sun and shade the top of his bald head. What hair he had was dirty blond and mixed fifty-fifty with snow white. A large full-lipped mustache blocked most of his nostrils and upper lip, so folks joked that the hair actually sprouted from his large, bulbous nose. Perched at the tip of his nose was a pair of bifocals that were so scratched and dirty it was a wonder he could see anything at all. Black pants that were about three inches too short exposed a pair of boots that had seen better days. The pants were held up with black suspenders and a once-upon-a-time white shirt soaked in sweat. To round out the ensemble, the remains of a cigar stub that was nothing more than a wad of wet tobacco was stuffed into the left corner of his mouth.

If first impressions meant anything, Doc Gibbons certainly didn't look like one to instill much confidence in the medical profession. But Jake knew better than to judge someone by outside appearances alone. In fact, he had bet his life on it more than once. Something, call it instinct, told him Doc Gibbons knew what he was doing and that Juneann was in good hands. The fact was, he was the best doctor within a thousand square miles and everyone in Delgado Station knew it. The mystery was why he chose this out-of-the-way town to hang his shingle. The simple reason was that he knew he was needed here and that was enough for him. The more complex reason had to do with what he had seen during the Civil War and his desire, need even, to get as far away from those memories as possible.

Doc Gibbons held both hands high and shouted to the approaching wagon. "Hold it right there, young fella! You don't need to go no further if you're the man young Pete was hopping up and down about." He glanced a look at Val and then leaned to his side and tried to stand up on his toes to catch a look at the inside of the wagon. He was too short and the wagon's contents too varied and plentiful to clearly make out anything from his current vantage point. From what he could make out, Juneann was covered up, as was the body of old Ben, whose feet stuck out from behind a bucket of nails. Any further examination of the wagon's contents would have to wait. Doc stepped off to the side and gave Jake the once over, then turned his attention and question to the sheriff. "Everything sit right with you about this fella, Sheriff?"

"I got his back, Doc," answered Val, as he threw a trusting glance at Jake. "He's all right. You got my word."

Doc gave a quick nod of his head and said, "That's good enough for me," then continued around behind the wagon and stopped at the back end. He addressed his direction to Jake, pointing to his left at a long flight of stairs to a second story. "My office is right upstairs."

Jake scanned his eyes to his left and noticed the long flight of stairs to the second floor that ran against the end of a building that housed a dry goods store. The stairs were narrow and steep. "Your doctor's office is up a flight of stairs?" His question was almost insulting in its tone.

The doctor was flipping back the blanket over old Ben's body, trying not to disturb Juneann when he paused at Jake's question. "You got a problem with stairs, mister?"

63

Realizing he may have insulted the doctor, however unintentionally, Jake immediately tried to backtrack his question. "Well, no... not me, but what happens if you've got a patient that can't climb those stairs?"

"Then I guess they'll die!" snapped the doctor. Jake wasn't sure if the doctor was kidding or not. He guessed not.

Jake set the brake and tied off the reins. Val defied his age and disabilities and quickly jumped down off the wagon and shuffled to the back where Juneann lay, still wrapped in Jake's bedroll. He quickly maneuvered the three horses to one side so the doctor could get a better look at Juneann.

Doc knew right away there wasn't anything he could do for Ben, barely even giving him a blink. His attention was reserved only for Juneann. As he pulled the blanket away from her face, he noticed she was sucking her thumb the way a two-year-old child might but was still sound asleep. Doc then reached for her hand to check her pulse.

"Jake says she ain't hurt real bad... physically," whispered the sheriff. "Least as far as he could tell. Just a few cuts and bruises is all, but nothin' serious."

Doc couldn't help but steal a quick glance at Ben's mortal wound before he then returned his attention back to Juneann. He was obviously moved by the sight before him and choked back his emotions by covering his mouth with a fist and a fake cough.

"Who did this, Sheriff?" Doc's question was filled with venom. He lightly moved a few stray hairs from Juneann's eyes and tucked them behind her ears.

"It was a couple of men down Tres Mesa way named Orin and Buck," said the sheriff. "You've seen 'em before, Doc. They been run out of town here more than once."

Doc pounded his right fist on the side of the wagon as if he was trying to hold back his rage. Under his breath, he said, "Dirty, rotten sons of bitches." Doc recovered his professional demeanor and asked, "You goin' after 'em, Sheriff?"

"Don't have to, Doc. Jake already took care of 'em. Buzzards are feeding on them now." Val stepped away from the back of the wagon and untied the horses and wrapped the reins around a hitching post in front of the dry goods store.

Doc patted Juneann softly on her shoulder and walked back around to face Jake. "For that, I am truly grateful, mister. I know it may not be very Christian or professional of me to say so, but the world is a better place without them two cancers taking up space in it. I'm sure you did the right thing."

"Can't say I disagree with you, Doc," replied Jake. "I'm just sorry I wasn't able to be there a little sooner. Might have been able to make things easier on her and save her friend here."

"Well, she's alive, thanks to you and that's somethin'." Doc came around the side of the wagon and stopped and placed his hands on the edge of the seat next to Jake. "Now I'm gonna ask you one more favor, not that you ain't done enough already. Since you've made mention of my stairs, and it should be pretty apparent that I'm old and fat and the sheriff here ain't much better, I'm gonna need you to carry Juneann up to my office all by yourself. You look young enough and strong enough. Would you do that so I can start doin' what I can for her?"

"Not a problem, Doc." Jake grabbed his Winchester off the seat and climbed down from the wagon and walked around the front where Val had just finished unhooking the singletree from Jake's horse, Teacher.

"I'll take your horse and these other two over to the livery, Jake," said the sheriff. "I'll leave mine tied up here for the time being. Once I get the horses squared away, I'll come back and

65

get the rest of your rig and take it down to the stable too. I'll take your Winchester back to my office. You can pick it up there when you're done." Jake nodded his agreement and handed his Winchester to his friend.

Jake gave his horse a gentle, thankful pat on the neck. Teacher nuzzled her nose against Jake's chest in appreciation. To Val, he asked, "You tell whoever runs the livery stable here to take good care of Teacher?"

"Sure will!" answered Val. Gracie McCall runs a nice stable down the street. I'll see to it your horse is well taken care of. Don't you worry."

Again, Jake patted Teacher on the neck again and rubbed her ears as he spoke appreciatively, saying, "I owe you something extra, Teacher." And once again, Teacher nuzzled her nose against Jake's chest, as if to signal total agreement.

Doc instructed the sheriff what to do with Ben's body, which was pretty basic. There was only one undertaker in town, Briggs Funeral Emporium, and they would take proper care of Ben. Money would not be a problem either. Old Ben was the town handyman for everyone within thirty miles. Affections ran high because he was reliable, good at just about anything he set his mind to, and honest. The sheriff was certain he could convince the town to put up the necessary money to give him a proper burial. It was the least they could do, he thought.

Before folding Juneann in his arms, Jake called out to his friend in a whisper. "Val, tell the stable girl to give her a good rubdown and some water too. No oats or hay until she's cooled down. Will you do that?"

Val tapped his hat with his left hand in something resembling a salute and said, "Consider it done, Jake. But Gracie ain't no stable girl. She'll peel your hide to the bone if you call her that." Val laughed at the thought of Jake seeing Gracie and realizing just how wrong he was. "But I'll make sure Gracie treats her special. No need to worry about that."

Jake gave a salute back indicating his thanks and appreciation and then scooped the innocent, tortured child up in his arms. Juneann stirred briefly in protest at being moved and only moaned a little before she buried her face against Jake's chest.

With some considerable and obvious effort, Sheriff Avery climbed up onto the wagon and took control of the now single-horse team, turning the animal around and heading them back up the street in the direction of the funeral emporium. He had to leave Teacher, and the two horses Jake had rescued, tied to a hitching post for the time being. Once old Ben's body was squared away, he would take all of the horses down to Gracie McCall's stable for boarding and some proper care.

Jake quickly made it up the stairs and inside Doc Gibbon's office and placed Juneann down on the examination table positioned against the far wall. Two oil lamps were already lit, illuminating a bowl of steaming water and fresh bandages placed at the ready on a small table just under a medicine cabinet. It was obvious the doctor was well prepared for his patient. Jake remained by Juneann's side until the doctor managed, with considerable and obvious effort, to carry himself up the stairs and into his office.

"You may be right, young fella. I'm going to have to move my office down to street level pretty damn soon if I'm to keep draggin' this much flesh around," huffed the doctor as he stood in the doorway to catch his breath. "You can head on out now. I'll take it from here."

Jake cautiously stepped away from his charge, placing the

back of his left hand on the side of her face and letting the back of his fingers gently roll across her right cheek. Part of him felt compelled to say something comforting to Juneann, while his other more natural instinct was to cut and run. The notion of caring for another human being was so alien to him that he was temporarily lost in the moment. Ultimately, his more familiar instinct won out and Jake spun around on his heels and headed for the door. He and the doctor crossed paths in the middle of the room, where the firm grasp of a seasoned surgeon's hand caught him at the elbow, halting Jake in his tracks.

"I don't know who you are, mister, but there's gossip about town already that says you're a famous gunfighter. The one they call Jake Benteen. I heard the sheriff call you Jake, so I'm guessin' that's who you are. That right?" The doctor's question was more one of genuine curiosity than an accusation.

"That is my name, yes," replied Jake, offering nothing more.

The doctor softened his grip on Jake's arm but still held on tight and said, "I don't know how you came by the reputation you brought with you, or whether it's a fair one," said the doctor with a stern, measured delivery. "Folks are already saying you're a bad one." The doctor paused before continuing. "But if what you did for Juneann and old Ben is what it appears to be, then my guess is that you are nowhere near as bad a man as people say." Then, he released his grip from Jake's arm and placed his hand on Jake's shoulder and added, "I sure hope I'm right."

Jake stood for a moment, absorbing the doctor's expressed observations. Choosing not to offer any reply, he just headed for the door. On the desk to his left, he noticed a cigar box which made him stop and turn back, facing the doctor. "Mind if I take a cigar for the road, Doc?"

Doc turned with a wry smile and said, "Help yourself, young

fella. Take as many as you like. The more you take, the less I'll have to smoke." With a wink and a nod, he added, "A good doctor I know told me I'm not supposed to be smoking them anyway."

"Would that 'good doctor' be you?"

"It would," answered Doc Gibbons.

Jake laughed slightly and, without hesitation, flipped open the lid and took a handful of sweet-smelling black cheroots and stuffed all but one in his pocket. He also grabbed a handful of matches sitting in a glass jar by the cigar box. Feeling somewhat like a thief, he quickly stepped out the door, closing it behind him. Once outside, he was startled to discover the once empty main street was now filled with about a dozen curious residents that stood, gathered in a silent mass about ten yards from the bottom of the stairs. He remained on the top landing, scanning the crowd for anyone that might pose a potential threat. Just because Doc Gibbons appeared to be on his side was no reason to get careless. By now, it was likely everyone in town knew who he was. Their opinions were also likely to cover the entire range of human emotions, from fear, curiosity, envy and even hate. He had to be ready for any or all of it.

Jake removed his Stetson and ran his fingers through his thick hair, which was matted down with sweat and the weight of his hat. Another sign that the stifling heat of the day was breaking came with a cool north wind that ran across the dampness of his brow. It felt good and he savored the moment. Then, he placed his hat back on his head and slowly descended the stairs. Before stepping off the wooden landing and on to the dusty street and equal footing with the town's people, Jake stopped and surveyed the scene. Staying on the slightly raised platform of the sidewalk gave Jake something of a stage from which to address his

69

audience.

"Something I can do for you folks?" His voice was low and deep in tone. Jake placed the black cheroot in his mouth and rolled it around to moisten the tip.

If the town's people thought their superior numbers would intimidate him, his confident demeanor proved otherwise. All remained silent until a heavy-set woman of undetermined age pushed a smallish man to the front of the pack.

"Well, go on!" she said, with another push against the man's back. "Ask him!"

The little man removed his bowler hat with both hands, holding it against his chest. He looked to his compatriots for moral, if not emotional support and was given several unambiguous nods of encouragement that seemed to bolster his nerve to finally speak.

"Is it true you're Jake Benteen... the killer?" A discernible groan rippled through the crowd at his choice of words. The man quickly corrected himself. "I mean, gunfighter."

"My name is Jake Benteen. What title you choose to give me is up to you."

Another voice called out from the back. "I say he was right the first time. You're nothin' but a killer. Back-shooter, from what I hear." The damning words brought an instant rise in tension to the crowd and made everyone surrounding the man who made the charge take immediate steps to distance themselves, not only from his words, but from his person as well. The sudden exodus left a lone figure standing in a circle of spectators. He was a large man in every way, with a full head of long blond hair that hung well past his shoulders. What little shirt there was covered only his chest. The sleeves had been cut off to allow room for his arms, which looked more like legs. The man also had a well-fed belly that hung over his belt and pushed his pants down past his waist. Thick wool pants with multiple holes and old patches were barely held up by two leather straps that resembled horse harnesses, which is exactly what they were. It was doubtful anyone made suspenders big enough to fit his needs anyway. His arms were crossed over his chest and his feet were planted wide in the dusty street. It appeared the man was completely unarmed, as no weapons of any kind were visible anywhere on his body. A smile grew upon the man's face as he repeated his claim.

"The Jake Benteen I heard of can't take a man in a fair fight, so he's got to shoot him in the back."

Jake showed no emotion as he reached inside his vest pocket for a match to light his new cigar. As he snapped the tip off the match with his thumbnail, another man in the crowd attempted to quell the increasing tensions by scolding the accusing citizen.

"Now, watch yourself, Amos. You got no call making charges like that." It wasn't clear who made the statement in Jake's defense, and it didn't matter. Random accusations and bold threats against him from loudmouths were a common occurrence for someone in his line of work. Usually, however, such claims came from someone carrying a pistol and looking to start a gunfight. Since this man was unarmed, his outward motivations were less apparent. Still, Jake knew enough not to push the fight from his end and chose to let the loudmouth make the next move.

"You got nothin' to say to that, back-shooter?" Amos rocked back and forth, bouncing up and down slightly on the souls of his feet and let out a chuckle of satisfaction. To him, it appeared he had Jake nervous because he didn't offer any defense to the scurrilous charges leveled against him.

To Jake, it was nothing he hadn't heard in one form or another, countless times before. Instead, he just lit his cigar and took a long, slow drag of the sweet, black tobacco, then blew out the match with a bluish-gray cloud of smoke. His silence only added fuel to everyone's jangled nerves. Still, as nervous as everyone was over what appeared to be an impending showdown, no one left the street just yet. Their collective emotions were a mixture of fear and curiosity.

The same man who spoke before tried again to persuade Amos to back off in his accusations. "Amos, you're just askin' for trouble. From what I heard, Mr. Benteen helped Juneann and Ben. We ought to be thankin' him, not callin' him names."

Amos turned his glare at the unseen voice and snapped his retort. "We don't know nothin' 'bout what happened out there 'cept what he claims!" Amos thrust a massive fist with a pointed finger at Jake. "So, I ain't takin' the word a no back-shootin' gunfighter. For all we know, it was him that shot old Ben and took Juneann for his pleasure."

A simple step forward off the wooden sidewalk and on to the street was all it took for the crowd to spread out and find cover. As Jake made his way directly to the imposing figure of Amos, still standing with arms folded across his chest again and legs planted firmly, the crowd offered even more room for the two men to stage their impending drama. Most onlookers just increased their distance from the two men, while others sought refuge under building overhangs. Some even stepped inside various businesses, choosing to view the drama through the safety of a windowpane.

Jake's advancing motion never slowed or even hesitated. He continued, on a straight-as-an-arrow path directly for Amos. The thumb of his left hand was tucked inside the waist of his pants. His right hand slowly rolled his cigar into the corner of his mouth. The fact that Jake's right hand was occupied with the cigar and not hovering over his Colt seemed odd to many, and even caught the attention of Amos, who mistook the move as a mistake on Jake's part, giving him even more confidence to push his taunts further.

"You gonna shoot me down in cold blood, gunfighter?" Amos was about twenty feet from Jake and holding his position. "I ain't carrying a gun ya know. Maybe you'd like me to turn around so you can shoot me in the back?"

Amos unfolded his arms and held them high as he began to turn his back on Jake. It was a classic sucker-punch move designed to confuse an opponent into relaxing his guard. Then, the supposed victim would spin around quickly and drive a fist into the face of the unsuspecting foe. First blood was always an advantage in a fistfight. The dirty move had an unusually high success rate for those that felt the need to gain the upper hand on a feared opponent. Why someone of Amos's imposing size would feel such a need probably had more to do with Jake's reputation than a fear of his own inadequacy in a bare-knuckle exchange. Jake had seen such moves before, although it was more often used to disguise the sneak draw of a gun or the pulling of a knife. It was what men did who weren't good enough. Just when Jake reached striking distance, Amos dipped slightly to his right, placing much of his considerable weight on his right leg. Pushing off and using the momentum of weight mixed with changing speed, Amos spun around quickly with his right fist cocked tight and swung wide and hard. Since Jake spotted the move early, he was easily able to dodge what surely would have been a devastating blow.

Now, Jake was able to use the very same factors Amos had tried to use against him, but to his own advantage. With Amos's body leaning in with a top-heavy, forward motion, his only chance of not losing his balance was in making contact with Jake's jaw which failed miserably. But Jake ducked under the blind haymaker, planted his feet, and pushed off hard, bringing an uppercut with his right fist firmly into the big man's jawbone. Although Jake was easily one hundred pounds under his opponent's weight, he was still of enough size and strength to stand Amos straight up with the blow.

The fact that Amos was also falling into the punch helped Jake's chances and increased the impact of the blow. The crowd released a unified gasp as the big man hit the ground. The blow didn't knock him unconscious, but left him dazed, sitting like a giant rag doll with his legs stretched out in front of him and his arms hanging limply by his sides. Jake stayed about six feet away, still holding his fist at the ready. Blood was spurting from Amos's mouth with every puff of air. He raised his head and looked about Jake, but it was clear by the glaze over his eyes that he was unsure of where he was or what had just happened. Suddenly, his eyes locked on Jake and instantly snapped into sharp focus. But before he could gather mind and body enough to get off the ground, Jake swung his right leg like a high stepper at a square dance and drove the heel of his boot dead center into Amos's face. The blow flattened his nose, sending sprays of fresh blood into the crowd. Women screamed and ran around in circles trying to wipe the blood spatters from their clothing. Men just stepped back, ignoring the blood, but stared, transfixed at the sight of Amos falling back, unconscious in the street.

There was a hushed silence all around as people gawked with disbelieving eyes at Amos and the man who brought him down. The silence was suddenly broken when a woman, wearing a white blouse now covered in red speckles of blood, charged forward screaming at Jake.

"Mr. Benteen!" She was a short, stout woman with a large

74

blue bonnet pinned to her hair. "Why… you just walked right up and… and kicked that man while he was already down."

"Yes, ma'am, just as hard as I could," countered Jake in a very matter-of-fact way. He took a long, slow drag on his cigar and released the smoke in a steady swirl which was picked up by the increasing late afternoon wind.

The woman was stunned even more by Jake's casual reply and blunt honesty. "But… why couldn't you have at least tried to talk to him?" she said. Her eyes were pleading as she looked at the bloody mess of human flesh known as Amos, now spread out like a dust angle in the street.

"Something told me he wasn't much of a conversationalist, ma'am," replied Jake, as he flexed the fingers of his right hand. They were beginning to swell from the impact on Amos's jaw.

"Well, then you're no better than the killer he made you for," she declared with great vigor and satisfaction as if she had just stated undisputed fact.

"If that were true, ma'am," said Jake, "he'd be dead." Then, he stepped forward, directly in front of the woman and stared down at her. "Now, if you don't mind – and even if you do – I'd like a hot meal, a drink and then a hot bath." Taking one step back, he addressed the rest of the crowd. "So, unless there's anybody else here with an opinion they'd like to share on the qualities of my character, I'll be going." He paused and waited, looking about the assembled crowd, making eye contact with many of them.

No one moved or spoke. "I thought not." Looking down at the unconscious mass that was Amos, Jake added, "You might want to clean that up. It'll attract flies." With that, he tipped his hat to the rest of the ladies of the group and walked off in the direction of the hotel.

Chapter Five

The only hotel in Delgado Station was the Bidwell Hotel and Restaurant, which sat squarely in the middle of town. It was hard to miss, so Jake felt no need to ask for directions or even suggestions on where he could get a room, that hot bath he'd been dreaming about, and right now, that drink. It wasn't likely anyone would have volunteered a suggestion anyway, given the discovery of his name and reputation, along with uncertainty over recent events.

Whatever good feelings he hoped would be offered his way for helping Juneann and Ben were apparently not going to be forthcoming. Just as had happened so many times in the past, people chose to assume the exaggerated legend and negative rumors surrounding him to be true and ignored any of the more positive and factual ones. The stories of the number of times he walked away from a challenge, or intentionally only wounded an opponent were always dismissed or never reported. They weren't as interesting and simply didn't fit with the image people wanted to believe. "So be it," he thought. "I'm used to it."

As Jake stepped up onto the sidewalk to enter the hotel, he heard the unmistakable click and snap of a key in a lock. The window shades over the double doors had been pulled down as well, covering the glass. But the sound of footsteps from within the hotel indicated someone was inside. A sign over the door read "Visitors Welcome." It was clear that the sign was meant for everyone but Jake.

Undeterred by the rude reception in the street, or total lack of one at the hotel for that matter, Jake continued on his path to the door. The thought of politely knocking had briefly entered his mind, but he decided it was a useless gesture. Instead, he lifted his right knee to his chest, then extended his leg straight out, kicking both doors open with the same foot he laid Amos out with. The doors popped open easily, slamming against the inside wall on either side.

Unusually elegant tables and chairs adorned the waiting area of the lobby. Fine curtains hung in all the windows. It was, by any level of comparison to other hotels Jake had stayed in, a very upscale establishment and seemed somewhat out of place in this small, New Mexico town. Oddly enough, the place appeared deserted. There were no patrons in sight, or even staff. Immediately to Jake's right was the restaurant portion of the hotel. Tables were set, awaiting the evening's dinner guests and the smell of what Jake thought was beef stew hung in the air throughout the room. The aroma of cooked beef with potatoes and vegetables started his stomach growling like a starving bear. Then, the rustling of clothing and the scuff of boots caught his attention. The sound came from behind the front desk. With his hand resting on the handle of his Colt, Jake crossed directly to the counter and cautiously peeked over the top. Crouched against the back wall was a man trying his best to fade into the woodwork.

Jake chose not to add to the man's already fear-weakened condition by shouting or making threats. Instead, he tapped lightly on the silver service bell on the counter. The hotel clerk jumped at the sound, banging the top of his head against the rim of the counter.

"Ow! Damn it to hell!" The man stood up, rubbing his head

and cursing continuously until he caught sight of Jake, which made the man freeze in position. With one hand covering his heart and the other still rubbing the fresh bruise on his head, he asked a question that made Jake smile.

"You're not going to kill me, are you?"

The absurdity of the question made him wonder just what sort of stories had been spread around town about him that would make a man assume his death was imminent over something so trivial as a locked door.

Jake couldn't help but laugh at the man's question and offered a calm question of his own in reply. "Any reason why I should?"

The man's eyes rolled a little as he pondered Jake's question. "Ah, no... no! No reason at all," answered the man with a nervous laugh.

"Then don't sweat it." Jake saw the hotel register to his right and pulled it over in front of him. "I'm going to need a room for the night." As he reached for the pen and dipped it into the ink well, he added, "And I'm going to want a large helping of whatever that is I smell coming from your kitchen. I've been dreaming of a cold beer all day too, but my taste has changed to something a bit stronger. Bring me a bottle of the best whiskey you've got. Something that won't rot my guts out." After he finished signing his name he walked behind the counter and pulled the key from its hook to room number 13.

"I'm not superstitious," he said with a wink to the clerk, who offered no resistance verbally or physically and just stepped back against the wall, trying to blend in again. "And bring me a full pot of coffee too, while you're at it."

Jake slipped the room key into his vest pocket and walked into the dining room. There was a small table at the far end of the room with just two chairs against the wall under a curtained window. The table offered a clear view of the entire room, as well as the street. He removed his hat, placing it on the table. After a moment's thought, he pulled his Colt from its holster and placed it on the edge of the table, within inches of his hand and then took his seat. It wasn't that he was expecting anything in the way of real trouble, but the sight of the gun at close reach was certain to send a clear message to anyone else in town that he was not in the mood for further foolishness. After he settled in comfortably, he pulled out another match to relight his cigar, which had gone out. He struck a match against the wall. The first drag of sweet tobacco felt good and tasted even better the second time. Now all he needed was that drink.

After a few minutes, Jake saw Sheriff Avery crossing the street, heading straight for the hotel. The clerk had only just left the counter area when he saw Sheriff Avery coming and moved quickly to meet him at the door. Jake couldn't make out everything that was being said, but it was clear by his body language that the clerk was telling the sheriff what had just taken place. How accurate the description was, Jake couldn't be sure. It was clear he was not happy with Jake taking a room, as well as his other demands and the clerk expected the sheriff to do something about it. His final question to the sheriff was loud enough for Jake to hear.

"What am I supposed to do, Sheriff?" pleaded the hotel clerk.

"If I was you, I'd do what the man said, Delbert. And I'd be right quick about it." Then the sheriff removed his hat and dismissively walked past Delbert and into the dining room and over to Jake's table. He spun his hat around in his hand a few times and then tossed it on the table next to Jake's. "I see you've been making friends in my absence." Both men chuckled a little at the sheriff's sarcasm. Then, the tone turned more serious when the sheriff caught sight of Jake's gun sitting on the table. "Expecting trouble?"

"I hope not," said Jake. "I didn't much care for the reception I got out there, so consider this a not-so-subtle warning."

"Can't say as I blame you much," said the sheriff as he leaned forward in his chair. "But believe it or not there are good people here in Delgado Station. They'll warm up to you if you give them half a chance."

Jake raised a quizzical eyebrow at his friend, and then leaned back in his chair until it braced against the wall behind him. "Did that hot afternoon sun cook you senseless, Val? The people in this town are no different from all the rest. It doesn't matter to them that I put my life on the line for that girl or the old man. They believe only what they read in those ridiculous dime novels or hear from drunken old barflies. I'm a gunfighter. To them, that means nothing but trouble."

"They said the same thing about me ten years ago," replied the sheriff. "Now, I'm workin' for 'em. That ought to tell you somethin'."

Jake leaned forward, settling his chair back down on all fours. He untied the holster leg strap to let it hang down, then took his Colt from the table and slid it back into its cradle. "Better?"

The sheriff smiled. "Every little bit helps, Jake."

"I hope you're right, Val. Like I said back out on the road, I'm tired. Tired clean through." Jake laced the fingers of both hands together on the table and hung his head low as he took a deep breath. "My head's been filled with uneasy thoughts and bad dreams lately, Val. It would be nice to stay in one place for more than just a few days at a time for once. I've got devils dancing in my dreams lately."

Val reached a hand across the table and grabbed Jake's forearm firmly. "You got my word, Jake. As long as you're in my town, you'll be welcome. Or at least, left alone. I'll see to it."

It was clear by Jake's expression that Val's words meant something to him. Although he didn't speak, Val knew his gesture and promise were appreciated.

"By the way, Jake, after I dropped old Ben's body off at the emporium, I took your horse and them other two sad-looking animals over to the livery stable and told Gracie to give yours a good rub down and a bag of oats once she's cooled down. Just like you asked."

"I appreciate that, Val. Thanks."

"I also asked her to do what she could for them other two." The sheriff shook his head from side to side in disgust. "Gracie was spittin' mad when she seen the condition of those two. But she'll bring 'em around in time. She's got a special way with animals. What do you want to do with them other two anyway? Technically, they belong to you, I guess. They ain't much to look at, but you might get a few dollars for 'em. Maybe a few more for their saddles and such."

Jake thought about it briefly, recalling the sorry condition he found Orin and Buck's horses. He took another tight drag on his cheroot and spit out some peeling tobacco leaf along with the smoke. "Tell that stable girl you mentioned to do what she can for them, then sell them and give the money to the girl and maybe that old man's family, if he has any. Or put it toward his burial if you think that would be better. Whatever you think is best. Do the same with the saddles and whatever else there is. I sure don't want any of it."

81

Val drummed his hands on the edge of the table, searching for the right words. Finally, he said, "That's good of you, Jake. A lot of people will be glad to hear you done that."

Jake turned away, almost embarrassed at the praise. "All that stuff is nothing to me. What I did, I didn't do for money or praise. That girl and old man have got more need for any money those things bring than me."

Sensing that Jake was feeling uncomfortable, Val quickly shifted the focus of the conversation. "That's a beautiful animal you got there, Jake," he remarked with obvious admiration, but with a sense of curiosity in his voice. "Smart too. Can't say I recognize the breed."

Jake smiled. "You don't recognize the breed because you've likely never seen one before. There are only a few of them in the whole country. It's called a Shagya Arabian."

Val tapped his fingers on the table as if a memory had just returned to him. "So that's what an Arabian looks like! I heard about them, but you're right, I've never seen one before."

Although Arabians were not entirely unfamiliar in the West, they were still relatively rare. A Shagya Arabian, on the other hand, was extremely rare. This particular breed of Arabian was bred in Europe with a variety of Spanish horses. This mix gave the breed the lines of an Arabian, but with the bigger bones of the more common European horses.

"Are they all that color?" asked Val.

Aside from the rarity of the breed itself, the color of Jake's horse was its most striking feature. People who saw it often described it as dripping in blood. Jake liked the image of the famed gunfighter riding a mare covered in blood, "in death" as others called it. He felt it only added to his reputation and gave him an air of mystery and danger that may have staved off more than a few gunfights.

"The man I bought her from said he had never seen a horse of any breed that color before. Said there was something different about her too. That she was smart, yes, but also calm. Too smart and too calm. Owning her made him uncomfortable, he said. So, I bought her. We've been covering most of the western territory for going on ten years now."

Val looked out the window and down the street toward the stable. "Well, she is a beauty and that's a fact," he said. "Gracie was right impressed I can tell you that. That girl knows horse flesh too. I think them two hit it right off."

Jake nodded in recognition of his horse's unique qualities and said, "She is something special."

"What do you call her again?" asked Val. "I think you said, Teacher, right?"

"That's right," answered Jake, with a matter-of-fact tone in his voice.

The sheriff gave his head a tilt. "Why, Teacher?"

"More often than not, a horse is a better judge of people than any other animal I've known." replied, Jake. "Dogs come in a close second. But Teacher… well, she's just got a way about her. I've learned a lot just by trusting her instincts."

Val shook his head with obvious amusement then chose to change the subject. "I took your bed roll and Winchester and put them in my office. Since it looks like you'll be spending the night here at the Bidwell, I'll have your things sent over. That all right with you?"

"I appreciate the courtesy, Val," said Jake. "It means a lot."

"Anything else I can do for you?"

"You wouldn't by any chance be able to persuade whoever's in that kitchen to hurry up and bring me out a plate of that stew

I've been smelling, would you? My stomach has been scratching my spine since I walked in here." Jake's eyes had the desperate look of a seriously hungry man.

Val slammed his right hand down on the table and said, "I'll see what I can do." Standing, he took a few steps into the center of the dining room and yelled to the hotel clerk. "Delbert!" There was no response. "DELBERT! Git yer sorry ass out here!"

The young clerk meekly poked his head around the edge of the doorway that lead into the kitchen. "Yes, Sheriff?"

"Didn't you tell me Mr. Benteen ordered his dinner?" commanded Val.

Delbert looked confused and stepped out into the room, even advancing a few timid steps toward the sheriff. "Well... yes, but I thought... "

"You thought what?" bellowed the man with the badge.

Delbert's confusion grew. He was sure the sheriff was going to side with him and ask Jake to leave. "But, Sheriff... "

"But nothin'! Move yer ass, boy!" The sheriff's voice boomed and made the clerk jump.

Delbert stutter-stepped backward and then shuffled from side to side, not knowing just which way to go first, the kitchen or across the street to the bar for the bottle of whiskey Jake had ordered. "Um... which should I get first, Sheriff? The whiskey or the stew?"

Val turned to Jake for a decision. "Whiskey first, or food?"

Jake smiled, enjoying the playful game both men were playing to toy with the hotel clerk. "Well now, I'm not sure. What do you think, Val?"

The sheriff scratched his stubbled chin as if pretending to consider giving serious consideration to the two possibilities, then looked back at Delbert, who squirmed as if he were about to wet his britches. "What do *you* think Mr. Benteen would like first, Delbert?"

Delbert's eyes danced back and forth, from the sheriff to Jake and back again. He finally decided the bar was the safest place to be and bolted out the door. Val turned to Jake and gave him a broad smile. "Looks like he decided to get you that whiskey first." Val tapped the brim of his hat to Jake and walked out the door.

Jake returned a salute of thanks and then leaned his chair back against the wall again in anticipation of his long-awaited, but well-deserved, dinner and a drink. He only hoped he would be able to finish it in peace.

Chapter Six

To Jake's delight, the beef stew and pot of coffee were brought out before Delbert returned with the full bottle of whiskey. His server was the cook, Berta, a short, stubby woman with a ruddy complexion and badly thinning hair. She brought out Jake's meal and slopped it on his plate in a grand display of courage and contempt, making a point of letting Jake know she was not the least bit happy about it either. She gave each dish an unceremonious slam or drop on the table in front of him and tossed what was clearly a dirty set of silverware in front of him. The clean and nicely arranged place setting Jake had seen earlier on each table was quickly removed with an obvious display of attitude, as if to suggest he was not worthy of the good stuff. Jake just ignored the childish display of attitude and offered a polite, "Thank you, ma'am," which Berta ignored.

Despite the less-than-polite manner of Berta's serving style, her culinary skills were impressive. It wasn't just that Jake was ravenously hungry either and would have been grateful for anything resembling decent food. This food was uncommonly good. The meal was consumed in an almost animalistic display by the gunfighter. After one full plate and a side of biscuits, Jake hollered out for more. "Ma'am, I have got to tell you that this beef stew and biscuits are some of the finest I have ever tasted. I would be most grateful if you would bring me another helping." When Berta brought out seconds for the gunfighter, it appeared as if her attitude had shifted a little in his favor. Any cook appreciates complimentary reviews of their efforts and Berta was no exception.

When he finally felt his stomach had reached its limit, he pushed both the plate and coffee pot aside and reached for the full bottle of whiskey Delbert had left near the end of Jake's first round of stew. Delbert tiptoed in and saw how Jake was devouring his meal and didn't want to get too close for fear of losing a finger. He left the bottle of whiskey on the far edge of the table and scooted for the perceived safety of the kitchen, leaving the front desk unattended.

It had been a long time between drinks and a lot of trail dust had built up in his throat that could only be broken up and washed down by a bottle of whiskey, and the smoother the better. He had told Delbert he wanted the best whiskey in town, and he was more than satisfied, surprised even, to see a full bottle of Jameson's Irish Whiskey sitting in front of him... and the seal had not been broken either. That was going to be his dessert. No cheap, rot-gut replacement whiskey had been slipped into an old, empty bottle, with an inflated price to go with it.

The first two shots washed down the food and a good deal of the tension Jake had been carrying since he rode that buckboard into town. The next two shots made a noticeable change in his demeanor. Pushing his weight against the back legs of his chair allowed him to tip back against the wall again and look out the window of the hotel. Another shot or two of this stuff, he thought, and he would sleep soundly tonight. The townspeople were sufficiently cautious, even terrified of him, so any chance of his being disturbed seemed remote. Val was an old friend who understood his life and would also make double sure that no one would bother him if he closed and locked the door to his room. The whiskey would give him a solid night's sleep and

Jake thought the hangover that would inevitably follow was worth the price.

As he leaned forward and settled his chair on all four legs again, he poured another shot and stood up. He wasn't drunk... yet, but he was well on his way to enjoying the pleasant numbness that was beginning to settle over him. Jake's comfort was short-lived and was immediately shoved back into mental oblivion by the shattering of glass. A large fragment of a building brick landed on the table Jake had just stepped away from. Shards of heavy leaded glass sprayed the room, some of it striking Jake on the left side of his face, leaving small cuts on his cheek and ear. Without realizing how or even when, Jake found himself standing full breast at the center of the window with his gun drawn and cocked. Instinct had pushed aside the creeping effects of the whiskey, replacing it with pure adrenaline. As he surveyed the scene before him, nothing immediately caught his eye that would indicate the origin of the brick. Then, a vocal challenge rang out from somewhere down the street and just out of sight of the hotel window.

"Come on out, gunfighter! I'm waitin' for ya!"

The voice was unmistakable, even though Jake had only had a brief acquaintance with its owner. It was Jeff, the boy who thought himself a man because he carried a gun, two in fact, and was foolish enough to try and use them. Even back on the road when he embarrassed the boy by ripping the packed holsters from his belt with two amazing shots from his Winchester, Jake knew he was going to have to face this punk sooner or later. It was a little later, but not as late as Jake was hoping. Tomorrow would have been a better time to face this boy, when his head was clear of whiskey and not battling the bitterness, he felt over the way many people treated him after all he had done. Now, the whiskey in him made things uncertain, even for Jake. He stepped back away from the window and waited for another challenge to be leveled at him.

"Ya hear me, gunfighter!" The boy's voice was pitched high and shrill. "I'm callin' you out! And this time you ain't got your Winchester to back you up. I saw the sheriff take it to his office. You'll have to face me with a hog leg tied to your hip, like a real man!"

It was true that Jake Benteen was known more for his uncanny ability with a Winchester, but only a fool would assume his skills with killing tools were limited to the power, distance and accuracy of a rifle. To survive as long as Jake had, mastery of all things in the gunfighter's trade was a necessity. Had the boy seen Jake's speed and marksmanship with a pistol earlier that day on the trail against Orin and Buck, he might reconsider his current course of action. But Jake knew that reason and logic were in short supply right now. This boy was trying to salvage a bruised ego and lay claim to something no man would pursue if he really knew the cost.

Jake released a deep sigh. On the table was a full shot of whiskey, while his right held his nickel-plated .45. With his left hand, he poured the full shot of whiskey back into the bottle that was sitting on the table. Not a single drop missed its mark. Then, he flipped his Colt into the now empty hand and opened the shell guard with his right to check his load. Five .45-caliber shells rested in their nests, with the receiving cylinder empty. Jake pulled a single cartridge from his belt and slipped it into place. He closed the shell guard with a snap and then plunged the gun into its cradle. The coffee pot he had pushed aside earlier in favor of the whiskey looked inviting. He touched the side of the pot. It was still warm, so he poured himself a small cup and tossed it down, hoping it would offset the whiskey he had been building up.

As Jake made his way out the door and onto the sidewalk, he noticed Val coming from up the street at a dead run. His stride bore the mark of a man in obvious pain with every step he took. His face, however, showed more concern for what was about to take place than for the obvious level of discomfort he was experiencing.

"Now you hold on there, Jeff," the sheriff shouted from about thirty yards away. Jake was about half that distance from the boy and off to one side, under the roof line that hung over the sidewalk of the hotel. "There'll be no gunfightin' today. Not while I'm sheriff."

Jake called out to his friend. "Val!" The sheriff stopped, standing even with Jake, glancing back and forth from his friend and the boy in the street. "Let me handle this Val. It'll never end otherwise."

The sheriff saw something in Jake's eyes that told him he was right. They weren't the eyes of a killer. Something was brewing inside the gunfighter that was calculated and showed a plan. The lawman took a few cautious steps toward his friend.

"You sure you know what you're doin', Jake?"

Jeff shouted his courage from his position in the street. "He don't need your help, Sheriff, and neither do I. This is our business, not yours!"

Val turned to the boy with a look of both pity and disgust. "Are you in that much of a hurry to die, Jeff?"

"I ain't the one that's gonna be eatin' dirt, Sheriff," replied Jeff with a giggle in his voice.

During the exchange between Jeff and the sheriff, Jake had moved several yards closer to his challenger. He was still under the sidewalk overhang but stopped at the edge of a support post on the corner that led down into the street. Neither Jeff nor the sheriff even noticed Jake's movement. Jeff turned his attention away from the sheriff and gave a jerky twist to his body when he realized Jake wasn't where he thought he was. It only took a fraction of a second to relocate him, but the realization that he had lost sight of his foe unnerved the would-be gunfighter and made him grab for his guns. Jake never moved, but remained motionless, then shifted his weight, leaning against the corner post. Jeff's guns were removed from their holsters, but not fully exposed or aimed at a specific target. Jake just raised his right hand up, as if to indicate to stop and then pointed to the inside of his vest pocket.

"Mind if I smoke?"

Jeff was suitably confused about what to do with his guns and even looked to the sheriff with plaintive eyes that asked for advice. Val gave no obvious signs that were of any help to the boy. Finally, in an effort to salvage his cool, Jeff slipped his guns back into their holsters and raised both hands to his sides and smiled.

"You want a last smoke before you die, gunfighter, that's just fine by me." The boy dropped both hands down on the handles of his Colts and then shifted his weight to one hip, striking a falsely casual pose.

By now, Val had pretty much assessed Jake's intentions and had decided he was going to let him play his hand. If his hunch was right, there would be no blood spilled in his street today. Not fatally anyway.

The burned-down cigar in Jake's mouth was tossed into the dirt, off to one side. As Jake reached inside for a fresh cheroot and a match, he also stepped down from the sidewalk and began walking slowly toward his nervous opponent. This was the same move he had employed against the oversized loudmouth, Amos, less than an hour earlier but a little further down the street. Fortunately, Jeff was still walking his way back to town when all that happened and he missed the ploy. Although the move was essentially the same, the intent was decidedly different. This boy was armed with two fully loaded Colts and was eager to prove he knew how to use them. The original pistol rig the kid wore earlier was slightly damaged by Jake when he blew them off the boy's hips with his Winchester. The leather was torn, and each Smith & Wesson had enough damage that couldn't be repaired in time for his showdown with the man who had humiliated him. The rig he was wearing now was his backup, the first set of guns he ever owned. They weren't as flashy as his other set, but Jeff was angry enough, cocky enough and just plain dumb enough not to care. Besides, it didn't matter how good or impressive the hardware for killing was. It was more about showing how skilled the man who used them was. This kid was an amateur. Jake was a virtuoso.

The gunfighter snapped the tip off the match with his thumb and lit the sweet-smelling cheroot as he continued his advance toward the boy.

"Is this your first time, son?" Jake tossed the spent match at Jeff's feet, bouncing it off the toe of his right boot. When Jeff's eyes followed the descent of the match, Jake pulled a long drag off the cigar and blew it slowly back into the boy's face. The cloud of smoke caused him to choke back a cough and squint his eyes.

The question was a simple, yet not immediately clear one. Jeff had to search his brain for what he thought was the appropriate response. "What?" The reply came out almost by accident and was not what he hoped for. It wasn't cool or defiant. But it was the best he could do.

For Jake, it was almost too easy toying with an immature mind like this, taunting and teasing the boy and playing with his nerves. The stakes were too high to be taken lightly, however, and Jake wasn't about to let this kid slip away or get the jump on him later. He was too headstrong and unpredictable, like an old stick of dynamite that's been sitting in the sun too long. Once it begins to sweat, there's no telling what might set it off, or when.

Jake took another long drag on his cigar and stepped in closer. He then spoke in slow deliberate tones, looking directly into Jeff's eyes, never blinking. The smoke trickled out at varying speeds and thicknesses, depending on the word. "Is this the first time you ever faced a man in the street intent on killing him?"

Jeff broke his hold on Jake's eyes and rubbed his own to clear the smoke. "You ain't scarin' me, gunfighter," said the boy. "I faced plenty of men before."

It was a lie, of course, and Jake expected nothing less, but just smiled and leaned in closer to the boy's face until they passed the same breath back and forth the way lovers do. The air was a mixture of sweet tobacco, whiskey and beer. The beer was Jeff's contribution, quickly tossed down with encouragement from other gutless wonders at the saloon down the street. It was likely they were all still hiding inside, some watching, others waiting and listening for the report of gunfire that would tell them who walked away and who lay bleeding or dying in the street.

"Did you ever look into their eyes like I'm doing with you?" Jake's voice was soft, almost soothing.

"You're talkin' crazy," whined the boy. "What kind of talk is that?"

Jake leaned in even closer. "You know what I see in your

eyes, boy?"

Jeff almost seemed hypnotized by the question and tried to turn his own eyes inside his mind as if to look in on himself. Finally, he spat out a sassy response that was supposed to show how confident he was. "No, gunfighter, what do you see."

"Someone who's about to piss his britches."

Jake pushed past the boy and walked about ten paces up the street, exposing his back to his opponent. He knew the boy was too stunned to be of any threat just now and he needed to reposition himself in the street to his best advantage. It took Jeff a few seconds to digest what Jake had said, then he noticed that Jake had turned around and was now facing him, but with the sun to his back and hanging low on the horizon. The boy had to squint to get a clear view of Jake.

"Anytime you're ready, son. I've got a hot bath, clean sheets and half a bottle of whiskey waiting for me." Jake relaxed his right hand over his .45 and was still puffing on his cheroot as he rolled it over and over in his mouth with his left.

Val had stepped off the street and up onto the sidewalk in front of a store with a sign that read, "Nana Beth's Fashions for Ladies." Inside, he could see curious onlookers peeking through the leaded glass or hiding behind store mannequins.

"What's it going to be, son?" Jake's question was firm but strangely cold. "Either draw on me or go home."

Jeff's eyes were filling with tears and his hands shook. Sweat was dripping down the back of his neck from under his hat. He looked desperately from side to side hoping to find someone to offer encouragement, even glancing over his left shoulder and back toward the saloon down the street. Val had moved closer, up the side of the street until he was standing parallel to Jeff. He could see by the boy's face that he was about to cry. It was over, he thought. Jake had played the boy like a cheap fiddle and gotten him to crack under the pressure. Any second now this boy was going to cut and run, Val was sure of it.

Suddenly, a voice from down the street in front of the saloon broke the silence. It was the worst possible thing anyone could have said or done, and the timing was sadly perfect.

"Don't let him run ya down, Jeff," came the call. "You can take him easy! He's all talk!"

Once the first declaration of support was heard, others quickly followed. Soon, a full chorus of saloon dwellers were shouting their own forms of encouragement, all of it aimed at either convincing him he was faster than the gunfighter and braver as well. Unfortunately, some even challenged the kid's nerves. The combination was too much for Jeff to bear. He took a deep breath, then shivered and set himself, shaking the fear from his hands and dancing his fingers over his guns.

Jake was instantly filled with disgust at the saloon harpies who were too selfish or too stupid to leave well enough alone. Now, it was almost certain that someone was going to die.

"Don't listen to those fools, son. Walk away and grow old." Jake dropped his cigar in the dirt.

"I ain't afraid of you, gunfighter," said the boy. Although his voice was still shaking, it was clear he was not going to back down. "Like I said, you ain't got your Winchester to back you up. That makes me the better man with my Colts!" The boy took another deep breath to calm his nerves. "Make your play!"

"If you're that eager to die, son, I'm not going to rush it." Jake folded his arms across his chest.

Jeff saw this move as an opportunity to strike first and jerked hard for his guns. The instant he made the decision to draw, he was convinced he had the drop on the gunfighter due to the distance Jake's hand was from his lone gun. That is why the shock of a .45 caliber slug shattering the thumb of his left hand was almost dream-like. It was followed by an identical shot that blew away the thumb on his right hand. Jeff stood, unable to speak. The real pain and agony were still moments away, waiting for his body to catch up to the reality of what just happened. He had barely cleared leather before the gunfighter found his mark… twice. Now, all the boy could do was stare at his bloody, useless hands. He dropped to his knees, still unable to absorb the horrific vision, the pain just beginning to sink in.

Soon, the street was filled with people eager to see the carnage many of them helped create or did nothing to stop. Val slowly made his way through the crowd gathered around Jeff and picked up his two blood-covered Colts. He then reached under Jeff's left arm and pulled him to his feet.

"Let's go see Doc Gibbons, boy, before you bleed to death in the street." He turned the stunned young man around and began walking him back down the street to the doctor's office. "The rest of you folks go on about your business. You've caused enough trouble for one day."

Jake picked up his still-smoking cheroot from the dirt, blew off the dust and shoved it back in his mouth, biting down hard. The townspeople now turned their attention to him. Some gave him glaring looks of hate, while others seemed genuinely impressed and nodded their approval over his decision to spare the boy's life. Jake was unmoved either way. He pushed past the crowd, ignoring all comments, good and bad, and made his way back to the hotel. The hot bath and clean sheets would have to wait a little longer. Right now, that half bottle of whiskey was like a siren calling his name, luring his tortured soul with the temptation of brain-numbing sleep and he was not about to fight it.

Chapter Seven

At the same crossroads where the two signposts stood, one pointing the way to Delgado Station and the other to Tres Mesa, two riders sat their mounts and scanned the horizon. One was a short, stubby little fellow without a trace of hair on his entire body. He stood about four and a half feet tall, weight approaching two hundred pounds, and rode a small pack mule named Sugar Pie. His name was Potch, a former circus clown who now worked as an assistant, of sorts, to the man riding the Appaloosa to his right.

A tall, solidly-built man with a broad-brimmed hat that shaded his pale blue eyes was a sharp contrast to little Potch. His hair was long and black as coal and pulled back in a ponytail. A braided strap with a silver buckle held it all in place. A leather vest was all he wore to cover his well-muscled chest. Buckskin pants laced up the sides with rawhide covered his legs. He even wore a loincloth, front and back, made of calfskin that had painted symbols on it with meanings no one understood. If truth be told, neither did he. He just liked the way it looked. On his feet were moccasins that had beautifully beaded calf-wraps that went up to his knees. His name was Wolf.

At first glance, many thought him to be Apache. He certainly looked the part. His real name was Anthony Bentino, born to Italian immigrants in Hell's Kitchen on the middle west side of Manhattan Island along the Hudson River. After a series of petty crimes ranging from burglary to street hustling, he graduated to the brutal murder of a dockworker. Witnesses claimed Tall Tony, as he was known then, simply walked up behind his victim and drove a grappling hook straight down into the top of the man's skull. When asked why he did it, he replied, with the cold assurance of a man convinced he was justified, saying, "I just got tired of him tellin' me what to do."

Escaping before the police could apprehend him proved simple enough. Within an hour of his first killing, he was signing on board an outbound cargo ship called *The Wayward Wind*, set to sail out of New York Harbor, bound for the Gulf Coast. Once word got out that he had made his escape aboard a ship sailing south, away from Manhattan Island, the authorities gave up any attempt at apprehending him and only put out a warrant, essentially a warning, to authorities outside the jurisdiction of the State of New York. He was no longer their problem, which was just fine by them.

While docked in New Orleans, he committed his second murder, this one a dispute over claims of a rigged game of dice, which was true. The dice belonged to Wolf. Just as before, he escaped the authorities by signing on to another ship that was making its way along the Gulf Coast, headed for Galveston, Texas. From there, he made his way further west, robbing and killing as he went. Eventually, he settled in Tres Mesa, where he soon took command of as motley a crew of outlaws and miscreants as the West had to offer.

"This is my town!" he often boasted, and equally as often killed anyone who disagreed with his claim. It wasn't that he was faster with a gun, more deadly in a knife fight, or stronger in a fistfight than anyone else. Rather, Wolf commanded obedience and an odd form of respect for one reason and one reason only; he was just plain crazy. That's why his men feared him. His erratic bursts of rage made him unpredictable and therefore, always dangerous. Aside from any perceived level of disrespect, he couldn't tolerate losing, at anything, regardless if it was a fair game, or a fair fight. Eventually, he would find a way to "even the score," as he perceived it.

Most men stayed in Tres Mesa because they were wanted in too many other parts of the country and had no place else to go. Letting Wolf rule the roost was easier than risking a run-in with Federal Marshals, Rangers or even the military, which could result in jail time, or hanging in some dirt water town over a crime committed somewhere else long forgotten. In Tres Mesa, they were close enough to the Mexican border to make a run for it should authorities get too close. Even the Mexican Federales couldn't touch them as long as they stayed just over the border. So, Tres Mesa was something of a neutral zone, the perfect location, as long as those who chose to stay showed blind obedience to Wolf. Although he was ruthless, Wolf kept them supplied with enough food, drink and women to make it worth their while. Stay on Wolf's good side and life was relatively simple, and profitable, however brief that life may be.

That is not what Orin and Buck were doing, however, when they came across Ben and Juneann's wagon, loaded with supplies from across the border. Initially, Ben had tried to discourage Juneann from riding along on such a long, hot journey, but she loved going into Mexico with old Ben, who thought of her as something of an adopted daughter. Juneann's mother knew Ben was a loving and trustworthy guardian for her daughter and spending the day with him was always preferrable to sitting home alone, even on a day as hot as this one. Since there had never been any significant problems with the men of Tres Mesa before, due mainly to the unofficial truce between the two towns,

99

everyone assumed both Ben and Juneann would be safe. Of course, they hadn't counted on Orin and Buck breaking the truce.

When the two brothers passed Ben and Juneann's wagon as it was heading back to Delgado Station, they noticed it was full of provisions, most of which were things they knew would be appreciated back in their own town. It was already a stiflingly hot day and due to get even hotter, so they both figured it was worth the risk. Orin charged his horse in front of the wagon, blocking the road, and ordered Ben to hold up and step down. At the time, they didn't see Juneann, who had been sleeping under a tarp in the back of the wagon to escape the intense heat of the sun. What neither brother was prepared for was that Ben was not about to give up his charge so easily when ordered to. Instead, Ben snapped the reins and tried to make a run for it off the road and around Orin, hoping he could get far enough away and close enough to town for Orin and Buck to back off. After a few gunshots, the wagon team bolted out of control and stampeded wildly off to a small, seldom-used side road. It was either Orin or Buck that accidentally shot one of the team horses, forcing Ben to pull up. From that point on, it was the futile shootout between Ben and the Wheatly Brothers that resulted in the carnage Jake stumbled upon less than a half hour later.

Wolf had sent his two boys out to scout around for food, women, whiskey and anything else that looked good. But they were late, a lot later than it should have taken them, by Wolf's reasoning. They were also supposed to stick to Wolf's cardinal rule and cut south across the Mexican border and do their hunting there. But Orin thought it was too hot and that crossing the border would take too long and decided to see if there was anything a little closer to home. That was when they spotted Ben's wagon heading back to Delgado Station. Orin figured Wolf wouldn't mind if he and Buck checked it out. If it had something worthwhile, what difference would it make where they got it from? But that was not true today, or any other day. They had a good thing going and Wolf had made it clear to all his men that they were only to raid on the Mexican side of the border. "Ya don't piss in your own britches," he would say. "It draws flies."

Most men saw the logic in Wolf's reasoning and did exactly what he said. Orin and Buck had barely enough brains between them, so it wasn't unreasonable to assume they would try for something easier. Wolf and Potch continued to look for signs along the horizon and down the road for any indication of Orin and Buck. No dust clouds were visible, but Wolf caught sight of about a dozen black specs floating in the air less than a mile west of the main road.

"Buzzards," Wolf said softly. "And lots of 'em. Way too many for a prairie chicken or a coyote. Must be something big."

Potch nodded his agreement with Wolf's assessment of the situation and squealed like an excited child at the prospect of opening Christmas presents. "Are we gonna go see what they's eatin' Mister Wolf?"

"Might as well see what it is," he said, with some suspicion. "It better not be anything those two juggle-heads did though, I can tell you that. If they broke my rule and stirred up trouble on this side of the border, I'll skin them to the bone." Wolf jabbed his spurs into his mount's rump and began to cut from the road in a straight line, heading for the buzzards.

Potch followed as quickly as his small mule, Sugar Pie, could go, squealing and giggling as he bounced up and down in his saddle. "You think maybe them buzzards is feasting on our boys, Mister Wolf?"

"If they ain't, I will be!" he replied. Another jab of his spurs and a slap of the reins sent his horse into a full gallop. Potch did the same to Sugar Pie, for all the good it would do, giggling and squealing louder with every bounce.

After about ten minutes, Wolf pulled up on the reins and choked his horse to a full stop. Potch was still several minutes behind, unable to keep up the pace on his mule. From inside a leather pouch made of human skin, Wolf pulled a brass spyglass he had stolen from a drunk Cavalry captain during one of his raids across the border. He had seen it hanging by a leather thong from the man's belt as he stood at a bar in a seedy saloon on the border in Juarez, Mexico. Wolf offered to buy it, but the man politely refused. Undeterred, Wolf waited outside the saloon until the man staggered down the street an hour or so later. His gait was clumsy and halting, the result of too much tequila and mezcal. As he crossed by an alley, Wolf stepped silently out of the darkness with a Bowie knife drawn and ready. With a sharp snap of his wrist, Wolf laid open the unsuspecting man's throat clear to the neck bone. The move was so smooth and fast that it left the man standing bewildered, unsure of what had just happened and totally unaware that his life had just ended. With another quick flick of the knife blade, the leather thong was cut, and the spyglass dropped into Wolf's hand as the man dropped into the dust. Wolf walked away, pleased with his trophy and unconcerned that another innocent life had crossed his path only to die in a pool of his own blood.

Through the haze of the afternoon sun, Wolf could make out three large shapes on the ground, smothered by buzzards. He was scanning the surrounding area for other signs of life or death when Potch and his pack mule finally caught up.

"What'chya see, Mr. Wolf sir? Any sign of our boys?"

Wolf continued to scan the countryside as he answered.

"Looks like Orin and Buck just might have met up with someone who wasn't very agreeable." He slipped the spyglass back into its gruesome sleeve. "Let's go see what's what." he ordered and drove his spurs hard into his horse's rump again, sending it squealing into a hard gallop.

Potch could only follow at half the pace but still managed to give off that God-awful giggle that could be heard echoing across the desert. "Oh, our boys are sure to be in trouble, yes sir! Sure to be in trouble." With frantic slaps with the reins on his mule's neck, Potch tried to catch up to his master. He didn't want to miss anything.

By the time Potch had reached the site of Orin and Buck's demise, Wolf had already dismounted and was pacing the area, looking for clues. Pulling a Remington .50 caliber from his belt, he fired into the flock of vultures that had been tearing away at the flesh of the dead draft horse and the two brothers. This was done mostly just to clear the buzzards away, but Wolf also did it just because he enjoyed killing… anything.

Although he wasn't an Apache Indian by birth, as many suspected, and was a myth he perpetuated, he had learned enough about tracking and reading signs to get a good idea of what had happened. It was likely a supply wagon from Mexico heading back to Delgado Station, but had gotten turned around, probably by Orin and Buck. The wagon tracks indicated it had come from the main road, then was stopped here. After what was done was done, it had been turned around and headed back to town. Not his town either.

The signs of a single horse and rider were also clear, complete with hoof and boot prints, as well as spent shell casings. This was enough for Wolf to know the basics of what went down. He also concluded that whoever it was that got the drop on Orin and Buck was no amateur. The bullet wounds showed an uncanny level of accuracy mixed with vicious intent. Something Wolf admired, as long as it was used to his liking. In this case, it was used against two of his own men. That made him spitting mad.

"I want the man who did this!" he screamed, as he fired two more shots at some returning buzzards, killing one instantly. Another had its wing shattered by the impact of the bullet and lay screaming in the dirt by Buck's ravaged body. Wolf walked calmly over to the agonized creature, staring down at it with blood-filled eyes. At first, he held his pistol over the bird, ready to end its suffering with one last explosion of lead. Then, he withdrew his aim and holstered the weapon. He couched slightly and then suddenly leaped into the air, crashing down on the wounded animal with both feet, kicking and stomping it into the desert dust until its blood mixed with Buck's. Even Potch was startled by Wolf's brutal tirade and instinctively pulled back on Sugar Pie's reins, backing the mule up several steps.

The air was still. Not a whisper of sound came from mule, horse, buzzard or man. Wolf kicked the dirt and scraped it with his bloody moccasins to remove some of the blood, then turned to face Potch.

"Haul your fat little ass back to town and get me as many men as we got in town and have 'em meet me at the saloon!" Wolf spoke in a voice that sounded more like a growl. It was so low that Potch had to lean in to be sure he heard him.

"What are we gonna do, Mr. Wolf?" Potch was looking at Wolf with concern because there was an expression in his face and a look in his eyes that he had never seen before, and it unnerved him. "We goin' after the men who did this to our boys?"

"It was only *one* man who did this... and I want him," growled Wolf as he paced in an agitated circle. "And when I find him, I'm gonna make new moccasins with the flesh on his back and feed his balls to my dogs!" Wolf looked up at the sky and scanned the horizon until he spotted the moon hanging low, but still clearly visible. "We got ourselves a Black Moon comin' little man. That's what they call providence."

"A Black Moon, Mr. Wolf?" Potch had never heard the term before and noticed that Wolf seemed transfixed on the daylight moon on the horizon. "What's a Black Moon, Mr. Wolf?"

"It's a special moon, little man," replied Wolf. "An extra one that comes in a month only once in a great while. We got one comin' and I think this one is made just for me. It's an omen." Wolf turned to Potch now and asked, "You know what an omen is, don't ya, little man?"

Potch quickly scanned his surroundings as if looking for a ghost. He was getting scared now. "An omen, Mr. Wolf?" Potch took his hat off and wiped his bald head of the sweat dripping down his face. "It's a sign of something bad, ain't it?"

"That depends on which side you're on." Wolf was doing something Potch had seldom seen. He was smiling. Oh, he had seen his boss break into something vaguely resembling a smile before, but it was usually about some sick and cruel thing he had done to someone, so that type of smile was common. The smile on his face this time was different and made him look... happy.

"The man that did this to two of my boys will die hard when my Black Moon rises." Wolf's smile grew wider.

There was already one man in the territory that Potch knew could send shivers down his spine and that was the man standing before him. He didn't like to think that there was another man out there capable of the same evil he often witnessed in Wolf. Potch's

105

next statement was a pathetic attempt at getting Wolf to change his mind and forget about the two worthless men whose remains were already rotting in the desert sun.

"You think this fella is still around, Mr. Wolf? You don't think he just robbed our boys and then run off?" Potch paused, hoping Wolf would agree. Wolf said nothing. "That's what I think. Yes sir, I think he just robbed Orin and Buck and then hightailed it north. That's what I'd a done for sure." Potch managed a little smile, displaying his rotting teeth, hoping Wolf would agree.

Still, Wolf said nothing. Instead, he took two quick steps toward Potch and his mule and grabbed the reins with his right hand and latched on to Potch's grubby shirt with his left. Then Wolf released the reins and grabbed Potch with both hands, pulling him from the saddle, holding him at eye level. "He's still here! Somewhere!" he growled. "I can smell him! And soon, I'm gonna *taste* him!" He then tossed Potch to the side, throwing him to the ground. "Now don't argue with me, you little puke. Just do what I say! Round up my men! Have 'em meet me at the saloon in three hour… no more!" Wolf reached down and pulled Potch to his feet and leaned in close enough for their noses to touch. "You hear me?"

Then, he threw the little clown to the ground again. Potch bounced hard and rolled under his mule. Sugar Pie bucked and kicked out with her hind legs, barely missing Potch's head. Scrambling to his feet, Potch quickly gained control of his mule and pulled himself back into the saddle.

"Yes, sir, Mr. Wolf! Yes, sir!" assured Potch, in his most obedient voice. "I'll get every man in Tres Mesa. I'll have 'em ready and waitin' for you right quick. You can count on it."

Wolf looked off in the distance again and drew a deep,

satisfying breath. "There's gonna be a party soon, Potch," said Wolf, as he stood motionless, sniffing the air. "I'm gonna enjoy myself."

For a brief moment, Potch sat on his mule, Sugar Pie, transfixed by the glare in Wolf's eyes and the calm in his voice. The eyes were filled with a flame of rage he had never seen before, yet the voice sounded peaceful. It scared him more than usual because this wasn't his typical display of anger. He had seen Wolf mad before, that wasn't at all unusual. There was the time Wolf got mad at one of his own men for failing to bring him a fresh bottle of whiskey fast enough. Plus, the man was a little insubordinate, saying something like, "Hold your horses," which brought a chuckle from the other drinkers in the saloon. Wolf felt it weakened his authority in front of his men, so he smashed the fresh bottle across the man's face and then proceeded to use the jagged remains to carve away his flesh as if it were a giant lump of cheese. The man lay on the floor moaning and coughing up blood for nearly an hour before Wolf finally shot him through the head just to shut him up. Potch thought that was the worst thing he had ever seen one man do to another. Something told him he was about to see something even worse.

Chapter Eight

Jake rolled over in his drunken haze until he was flat on his back staring at the ceiling. For a brief moment, he was numb and unsure of where he was. The bottle of whiskey had done its job all too well. As he rubbed the sleep from his eyes, he noticed an odd pattern that was stained into the ceiling directly over his head. It resembled a flower, a Texas Rose, he had seen on a windowsill in Huston, some years back. He couldn't remember when. When he swung his legs over the side of the bed, he popped up into a sitting position that left him staring directly into a wall about ten feet away. There were cracks and odd patterns in the plaster and paint that resembled a kind of road map. It was all a bit confusing and hard for Jake to absorb given his condition. A hangover on bad whiskey was a true horror. Reasonably good whiskey didn't offer one much better, especially if one were to drink the entire bottle, which Jake came close to accomplishing, but not quite. He still had a few healthy shots left of the Jameson's before he passed out.

On the washstand was a fresh bowl of water and a clean towel that cradled a bar of soap. As bad as he felt, the thought of scraping some of the road off his body was a welcome diversion to his throbbing head. He would have preferred a hot bath, but this would have to do. When he made it to his feet, the pain in his head increased tenfold. It was enough to make him sit back down again. Why had he gotten himself so drunk anyway? Then the memory of that young punk looking to make a name for himself came flooding back, making its way past the booze. He remembered now. A sudden flush of anger at the memory shot through his body but was quickly pushed aside. He gave the boy plenty of chances to walk away. It was his own damned fault he chose to call him out. This was no time for guilt and self-recrimination. Any other man would have used the opportunity to put another notch on his gun handle and add to his reputation. Jake Benteen was a lot of things, but he was never that cold.

Grabbing the brass bedpost, Jake pulled himself up to his feet and staggered his way over to the washstand. There was an oval-shaped mirror on the back of it that was tilted slightly upward. He pulled it level until he saw his image clearly reflected. What he saw was a very tired man. His own eyes looking back were unsettling, forcing him to look away... from himself.

When he plunged his hands into the bowl of water it was so warm it felt more like a bowl of sweat. Cupping his hands, Jake pulled the tepid liquid to his face and through his dusty and dirty hair. Rinsing the dirt from his face and eyes seemed to bring him back to life a bit. He grabbed the pitcher of water on the washstand and leaned over the bowl and slowly poured the remaining water over his head. He could see the dust and dirt rinse out of his hair and into the bowl. He repeated the rinse until the water was gone. Jake peeled off his shirt and embraced the idea of scrubbing himself clean with a vengeance. When he finished, the bar of soap was reduced to a sliver and the wash towel a blackened, soiled rag. But the transformation was striking. What looked back from the mirror now was a ruggedly handsome man who had clearly seen better days but was considerably more presentable. The scars, both physical and mental were still visible though.

On his left shoulder, just below the clavicle, was a perfectly round scar about the size of a five-dollar gold piece. It was from a bullet fired by Tate Barlow in one of Jake's most notorious gunfights. Similar to the gunfight his friend Val had witnessed, where his opponent beat him to the draw and the bullet passing under his armpit, this was strikingly similar. In this case, witnesses were convinced Barlow had beaten Jake to the draw that time too… and they were right. Had the gunman been a couple of inches lower and closer to center, Jake would have been the one to fall into the dust of the Loredo street. As it was, Jake's bullet, though fired a fraction later, hit Barlow square in the center of his chest, shattering his sternum and obliterating his heart, killing him instantly. Spectators mistakenly assumed Jake had beaten his opponent to the draw simply because he was the only one who remained standing. No one knew he had actually been hit. Fortunately for Jake, the bullet only struck meat, passing completely through, missing anything vital and buried itself in the dust of the street behind him. Jake was able to make it to his horse with what amounted to a casual stroll. Once he was safely out of town, he made camp along a secluded riverbank where he tended to his wound by pulling the slug from a fresh .45 shell and pouring the gunpowder into the bullet hole. He lit the powder with his cigar and then passed out from the pain. Teacher stood guard over Jake like a watchdog, never moving until he saw him begin to stir back to life more than an hour later. Jake drank as much water as he could hold and poured some whiskey over the wound, which made him scream in agony before he passed out again. If anyone had come by while Jake was unconscious, it's not likely Teacher could have done anything tangible to stop them from hurting him, but there was no doubt she would have died trying. When Jake awoke, a full day later, the wound was cauterized and healing nicely.

Staring at the scar brought back a flood of memories that forced Jake to take a personal inventory. Noticing all of the other brushes with death, the other scars that marked his body like a road map of his life, made him hang his head. How, from where it all began, he thought, did he ever end up here, and still breathing?

A knock at the door startled him out of his trance, allowing his instincts to take over. As often happened, Jake found himself positioned, gun in hand at the ready, before he really even knew the reason why, or even if it was justifiable. Stepping to the latch side of the door, he placed his left hand on the door handle but pressed his back to the wall. As he spoke, he cocked back the hammer of his Colt with a cupped hand to muffle the sound. "Who is it?"

"Gracie McCall," came the reply. "You owe me twenty dollars, assuming you're the owner of that Arabian I've got eating all my oats and hay."

The voice was strong, yet obviously feminine. Jake turned, facing the door, but still kept his left hand on the knob, with his right hand manning the Colt, but lightly pressed up against the wall, out of sight. He opened the door slowly, just enough to see the person on the other side but blocked it with his left foot so the door couldn't be pushed open further without considerable effort.

"That would be Teacher," said Jake. "She's tired and hungry and she's earned it." He stepped back, allowing the door to open fully into the room. Jake stood clear, framed in the opening, his eyes fixed on a small, but sturdy woman dressed in men's clothing and covered with all the makings of a livery stable. Her hair was long, with a mix of brown and gold, all pulled back and tied with what looked like a strip of leather. She wore a man's checkered shirt that was obviously two sizes two big. The sleeves were rolled up to the elbows, but the body of the shirt was filled out as much as the buttons could handle. It was tucked in at the waist.

Jake gave a quick, cursory glance at the young woman before he answered. "Can't say I care much for your customer relations, Miss McCall," he said with a sly smile. "Most livery hands don't come callin' for the bill before it's due."

Gracie McCall took a defiant stance, folding her arms across her substantial chest and cocking her head to the right. "Don't much care what you like, mister, just so long as you pay your bill. And given who you are, I'd just as soon get my money upfront." She unfolded her arms and pressed her hands on her hips. "Besides, I ain't no stable hand neither. McCall's Livery is my place you boarded your horse at. I own it, free and clear, and I make my own rules. You don't like 'em, you're free to take Teacher someplace else."

"*Is* there someplace else?" asked Jake rhetorically.

"No. Tough luck for you, huh?" She shifted her weight from one hip to the other, then held out her right hand. "Twenty dollars."

Jake released the hammer on the Colt, pulling it away from the wall and slipped the gun into the front of his waist. The whole movement did not go unnoticed by Gracie McCall, whose eyes popped as wide as a child's at seeing something that was more awesome than frightening. As he crossed over to his saddle bags to get his money he said, "Come on in. I'll get your money."

The young woman cleared her throat to disguise any sign of fear… or interest. "I'm fine right here," she said, folding her arms again with a snide chuckle as if to let Jake know she wasn't going to fall for an old line like that.

"What's the matter, afraid I'll bite you?" Jake let out a small chuckle as well, just to let her know he wasn't intimidated either.

"I bite back," she snapped. "You best believe it if you know what's good for you."

Jake pulled out a small roll of bills from one of his saddle bags and peeled off a twenty note and extended his hand. It was time for her to go. "Here ya go."

"Not paper, mister. Gold."

Her attitude was beginning to wear thin with Jake. He pulled back the paper offering, wrapped it back into the roll and tossed it back on the bed. As he turned to face her again, he stepped toward the door and reached into his right front pocket for some hard currency.

"You got a lot of hard bark on you, lady," he said as he scanned her figure from head to toe again, but with a more discerning eye. He was impressed. "Did I do something to rub you raw under the saddle?" He found a twenty-dollar gold eagle a flipped it into the air.

The unfazed young woman snatched the coin out of the air without even taking her eyes off Jake. "Don't flatter yourself, mister. I'm not as easily impressed as the women you're likely used to."

Jake took another step closer to her. She tensed up but didn't back away. "*Is* there a woman under all that dirt and horse shit?"

The young woman's eyes flared and her face flushed red. She snapped her right hand high and fast, catching Jake off guard and slapped him hard and flat across his right cheek. Before the blow even had a chance to take effect, Jake returned the slap. It wasn't a hard blow but was sudden enough and so totally unexpected that she fell back a step, more shocked than hurt.

"Don't do that again," warned Jake, his voice was still and

calm but not really threatening. "I don't hold with hittin' a woman, but I won't take it from one either. Especially when I haven't done anything to deserve it."

She was fighting back tears now. "Done nothing, you say? You called me a pile of dirt and horse shit! You think I'm just going to stand here and take that?"

She had a point. Jake felt a little ashamed now, not only of his comment but her rebuke as well. What he said was crude and insulting, even if it was an accurate physical description. He stepped back a pace and leaned against the door frame. "You're right, ma'am. That was uncalled for. For that, I'm sorry. Please forgive my rudeness. My fuse is a bit short lately." It was obvious his apology was honest and sincere, which seemed to have an impact on the woman he had just insulted.

Gracie McCall became restless and paced in a tight circle, searching for something to say. She was also tossing the gold piece from hand to hand without much significance, then stopped, facing Jake. "Apology accepted."

"Thank you, Miss McCall," offered Jake. "I honestly meant no offense. I respect anyone, especially a woman, who runs her own business and stands up for herself."

Gracie McCall blushed enough to make her hang her head to try and hide it. "You don't really owe me twenty dollars," she said, a little ashamed. "Leastways, not yet. I just wanted something in advance in case you… " She paused, realizing she had talked herself into making an awkward prediction.

"Get shot dead?" Jake smiled. He wasn't offended in the least. It was an honest consideration and all "matter-of-fact" as far as he was concerned.

"Well… yeah," she replied. "You gotta admit, there's a pretty good chance of it the way things are going."

Jake couldn't help but laugh. "Fair enough," he said. He stood straight now, both feet planted squarely, facing the young woman, who had suddenly taken on a much more attractive appearance and demeanor in Jake's eyes. "I'll tell you what, Miss McCall—"

"Gracie" she said, cutting him off. "I prefer folks call me, Gracie."

Jake offered an accepting smile. "Well... Grace... why don't you take..."

"Gracie!" she corrected quickly. "I prefer Gracie instead of Grace."

"My apologies again... Gracie," answered Jake. "Please take that twenty on account. If I die owing you anything more, you can take my gear and sell everything outright. Or keep it, whatever you like."

"What about your horse?" Gracie's voice broke into a higher pitch than she would have liked, giving away her obvious interest in Teacher.

Jake could tell she really like the sound of that deal, especially Teacher. "That'll be up to Teacher," he said. "She pretty much goes her own way. If she takes to you, she's yours. If she doesn't, I'd say cut her loose."

"Just let her go?" Gracie was stunned. "Mister, that makes no sense. A horse like that is something special. Her color, her build; I've never seen one like her, ever."

"And like as much you never will," Jake replied with pride. "Teacher is, indeed, something special. My point is, even if you wanted to *try* and keep her, she wouldn't stay unless she wanted to. Sooner or later, she'd bolt." There was a noticeable shift in the level of tension between them. "Besides, we're getting a little ahead of ourselves, aren't we? I'm a long way from dead just yet." Then, for the first time in a long while, Jake actually offered a smile that was easy and natural, relaxing his body a bit more. Then, he winked his right eye.

Gracie was disarmed by Jake's unexpected charm and felt a sudden release of air escape her lips as her cheeks flushed red. She smiled back, then tried, almost unconsciously, to straighten her hair and wipe some of the mess from her face. If she had seen herself do it, she would have been angry and tried to stop. Falling all over herself and fussing about her looks would have made her spitting mad. But she couldn't help it. She stepped back and looked from side to side again, nervously, and cleared her throat. The gold eagle was being fumbled about from hand to hand again and then was tossed in the air back to Jake, who never took his eyes off Gracie and let the coin fall into his open left hand.

"You can pay me when you leave," Gracie snapped back at Jake, playfully. "I guess you're good for it." As she back peddled her way down the hall away from Jake she added, "You can stop by and check on Teacher and your rig anytime. You'll find I run a good stable. I washed your saddle blanket and gave the saddle some soap and beaver oil to clean up the leather some." She then added a wink of her own before turning away and sprinted the rest of the way down the hall and down the stairs.

Jake slipped the coin into his pants pocket and rolled his body against the doorway before pushing off and stepping back into the room. With the heel of his boot, he hooked the base of the door and flipped it closed. Just before the door latched shut, Jake felt a genuine smile cross his face again. It was his second smile in less than five minutes and he liked how it felt.

Chapter Nine

"I WANT 'im!" screamed Wolf at the top of his lungs. "I don't care who he is, or what it takes, but I want 'im and I want 'im DEAD! Ya hear me?"

Although the bar room was filled with over twenty men and at least as many women and assorted workers, all were frozen in place. There wasn't a breath of air to be heard.

"WELL? Somebody say something, damn you! Are ya with me or not?" Wolf scanned the entire room, looking into the eyes of each man. As his glare met each pair of eyes, all turned away, left or right, up or down, but no one held his gaze with Wolf.

Finally, the tension was broken when one man dared to speak. His name was Dabs Greer but most just called him Dabs. He wasn't a large man, by any means, but he was lean and mean where it counted. "But Delgado Station is on this side of the border, Wolf."

He quickly looked about the room, hoping for some support or at least agreement with his point. No one spoke. It was clear he was on his own. After clearing his throat, he decided to trudge on. "Thing is, you always told us not to do nothin' on our side that could get folks or the Rangers riled up enough to come after us. That was your own rule. And it's a good one. We leave them alone... they leave us alone."

Wolf took his own deep breath and walked casually over to where Dabs was seated and stared down at him. "So?"

Dabs gulped some air and continued. "Well... I'm just

askin' is all. 'Cuz if this fella, whoever he is, is from Delgado Station, or went back there fer some reason, then ain't we just askin' fer trouble with the Texas Rangers or US Marshals if we go in there lookin' fer him and… I don't know, maybe kill some folks?" Dabs looked around the room again, hoping for some support. Again, everyone remained silent. As far as they were concerned, Dabs was on his own. He looked sheepishly at Wolf as if he were about to apologize for even bringing it up when another voice finally broke the tension.

"Dab's got a point there, Wolf," said a man about equal size to Wolf, but maybe carrying another fifty pounds of solid muscle. His name was Pierson, and he had a woman sitting on each knee. His friends called him Spud because of how a potato has eyes all around it. Spud had something of a sixth sense for trouble and the other men always liked that about him. That's why, when he spoke up, the other men listened. He pushed both women off his lap and leaned back in his chair. "The truth of it is, Dabs is dead right. It's always been your rule, Wolf, and we've been left alone as long as we never broke it. Now you want us to break it over the likes of Orin and Buck; two of the most useless pieces of human flesh this side of hell. The two of them together don't make up enough brains for a mule. So, it's a fair question to be asked."

Finally, there were enough voices at least raised to supportive murmurs leaving Wolf no choice but to answer them. Wolf stiffened his posture, arching his back. He then put both hands on his hips and arched his back again and even gave his neck a twist from side to side making a cracking sound that seemed to echo around the room with each turn of his head. His actions were clearly designed to draw out the tension in the room and build anticipation for what he might say or do. It worked.

118

"I hear what you're saying, boys. I truly do." His demeanor was uncharacteristically calm and very different from what anyone expected. He took two steps forward, more like marching steps, then spun quickly on his heels heading back the opposite way he came, but this time doubling his steps and then stopped, spinning around again to face the room. No one breathed. Even the flies stopped buzzing about. "But here's the thing you boys ain't taking into proper consideration. The rule is WE leave THEM alone..." He took two more steps forward, back to the middle of the room. "... and THEY leave *US* alone. That was the deal! It works both ways. But it was THEM who broke the deal first! Not *US*! So, now we gotta answer back! Otherwise, they might get to feelin' uppity! Like they aren't afraid of us no more." Everyone looked at one another, but no one spoke. "You get what I'm trying to say here, boys?"

There was an obvious shift in sentiment at Wolf's pronouncement. He continued to flesh out his reasoning. "Besides, things have been..." he searched his brain for the right word, "... tight lately, wouldn't you say?"

There were more murmurs of agreement this time. Wolf could tell he was beginning to win a few of his men over but pressed on to solidify his point. "Let me make this perfectly clear. This ain't for Orin and Buck. Spud's right on that score. I couldn't care less about those two... or any of you neither, if it comes to that! What I'm talking about here is the principle of the thing. If we let this go unanswered, they just may feel like taking another step in our direction. And we can't let that happen." Wolf mentally polled the room to see if he had won them over yet. Things didn't look definitive until Spud spoke up again.

"He's right about one thing, boys," said Spud with a smooth, rational tone. Everyone turned to face him. "It has been a might tight around here lately. Pickins have been a bit slim across the border too. It may be time to rethink our peace treaty. Especially since, as Wolf pointed out, it was them that broke it first."

Wolf clapped his hands together in a loud, raucous form of applause that seemed to revive the entire room. Soon, everyone followed in concert until the entire room echoed with thunderous applause.

"*THAT'S* what I want to hear!" he screamed. "We've gotten soft and lazy, sitting on our asses. It's time we reminded everyone in the territory, not just who we are, but just how dangerous it is to cross us. So..." He suddenly leaned into the room and gave everyone a smile they had never seen before. It was enough to make every hair on a man's body flutter, like the feeling of a thousand ants crawling all over from head to toe. Then, in what was more of a whisper, he said, "So... are you with me, boys?" No one responded at first. Then, Wolf turned with a twisted smile that covered every man in the room and added; "'Cuz if you ain't... I'll have to slit the throats of every last one of ya that says no." There was another deathly silence in the room that lingered for several seconds until Wolf broke it with a screaming, banshee of a laugh.

The room let out a collective gasp of relief that was followed by mixed levels of laughter. Then, it suddenly hit each and every man in the room that maybe Wolf wasn't really kidding. Wolf turned his gaze back again across the room, slowly, purposefully, from man to man and growled his last words of the evening. "Now, get some sleep. Then, gather your rig and make it ready for killing. We got ourselves a Black Moon comin' boys, and I aim to make use of it." Most everyone in the room, like Potch before, had no idea what Wolf was talking about. A Black Moon meant nothing to them. Wolf liked to think of himself as something of a medicine man, a shaman who dabbled in the black arts. It was part of the mystique he had created around his image. Most of the men just shrugged their shoulders as if to say, "Black Moon? Eh, whatever." The only thing that mattered to them was that they were going on a raid to a town that was beginning to show promise. Delgado Station was becoming more and more prosperous and, if they were going to strike, it might as well be now.

"We meet outside at first light." Everyone in the room remained still, frozen in place like they were carved in stone. "GO!" screamed Wolf so suddenly everyone tripped over themselves and each other, clearing the room in a matter of seconds. Wolf turned to leave but then noticed one man had remained seated. It was Spud.

"You got somethin' else to say, Spud?" asked Wolf, with some venom in his voice.

"Just wondering what the plan is, Wolf." Spud was the type of man that always bothered Wolf. He couldn't be pushed and didn't scare as easily as the others.

"Ain't it enough that I just give the orders, Spud, and expect everyone to follow them, including you... without question?"

Spud burst out with a belly laugh. "*HA!*" He leaned forward in his chair, pulling it away from the wall and dropping it down on all four legs that creaked under his weight. "You know me better than that, Wolf," he said, as he reached for the half-full bottle of whiskey in front of him. As he poured himself a shot he said, "I ain't like those other pups, Wolf. I like to know who's doin' what, and when, where and how they're doin' it. That way, I stand a much better chance of comin' out alive."

"You don't like the way I've been runnin' things, Spud?"

"Didn't say that, Wolf." Spud tossed back the shot of

whiskey and then resumed his previous position of tipping his chair back against the wall. The move also exposed his gun, a .44 caliber, Smith & Wesson Double Action Frontier Model. It was light and fast, but also packed a wallop. He lightly rested his hand on the pistol grip. The move was not meant to be a threatening one, but it was meant to convey the not-so-subtle message that he was ready for anything Wolf might decide to try. "I just prefer to have some sort of plan," stated Spud plainly. "We usually don't gather more than a half-dozen men at a time for a job. Taking this many along on one raid could get out of hand and is bound to attract a lot of attention. A whole lot more than we need. I just want to know what to expect. You owe us that much."

"I don't owe you or them nothin'!" Wolf replied, almost spitting his answer. "If you don't like the way I been runnin' things, you can pack up and leave and go your own way…" Wolf took a threatening step forward, placing his right hand on his own gun and his left on his knife. "… or take me on now."

Spud smiled, then leaned forward and settled all four chair legs back on the floor again. It was clear he wasn't the least bit intimidated by Wolf's bluster and challenge, which irritated Wolf even more than anything else Spud might have said or done. Spud reached for the bottle of whiskey again and slowly poured himself one more shot, finishing the bottle. This time, he didn't toss the shot down in one swallow, but sipped it slowly, until it was all gone. Once the contents were drained dry, Spud turned the shot glass upside down, placing it over the top of the empty bottle. He then slowly stood, never taking his eyes off Wolf.

"I don't want to fight you, Wolf," replied Spud, his tone showing no signs of fear. He pulled both shoulders back and placed both hands on his hips, just above his Smith & Wesson, then relaxed his posture. "And you don't want to fight me." Wolf looked momentarily confused, unsure if Spud was challenging him or not. Spud continued, "We've had a good thing goin' here and that's mostly thanks to you. I'll give you that. But the truth is most of these men don't have the brains of a sack of wet mice, and they'll follow any leader that gives them cause, or scares them shitless. That ain't me."

Wolf wasn't sure what to say or do. Of all the men in his outfit, he feared Spud the most, simply because he never showed a drop of fear of Wolf or any of his threats and that always bothered him. He also knew that, if there was anyone in the outfit that just might be able to take him in a fair fight, or even an unfair one, it was Spud. That made him doubly nervous.

Wolf relaxed his stance as well and folded his arms across his chest. "Then why are you comin' along?"

"It's simple," answered Spud. "You're going into Delgado Station whether I go or not. Whether I agree with you or not. Your reasoning is horseshit, as far as I'm concerned, but it could also be a very profitable score. So, I might as well get as much out of it as I can. But just so you know, once we take that town for all it's got, I'm gone. There's no way the Rangers or US Marshals won't be on our trail after that. Hell, they could end up sending out the whole damned Army too. So, I'm goin' in for me, and only me. I'll take what I can and kill anyone who gets in my way… including you."

Wolf didn't like that last part, but knew he needed to remain calm. "So, it's one last hurrah for you then, huh? Then what?"

Spud shrugged his shoulders. "Depends on how it all works out in the end, I guess. If I make it out clean and clear, I'll likely head south, across the border. Or maybe even up Canada way. Any place but here."

"Sounds like you got it all planned out," said Wolf. He

almost seemed relieved to hear Spud might be leaving.

"Just being practical," answered Spud, with a tone of resignation. "You've been taking too many chances lately, Wolf. Something is eating at you and I'm afraid that, sooner or later, it's gonna get me killed, one way or another." Spud stepped away from the table and fully into the room, allowing his body to lean in the direction of the door and then stopped. He had more to say and took another deep, thoughtful breath. "I've made it thirty-eight years on this earth up to now. Been shot six times with only one of 'em serious enough to make me think I was through." He paused again, taking in another deep breath. "Spent eight years inside prison walls too." It was clear the memory of his imprisonment still tormented him. "Gettin' shot is part of the life I chose, and I don't mind taking that risk again if I thought I could maybe make it out alive... if I'm lucky, or die trying. But prison?" He paused again, taking in another full breath, then released it slowly, shaking his head from side to side. "Prison ain't something I could handle ever again. That I can tell you. So, if I come out of this one walkin' and talkin', kickin' and screamin' I plan on spending whatever time I got left, livin' easy and stayin' free. And that ain't likely anywhere around here."

Wolf decided to test his power and leadership position by posing a pointed, mildly threatening question. "What if I say you ain't comin'?"

Spud smiled and replied, again without threat or malice, "That would be foolish, Wolf. Fact is, you need me more than you know."

Wolf saw something in Spud's eyes that told him he knew something he didn't. That made him curious. "Oh, and what might that be?"

Spud turned to face Wolf directly. "I've been asking around, talking to some of the locals that are brave enough to travel back and forth, bringing us supplies we can't steal. I asked one of the stable hands that came back from Delgado Station just after you and Potch got in. He was comin' back with some horse tack and shoes, so I asked him what he may have seen or heard about who might have been responsible for taking down Orin and Buck."

Wolf's curiosity was piqued, but he tried not to give too much away. "And?" he asked, calmly, as if he didn't care.

"They said people are talkin' about a lone rider, who wields a Winchester like nobody ever and rides a blood-red Arabian that's smarter than most humans." Spud paused to let that description sink in for Wolf. "Any of that sound familiar to you?" Then Spud saw that flash of recognition cross Wolf's eyes, telling him he just might know who the mystery man was. "Yup."

"Jake Benteen?" answered Wolf in a whisper. He turned, taking a few steps away from Spud, then slowly turned back around, facing him again. "You sayin' it was Jake Benteen that took down Orin and Buck? Are you dead sure on that?"

"Has to be," replied Spud. "Ike Basset, the driver for our delivery wagon that brought back our stable hand overheard some young kid bragging about what he seen out on the road. He said that a man, sittin' on a wagon seat on the road just outside of town, shot the guns right off the hips of some young punk he was out ridin' with who was tryin' to pick a fight with the man in the wagon. He said the kid claimed the man blew the guns right off his friend's hips with a Winchester. Said the kid was still sittin' on his horse when he did it." Spud shook his head in admiration and even laughed a little. "Later, that same kid tried to take this gunfighter on again in town, only this time, the man shoots off both the kid's thumbs with a Colt, when he could have just killed him outright, and be done with it." Spud laughed again in disbelief. "He spared the kid's life when he didn't have to! Can you believe it?" Spud paused again and looked closely at the expression on Wolf's face. "There's only one man that fits that description. Winchester or Colt. He's a dead shot with both, and it don't matter which. That man is Jake Benteen." Spud paused once more to read Wolf's mood. "That puts a different spin on things, Wolf, at least for me."

Wolf looked down at the floor and whispered Jake's name again, almost as if he were afraid to say it out loud. "Jake Benteen." Looking up at Spud, Wolf smiled, showing all his remaining teeth, then tipped his head back, looking to the heavens and raised both fists to the ceiling and screamed.

"JAKE BENTEEN!" Ha. HAAAAA!"

Chapter Ten

By midday, the New Mexico sun was proving too hot for most folks to handle, so finding shade to escape the blazing heat was a typical routine for everyone except those who had no choice but to go about their daily chores.

Howard Lynde, the owner of the only dry goods store in town, was busy laying out some of the newest goods that had just come in off the morning supply wagon from Santa Fe; some farm supplies like shovels, pickaxes and garden rakes, a dozen bundles of barbed wire, two kegs of salt pork, a case of Humphries Homeopathic Veterinary Specifics, the accepted treatment for any horse ailment, or humans either, for that matter, as well as a healthy supply of assorted candies.

Down the street, Nana Beth's Ladies Finery was unloading the latest in women's fashions, delivered all the way from Chicago. Despite the stifling heat, many of the town's women folk were already waiting to get a look at the newest trend in ladies wear, pressing Nana Beth and her granddaughters, Kennedy Ann and Ava, to hurry up and unpack the hats, dresses and fabrics they had been waiting for months to see.

Down at Lou Hudson's Barber Shop, men were sitting in the two barber chairs, with big Eric Bonawitz, taking one, getting his head shaved bald, as was his usual. The irony was that he wasn't naturally bald, but just hated his hair getting in his face and dripping with sweat, yet he let his beard grow so long it touched his chest. Eric was the tallest man in town, at six foot five, so Lou had to stand on a fruit crate to reach his head, even as Eric sat in the barber chair.

The other barber chair was filled with Pete Adams, the editor of the town newspaper, *The Blazing Sun*. He wasn't there for a shave or a trim but just to join in the local gossip and to see if there were any legitimate local stories he might write up for his paper. Most of the articles he printed came from the telegraph service. The relay hub had been set up in his office because he was the only man in town that knew how to read Morse Code. People were eager for news on what was happening back east, while regional news often concerned the quest for statehood being waged for both New Mexico and Arizona.

Opinions on statehood were largely split among the ranchers and some of the larger landowners who wanted New Mexico to be left as a territory, while the people of the growing cities and towns wanted statehood. The issue wouldn't be settled for a few more years, when both New Mexico and Arizona would be ratified as states in 1912. Such news and the endless debates that followed were the usual topic of conversation everywhere, especially in Lou Hudson's barbershop. Today, however, the only conversation to be had involved poor Juneann and what happened to her, and the murder of old Ben. Naturally, the conversation came around to Jake Benteen and his role in that sad event, as well as what he did to young Jeff Wade out in the street the day before.

"I still can't believe what I saw," said Eric. "I was dead certain Benteen was goin' to drop that boy dead in the street."

"He had every right to, as far as I'm concerned," replied Lou. "Jeff's been looking for trouble since the day his father gave him those Colts for his sixteenth birthday. Something like this was bound to happen to him sooner than later. He's just lucky it was

128

Benteen that faced him."

"I always thought Benteen was a cold-blooded killer," offered Eric. "That's the skinny on him that I always heard anyway."

Pete Adams leaned forward in his chair. "Boys, I can tell you from professional experience that what you read in the dime novels is almost always a bunch of horse manure, written up by men who only want to sell their books, with no regard or respect for the truth. It's just sensationalism and exaggeration, masquerading as the truth. Nothing more."

Lou stopped shaving Eric's head and stepped back to address Pete directly. "Are you tellin' us that Benteen is some sort of saint or somethin', just 'cuz he didn't kill that boy? He shot both his thumbs off, fer Christ's sake!"

"Right!" bellowed Pete back at him, "And just like Eric said, he could have just blown his damn-fool head clean off. Instead, he let him live! That tells me that what I heard most is that this gunfighter is not like a lot of the others we've all heard about, like Holiday and Hardin or Billy the Kid. I talked to Val, who has known him for years, back in the day, and he tells me Jake's about the most decent of the lot of them. Said he became a gunfighter more or less by accident. Never wanted it but said it's not so easy to just walk away once you get tagged with a reputation. There's always someone out there looking to make a name for themselves by taking you on. That's all Jeff was looking to do, and it could have cost him a hell of a lot more than just his thumbs. I'm not saying Benteen's a saint, but he's not the Devil either."

Lou finished shaving the top of Eric's head and was wiping his dome with a damp towel. "Well, maybe that's true," he said as he reached for a bottle of scalp lotion and poured a dribble into

129

his left hand. "It was a good turn of luck for Jeff I suppose but it still makes me damn sure uncomfortable having a known gunfighter here in our town. It just invites more of his kind to come gunnin' for him." He patted both his hands together, letting some of the lotion air dry before he patted the top of Eric's head, signaling the completion of his weekly head shave. "There ya go, Eric," he said, as he stepped back to admire his work and gave his hand towel a flick and a snap. "You're clean as a baby's bottom now! That'll be two bits."

Eric stood up and leaned into the mirror to examine Lou's handiwork. He was pleased, as always. "Nary a nick on my scalp, as usual, Lou." Reaching into his vest pocket, Eric pulled out a half dollar and tossed it into the air, which Lou immediately snagged on the way down. "Keep the change."

"Always do!" replied Lou. "See ya next week!"

Eric strolled toward the front door, stopped and turned to the two men. "I got a feelin' boys and it's somethin' I just can't shake." His voice was oddly soft, even wistful. "Somethin's comin'... and it ain't good."

Pete turned in his chair to catch Eric's reflection in the mirror. "Care to share it with us?" Both Pete and Lou shared a suspicious laugh at Eric's expense.

Eric stepped across the threshold, then stopped and turned back around, facing the two men. He gave both men a stern look and said, "You can laugh all you want, boys, but you know that when I get one of my feelin's, I'm almost always right and they are almost always about somethin' bad."

Pete turned away from the mirror to look directly at Eric. "I'm not laughing at you, Eric. My grandmother, Lena Maude, used to get feelings like that too and she was always right. She said such feelings were a warning. Like the Lord's way, or the spirit of a deceased family member looking out for you and they best be listened to." Eric and Lou just nodded in agreement. Pete continued, asking, "So, are you saying that this feeling of yours is a bad one?"

Eric ran his right hand across the top of his clean-shaven head. "Not sure, exactly. Sometimes, I get the feeling that a storm is comin' and I just tell the wife, Mariah Ann that we got to just get ready to hunker down and ride it out. I had one like that jest before that dust storm that damn-near wiped this town off the map. You remember? It was 'bout twenty-five years ago. I was just a pup then, but I'll never forget the feelin' of ants crawlin' up my spine. Another time..." he paused, searching his memory, reluctantly. "Another time... it felt... well it was just... different."

"Different how?" The newspaperman took pencil to paper like he was going to write down Eric's description and then changed his mind and put the pencil and paper down on his lap.

Eric scratched his beard and seemed to be debating with himself again about whether or not he wanted to continue. Finally, he said, "It wasn't just a bad feelin' about the weather, like before. This one is like the time I was having breakfast with my ma'am and pap and they was just talkin' about the chores for the day. My pap got up, gave my mam a kiss. He patted me on the head and walked out the door. Then my guts just turned over inside, like I had just drunk me some sour milk. Pappy died that morning when our mule kicked him in the chest and stopped his heart."

"I recall hearing about that, Eric," said Pete Adams. "The whole town talked about it. Your Paw was a good, hard workin' man."

"Thanks," replied Eric. "He was that." The room stayed

131

quiet for a moment. "The point is, gents, when I get these feelin's... I listen to them. I ain't never been wrong."

Lou showed obvious concern when he stepped back a few paces and put his left hand on the back of Pete's chair. "And what's this one feel like? Just a bit of trouble, like a storm coming... or worse? Like... death, maybe? Which one is it?"

Eric stared at the floor for a moment, then raised his eyes to meet both men. "Both." He stepped back out onto the porch and closed the door.

Chapter Eleven

Jake was restless, with the afternoon heat making it impossible for him to close his eyes for anything resembling a nap. Thoughts of Gracie kept creeping into his brain and how good it felt to talk with a woman who wasn't interested in turning her charms to him only for money, or to get him to buy her drinks. Gracie was a tough, independent young woman that gave as good as she got, and that made her all the more attractive to Jake. It helped that she was also a fine-looking woman whose beauty wasn't painted on but shown through in the way she held herself. Yes, the hair and clothes were a little messy, and she could have used a bath too, but that was because of her job and how hard she worked. No shame in that. But there was also something refreshing about her blunt honesty that made Jake restless. She was confident and strong without putting on false airs. Clearly, Gracie was a woman who could take care of herself and that was, perhaps, her most appealing quality.

Jake rolled off the bed and walked over to the washstand. He had gotten a fresh pitcher of water earlier, but when he poured the contents over his hands, it was just as warm as before. Still, Jake splashed some over his face and across his chest to wash away some of the sweat and to try and cool himself some. After he toweled off, he put on his last clean shirt, combed his damp hair with his fingers and walked back over to the bed, where he sat down to put on his boots. Just then, there was a knock at his door.

Once again, more out of reflex as well as habit, Jake reached for his Colt, which was hanging on the bedpost in its holster. He stood, with one boot on, shirt unbuttoned, but Colt in hand, ready and waiting.

"Who is it?' Jake called out firmly, but not threateningly.

"It's me, Val. Put the gun down, Jake, and open the door." There was something of a tease in Val's voice when he told Jake to put down his gun. He knew how Jake would respond to a knock at his hotel room door. "We need to talk. I got news that ain't gonna sit well with you."

Jake crossed and turned the key, but left the door closed. He stepped back into the center of the room and off to one side, away from the center of the door. Not out of fear. Just habit.

"It's open," answered, Jake. He did not put down his gun, but just held it down at his side.

Val opened the door but stayed in the framing and held his hands up in surrender. In a mocking voice of a scared victim he said, "Please don't shoot, mister! You can have all the money I got!" He snickered at his pathetic little performance, as he pretended to be especially scared by shaking his knees.

"Come on in and close the door, you old fool," said Jake as he walked over to the holster and slipped the Colt back into place. "Now what's this about news I'm not going to like?" He began to finish buttoning his shirt.

Val pulled the only chair in the room away from the side of the washstand and straddled it. "You remember me asking you about the leader of that outfit in Tres Mesa, Wolf, and if you had ever heard of him before?"

Sometimes, hearing a certain name causes a man to pause his breath. Hearing Jake's name has done that to many a man over the years, just as it had for Wolf. Now, it was Jake's turn,

134

and that name was Wolf, and he was hearing it again. Jake ran his fingers through his hair once more and sat down on the edge of the bed to put on his remaining boot.

"Yeah," said Jake. "I told you I had heard of him but never met him, or even seen him as far as I know." Jake stood and stomped his foot down into the other boot. While reaching for his holster and Colt, he said, "Why?" He swung the buckle end of his holster around his waist, catching it in his left hand then slipping the tongue of the belt through the buckle and the pin through the well-worn hole. As he tied down the base of the holster to his leg he added, "You were saying he's full-on crazy and kills just for the fun of it. Ruthless and unpredictable. Crazy. Again, why is Wolf any concern of mine?"

Val sat upright in the chair and said, "Well, it's like I was tellin' you before, Wolf keeps a tight rein on his bunch and word is he's rabid mad and out for revenge... against you."

Jake leaned to one side, locking on one hip and folded his arms across his chest. "Me? Why me? Like I said, I've never met or even seen him before. Besides, how does he know it was me that took down those two men and not someone else, or some authorities, like the Rangers, maybe?"

Val stood and slid the chair back against the wall by the wash table. "We don't get Rangers this far south unless we wire them ahead of time. Besides, your name carries a lot of wind in the wires, Jake. The telegraph lines were buzzing before you even got to town. So, once word got back that it was you who took down his two boys, he got to thinkin' maybe the people in this town hired you to take him and his gang on."

"That's crazy," cracked Jake. "I came across those men and that wagon totally by accident, like I told you. I heard the gunfire and Teacher just turned that way on her own. I've always trusted her instincts, so I just let her lead the way."

Val raised both hands, palms up and shrugged. "What can I say? Orin and Buck were about as sharp as a sack of drowned mice and together they barely made up one brain, but they were Wolf's men just the same and he feels he has to make an example of you for breaking the truce." Val stood and stretched his back.

"What?" Jake roared. "Breaking this truce of yours was the last thing on my mind, Val." He was beginning to get angry and began pacing in a tight circle in front of the window. "I didn't even know there was such a thing! Besides, if we wanted to get technical about it, it was Orin and Buck, Wolf's men, that broke the truce, not me!"

"I totally agree, Jake," reasoned the sheriff. "No argument from me on that score. Orin and Buck were likely too lazy to keep headin' south and decided to search for somethin' closer our way," theorized Val. "It was the sad misfortune for Juneann and old Ben that they crossed paths with them, but good for Juneann you came along when you did."

"How is she doing, by the way?" asked Jake, with genuine concern as he changed the subject.

"Doc says she's comin' around, little by little," answered, Val. "She's able to eat some and even sleep a little, although Doc says she keeps wakin' up screamin' and callin' out for Ben, or her mom. She's got her mother staying with her at Doc's place for the next few days until Doc feels she can go home. He said it will likely take her some time to come through it. But she's young and the doc thinks she'll make it in time."

Jake nodded in agreement, adding, "True enough. The wounds we can't see are usually the ones that take the longest to heal." Jake took a long, deep breath and held it for a beat, then released it slowly. Finally, he said, "Okay, so what do we do about Wolf? Are you running me out of town before he gets here?" Jake took a step forward. "I'll leave right now if that's what you want?"

The sheriff looked directly into Jake's eyes. "If I thought it would help, I'd have asked you to leave the minute I walked in here. But I'm afraid running you out of town would only make things worse, Jake."

"Worse?" Jake shot back in disbelief. "How would my leaving make things worse? You just said he was after me for revenge. If he gets word that I'm not here, that I left for parts unknown, like toward Taos or Tucson, won't he try to follow me?"

"That's what most folks in town are thinkin' but I'm not so sure," countered Val. "We still got people that can come and go pretty easy, delivering the things Wolf and his people can't steal easily, so they hear things and pass them on to me if they think I need to hear it."

Jake cocked his head to the left with a quizzical look and asked, "And you heard what, exactly?"

"That it don't matter where you go or where you've been, or whether you're even here now, Jake," answered Val with a stern tone in his voice. "Like I said, he thinks I or this town hired you, and he plans on takin' his revenge out on all of us, whether you're here or not. He'll come lookin' for you later, if you're not here."

Jake was both surprised and even angry. "That's insane!" he bellowed.

Val showed a wry smile and said, "I think we've already established that, Jake." He crossed to leave and took a hold of the knob but didn't open the door. Instead, he just stood, facing the door and said, "So, the way I see it, you might as well stay and see this thing through." He turned to face Jake and added, "It's a

137

damn sight better than having them track you down on the road somewhere and bushwacking you." He looked his old friend in the eyes and concluded, "For what it's worth, I won't leave you to face him alone, or his men, however many there may be. You stand a better chance that way and, frankly, so does this town."

Jake was obviously touched by Val's promise, but couldn't hold him to it. "Thanks, Val, but there has got to be a better way. Can't you call for the Federal Marshals or the Rangers?"

The sheriff gave a cynical look at Jake and said, "I ain't some rube who doesn't know how to do his job, Jake. I already tried sending out telegrams to Tucson and Taos, askin' for help but nothin' got through. The wires had been cut in a few places, up and down the line." Val shrugged his shoulders in defeat but continued. "I sent out riders this morning but that's a two-day ride, one way. So, even if they agree to send help, it won't do much good unless it's a small army, even if they could get here in time, which they can't. Wolf's got more than thirty men, from what I hear. Some don't want any part of a full-on raid on a town this side of the border and are plannin' on deserting once they know Wolf can't catch them. Others think of this as their last hurrah and are plannin' on taking as much as they can carry, then head out for parts unknown."

"Sorry, Val." Jake was obviously sorry and regretted doubting his friend's skills. "So that leaves just you and me... right?" asked Jake. He had a resigned look on his face that seemed to indicate he was accepting his fate but was still uncomfortable with asking his friend to join him, even though it was technically his legal responsibility to do so.

"Kind of looks that way, don't it?" Val added with another wry smile. "I might be able to convince Eric and maybe Pete to lend a hand. Lou and Howard too, maybe. Possibly a few more men here and there, especially if they know they don't really have much choice if they want to stay alive and have much of a town to come back to." Val thought a bit more and added, "I know it's against that oath doctors take about not doing any harm. I imagine not killing people is in there too, but I wouldn't be surprised if old Doc Gibbons picked up a rifle and stood his ground." Then, Val got another idea that didn't sit well with him. "Come to think of it, Gracie is more than likely to pull out her scattergun or deer rifle and drop a few. That girl is a crack shot when it comes to huntin' for wild cats, deer and rabbits. Defending herself and this town is somethin' she won't have to be asked twice to do if it comes to that."

Jake wasn't surprised to hear that about Gracie but didn't like the idea of seeing her get hurt or killed or knowing that he was responsible for her taking part in the killing of others. It was bad enough he had done it for so long and so well, but asking others to carry that mark on their souls was something he didn't even want to think about.

"I appreciate the help, Val," offered, Jake, "but I never meant for anyone to get hurt by my taking out those two men. I was just trying to stop a wrong I couldn't stomach riding away from."

"I know, Jake," said Val, "and that's why I can't let you take this on alone. Besides, it's what I signed on for when I took this badge. I can't very well run away now just 'cuz things have gotten tough."

Jake stepped forward and stopped, standing toe to toe with Val. "Sorry, Val, but I'll handle this on my own. I can't have you getting killed on my account." He placed his right hand on Val's left shoulder and patted it twice. "I'll take it from here."

Val just laughed and said, "Sorry, Jake, but I'm joining you, just the same and there ain't nothin' you can do to stop me. Fact is, Doc says I ain't got that much time left anyway, so I'll make my own decision, thank you very much."

Jake's eyes popped open wide, but he remained speechless. The sheriff could tell he caught his friend off guard with that comment. By way of explanation, he continued. "Somethin' about what's goin' on inside here." He slipped his right hand across his stomach and then patted his belly. "Whatever it is he says can't be fixed. The end won't be pretty either, so if I have a say in how I 'shuffle off my mortal coil'… that's Shakespeare, you know," he added with a wink and a smile. "Bet you didn't know I knew any of that smart, educated stuff, huh?" Both men shared a gentle laugh. "Anyway, if I have a say, and I do, I want to go out on my terms. So, like it or not, I'm standin' with you."

Jake was stunned into continued silence. All he could do was extend his hand to his friend. Val grasped Jake's hand firmly and both men struggled to bring their eyes to meet. As he turned to leave, he paused and said, "Jake, it's been a pleasure knowin' you. I'd say, even an honor." As he opened the door, he turned back to Jake and added, "I'll see who else I can round up and let you know what our numbers are. Then, I'll order a town meeting down at the church to let everyone know what sort of trouble is comin' their way… maybe tell folks to head for safer ground if they can." The sheriff stepped into the hall and walked away from Jake, talking as he went. "Come on down to my office when you can, and we'll put together some sort of plan or strategy depending on who and how many other guns I manage to get." Without ever turning back around to Jake, Val just raised his right hand and gave a gentle wave of goodbye.

Jake watched as his friend faded away down the hall, then stepped back inside his room and slowly closed the door.

Chapter Twelve

Gracie was just finishing up putting fresh straw down inside the stall she had given to Teacher. She had always loved taking care of horses, but Teacher was a particular pleasure for her. There was something special indeed about this animal that made her both admire and yet still show some caution when she was around her. It wasn't fear, exactly, but more a matter of guarded respect. Teacher was wickedly smart by any level of comparison with other horses she had dealt with, and if there was one thing Gracie knew well it was horse flesh.

All horses have their moods and quirks but sometimes a horse gave her clues about what type of man the rider was. It had to do with how the horse was treated. Some clues were subtle, more about how the horse moved, if it was skittish and how it responded to sound and sudden movement. Other clues were more obvious, blatant even. One horse she had been boarding for a few days belonged to a drifter she took an immediate dislike to when he dropped his horse off for boarding and care. The horse showed signs it had been whipped, likely as a continuous form of control, which usually meant the rider didn't know how to ride, much less how to handle a horse. She also noticed scars from the repeated jabs of spurs into the horses' haunches. She hated spurs and felt they were unnecessary, especially when they were used to extremes, as appeared to be the case with this poor animal. When Gracie spotted the saddle tramp from across the street, she called out to him, asking if she could have a word with him. Having a pretty, young woman, however disheveled from barn work, ask for a private conversation sent the wrong signal to this cowboy. He was a stranger, after all. She must want something special from him, he thought. He immediately changed direction and hustled across the street to the livery.

"What can I do fer you, little lady?" asked the cowboy. His tone and body language indicated he was under the false impression Gracie was interested more in him than in anything to do with his horse.

"I wanted to talk to you about your horse," she said with some scorn in her voice and a displeased manner that was hard not to notice.

"What about it?" asked the cowboy. He seemed confused now, since her first words were not the least bit flirtatious. "Is it sick, or somethin'?"

Gracie folded her arms across her chest. "You could say that," she answered firmly. "Your horse has been abused, cowboy." By her words and manner, it was obvious she wasn't interested in anything to do with striking up a relationship with him, and the cowboy's attitude changed noticeably.

"So what business is that of yours, little missy?" The cowboy's attitude was snarky and dismissive.

Gracie could tolerate a lot from the men she dealt with, and did, until they realized she knew her business and was especially good at it. But taking sassy, demeaning name-calling was not one of the things she was inclined to put up with.

"My business is taking care of horses, mister, and anyone here in town will tell you straight out that I am damn good at it." Gracie's voice was strong, yet low in volume and her pitch was sharp. "By the looks of your horse, you treat it worse than any of God's creatures deserves. She is underfed and has saddle sores and spur scars that are infected and need treatment. That bothers me and I thought you should know it."

The saddle tramp's temper flared instantly. He didn't like being chastised or called out by anyone, especially a woman. He took a bold stance, facing Gracie directly and went to slap her with the back of his hand. Big mistake.

Gracie anticipated he might not take kindly to being scolded or challenged by a woman and was ready for such a move. As he swung his right hand around, aiming for the side of her head, she side-stepped to her right and ducked under his open hand. With the toe of her boot, she kicked as hard as she could, which was considerable, down on the inside of his left leg, just behind his kneecap.

The cowboy let out a scream and dropped down to his knees. "OW! You little bitch! I'm gonna…"

Before he could finish his threat, Gracie grabbed a full manure bucket from the back of the stall and brought it down on his head. The bucket broke open, spilling the fresh manure over the man's head. He hit the stable floor, face first, with a resounding thud and was out cold. Knocking the man unconscious was not exactly her intention, but the result didn't bother her much. Seeing his face buried in horse shit seemed fitting.

Gracie swore the man's horse let out a whinny that seemed to indicate its approval, even turning its nose into her to nuzzle against her chest. She patted the grateful animal gently along its neck and said, "I figure he had that comin', don't you?" Again, the horse whinnied in agreement.

While the unconscious cowboy lay spread out, face down in the straw and manure, Gracie walked out the barn door and headed to Sheriff Avery's office. He had just left Jake's hotel room and was about to head over to Lou's barber shop when she called his name.

"Sheriff Avery! Can I have a word?"

The sheriff, as well as everyone else in town, respected Gracie and tended to be more protective of her than she would have liked. Although she quietly appreciated their concern, she also felt she didn't need it. She could take care of herself. The sheriff immediately changed course and sprinted across the street, as best he could anyway, which wasn't much. Seeing him wince and grunt as he hobbled to meet her made her feel guilty.

With a few huffs and puffs of air, the sheriff asked, "What's wrong, Gracie?"

She told him her side of the story, which he believed without question. By her description, he was aware of who the cowboy was and had been looking for a good reason to run him out of town anyway. Although he had not, in fact, broken any laws, he was still enough of a pain in the ass to everyone he met to not want him around anymore, especially when Wolf and his men came riding into town. Gracie may have given the sheriff sufficient cause now to run him out of town, for his own good, whether he knew it or not.

His name was Larry Budwing, a drifter with no plans or direction in his life. The West was filled with men of his sort. Often, they would pass through a small town looking for work of one sort or another, anything to make enough money to afford food and shelter for a few days or weeks. If they didn't click with something that made them want to stay, they usually moved on. Many often got bored or too lazy for honest work and eventually got themselves into serious trouble that landed them in jail or a cemetery. Larry Budwing was headed for an early grave at the rate he was going. The only man in town he managed to make friends with, however briefly, was Amos Lubic. Basically, Amos was the only one who would put up with him for more than five minutes, if one could call that a friendship. They were two peas in a pod. Like Amos, Larry Budwing wasn't particularly dangerous or threatening, just obnoxious and unpleasant, showing disrespect to women in general and always claiming he was being cheated or disrespected. But it was all bluff and bluster when it came to backing up his claims and silly threats because he didn't have the imposing physical proportions of Amos. It was his misfortune to run up against someone like Gracie, who wasn't impressed or intimidated by him, nor any man, for that matter. He was just another dumb cowboy.

When they returned to the stables, the cowboy was moaning, but still largely unconscious. Sheriff Avery noticed a pail of water hanging on a hook on the stable door and took it, dumping the contents over the man's head. The liquid brought him around a little, so Sheriff Avery grabbed him by his belt and the back of his shirt at the neck and dragged him to his feet, propping him up against the door of the stall.

"What's he owe you for boarding his horse and for the treatment, Gracie?" the sheriff asked, as he watched the man's eyes begin to clear and take focus of his surroundings.

"Three days of feed and board, plus medicine for cuts and sores comes to six dollars," replied, Gracie with clarity and determination. "Cash."

Val pressed the man's body harder against the stall door and asked, "You got six dollars on you, boy? Cash?"

By now, the cowboy was wide awake and able to comprehend where he was and what was taking place. "Six dollars?" he shouted as he struggled against the sheriff's grip. "No, I ain't got no six dollars! Besides, I didn't ask her to doctor my horse! I ain't payin' her fer that! I ain't payin' her nothin'!"

"Is that so?" asked the sheriff.

"Yeah, I ain't!" He tried to pull the sheriff's hands free from his shirt collar, but the sheriff held tight. "She attacked me fer no good reason! You should be arresting her!"

Although Gracie had already explained the events in question, and he had every reason to believe her, the sheriff decided to play along and see just how far this fool would go.

"Really?" said the sheriff, sounding a little melodramatic and pretending to maybe even be a little supportive of the man's claims. He turned and looked over his shoulder at Gracie and winked. She was easily a full head shorter and eighty pounds lighter than this sad excuse for a man. He turned back to the cowboy and asked, "So… what you're tellin' me that this slip of a girl beat the tar out of you?" The sheriff let out a hoot of laughter. "Haaa!"

"No… NO! It wasn't like that," he pleaded. "Really!" The man stuttered and tried to fabricate another version of the events. "Hones… she… she must have come up behind me when I came to check on my horse and hit me with something. This whole thing is nothin' but a bunch of bullshit."

"Well, he's right about one thing, sheriff," responded Gracie, with a sarcastic tone. "There is a whole lot of shit being thrown about here, but it's all comin' out of his mouth. To be fair, I did hit him over the head with a bucket of horseshit though. But like I told you, that was after he tried to hit me."

The sheriff gave a sardonic laugh, then said, "Well, it seems we've got something of a 'he said, she said' goin' on here." The sheriff pretended to be pondering a solution. "Now, what do I do about that?" He pretended to pause and think harder for a solution. "Hey, I know! How about we go over to the saloon and you can tell everybody there how little Gracie here cut you down to size all by herself with just a bucket of horseshit? I'm sure they could all use a good laugh. Let's go." The sheriff tugged the cowboy away from the stall and toward the barn door.

The realization of the humiliation the young man was facing sunk in instantly. "Uh... no wait," he said, with a plea that had defeat etched in every word. "I was... I mean... well, maybe I was..." He took a defeated breath. "It's just that, well, I ain't got more than two dollars left on me. I can't pay her six dollars."

"Hmm, can't pay your debts, eh?" The sheriff gave another wink to Gracie indicating he had an idea. "I guess that means you'll have to work it off, cleanin' out these stables and feedin' the rest of the horses. Right, Gracie?" asked the sheriff while never taking his eyes off the cowboy.

"WHAT?" cried the man. "That ain't fair!"

Gracie decided to play along a bit, just to see the man squirm a little longer. "Gee, sheriff, I don't know if he can handle such hard, physical labor. It takes a man with a strong back and a delicate touch to handle horses." Then, Gracie suddenly changed her tone. "So, I guess I don't think I want him in my stables, Sheriff," replied Gracie, defiantly. "Maybe you should just throw him in jail for a week or so. Whatever you think is best."

"What... and have the town foot the bill for his feedin' and care?" said the sheriff, in mocking protest. "No thank you!"

"Well, what do you think we should do with him, then, Sheriff?" Gracie pretended to pace back and forth as if she were trying to come up with an idea. "Hey, I've got an idea!"

The man's eyes brightened.

She stepped in closer to the cowboy and offered a solution. "I'll make a deal with you cowboy." Gracie walked over to the man's abused mount and ran her right hand down its neck, then tousled its main around the ears. Looking at the poor fool still held in the sheriff's grip she added, "I'll pay you twenty dollars for your horse and we'll call it clear."

"What?" protested the drifter. "That horse is worth twice that!"

The sheriff interjected a little more information for the man to consider. "You been stayin' over at the hotel since you rode into town, haven't you?"

The man's eyes darted from side to side as he searched for a way to answer a question he clearly didn't have an answer to.

"Well... um... yeah, I been stayin' there," he said, with some self-pity in his voice.

"Then, am I to assume you ain't got the scratch to cover that bill either?" The sheriff twisted his grip on the man's collar even tighter.

At this point, the man was on the verge of tears, so the sheriff decided the point had been made. "Gracie, you said twenty dollars for the horse?"

"Yup! Twenty dollars cash," she repeated. The saddle, blanket and rig were straddled over the wall of the stall. She gave them a glancing, dismissive look and added, "He can keep the rig. I got better and don't want his scrub." She pulled a small roll of bills from her hip pocket. "I'll even make it twenty-five dollars. That is more than a fair price. Take it or leave it."

Before the man could answer, Sheriff Avery settled the impromptu auction. "Sold!" he said, snatching the paper and stuffing it into the man's shirt pocket. "That ought to be enough to pay off your hotel bill and give you a fresh start... in another town." He spun the man around, putting him in front and started guiding him out of the stable. "Let's go settle your bill."

"But... where will I go without my horse?" pleaded the man

as he was being shuffled out the door.

"There's a noon stage for Tucson," answered the sheriff. "You got just enough time to gather your things and get on it! The town will even pay for your ticket. Think of it as a going-away present."

"But... but!" were the only words the defeated man could utter as the sheriff escorted him across the street to the hotel.

The man's horse took a step forward and nuzzled its nose against Gracie's back. She turned and reached up with both hands and lightly scratched behind the horse's ears, then leaned down and placed her head against the grateful animal's long nose. "Looks like you've had a reprieve," she said. Then, a thought occurred to her. She raised the horse's head and looked into its eyes. "I don't know if you ever had a name, but I kind of like the sound of that word. Reprieve. How's that sound to you?" The grateful horse lowered its head and rested it against Gracie's chest. Nothing more needed to be said.

Chapter Thirteen

Whenever the church bell rings on a day other than a Sunday, it usually indicates a wedding, a funeral, a fire or, in this case, an emergency town meeting. Today, it was the latter of the possibilities. Regardless, anyone within earshot usually dropped whatever they were doing and came running. On this occasion, Sheriff Avery walked into the church and said to Preacher Mitchell Lee, "I'm gonna need to ring your bell, Preacher." His voice was deep and serious and not to be questioned.

"Is this about that group of men down in Tres Mesa, Sheriff?" The Preacher had been hearing rumors and had also been listening to more than the average number of confessions ever since Jake brought in poor Juneann and the body of old Ben. "Folks are saying trouble might be coming up our way."

"Afraid so, Preacher," replied the sheriff, reluctantly. "I wish it weren't about that, but it is and folks have got to know what their options are."

"I understand, Sheriff," the preacher answered, with equal reluctance. "Why don't you give it a tug and I'll stand at the door to greet folks as they come running. Maybe I can keep everyone calm and get them seated in an orderly manner."

"I'd appreciate that, Preacher. Thank you." He went to tip his hat, but then realized he should have removed it when he entered the church. "Oh, sorry, Preacher," he said, with a childlike embarrassment. "I don't make it to church much and forgot my manners."

The preacher just smiled and placed a welcoming hand on the sheriff's shoulder. "No need to apologize to me, Sheriff," he said. "The good Lord understands your mind was occupied with more pressing concerns." The sheriff pulled his hat to his chest. "Maybe after this is over, you'll find the time to stop in for a Sunday service, or maybe even a confessional?"

Sheriff Avery did something of an "Aw, shucks" shuffling of his feet and said, "Well, I appreciate the invite, Preacher, but me and God have been at odds for a good number of years now, so maybe I best stay home as always. And as to your invite for a confessional, I'm afraid neither one of us has got much time to spare for that right now."

"As you wish, Sheriff," came the preacher's reply, without judgment. "Just know that you are always welcome. Besides, I'm sure God has heard everything you've got to say, whether it is inside these walls or out." He ended his advice with two firm pats on the sheriff's shoulder. As he turned toward the front door to greet the townsfolk that would be coming in, he stopped and turned back to the sheriff. "Oh, be sure to take a good, strong hold on the rope and plant your feet firmly. That bell can pull a man right off his feet if he's not ready for it."

Sheriff Avery laughed. "Ha! Is that something of a... whataya call it... a metaphor, Preacher?"

The preacher laughed equally, not intending his comment to be a metaphor of any sort. "Not at all, Sheriff. Just fair warning is all." Both men shared a knowing smile. "I'll go get ready to greet people. You pull that rope hard and make that bell sing loud and clear."

"Will do!" replied the sheriff, as he plopped his hat back on his head and headed for the bell tower.

When the bell began to ring, sending out its ominous signal, the reaction of the townsfolk was one of advanced expectation rather than shock or concern over some unexpected emergency. Everyone in town knew why the church bell tolled this time. People stepped slowly outside from the various buildings and shops. Some, who were already walking the covered sidewalks and side streets, just stopped and looked in the direction of the church and, in what resembled an almost trans-like state, began to head toward the church.

"No cause for alarm, folks," yelled the preacher, in his best fire and brimstone voice. "Please stay calm and enter into the Lord's house and take your seat. The sheriff needs to have a word with you."

"We know what he's gonna say, Preacher!" yelled big Eric Bonawitz. Behind him was Pete Adams, with paper and pencil in hand, ready to take down whatever information was needed for his newspaper.

Old Doc Gibbons popped his head out of his office to see what the fuss was all about, not that he didn't know, then looked back over his shoulder to check on Juneann, who was still asleep, but with her mother seated close by. "Ellie," he whispered softly to Juneann's mother, "I'm going down to the church to get a handle on the calling of the bell. You stay with Juneann here and tend to her needs if she wakes up or stirs any. I'll be back as soon as I can." The distraught woman, who was still holding tightly to her daughter's hand, just nodded her understanding before returning her sleepless eyes back to her only child.

Dan MacNeil, the town banker and likely the richest man in Delgado Station, stood in the doorway of the bank, assessing the crowd approaching the church. He was curious about just who was going to answer the call, both from a general sense of curiosity over which neighbors and townspeople were going, as

152

well as a professional one. If they were depositors, well that was one thing, but if they were people that his bank held mortgages on, he was doubly interested. Once he saw that the assembling crowd was thinning out and had largely settled inside the church, and he had made his calculations as to who was attending, he closed and locked the bank's front door and headed down to the church.

Preacher Lee poked his head around the door frame to the lower level of the bell tower where Sheriff Avery was puffing away pulling down on the church bell rope and called out to him over the deafening tone of the bell. "Sheriff!" he yelled just loud enough to be heard in between each clang of the bell. "Sheriff! You can stop ringing that bell now. I think everyone's here that is likely to show up!"

Sheriff Avery looked back over his shoulder and released a sigh of relief. Pulling down on that church bell rope was more exercise than he had allowed himself in years. "Thank the Lord for that, Preacher. I was about to burst a lung!" He let the rope slack, just as it managed to tip the clapper one last time, for a soft touch on the interior dome of the bell.

"If you need the exercise, Sheriff, I'd be happy to let you ring it every Sunday," offered the preacher, with a teasing smile.

The sheriff removed his hat again and began to fan his face to cool the sweat he had generated ringing that bell to call the townspeople for the emergency meeting. His eyes spoke loudly to the preacher's obviously sarcastic offer, clearly indicating he was rejecting it, but choosing not to verbalize it. Instead, he said, "Let's go tell the folks the bad news."

After a few more stragglers managed to find their seats, Preacher Mitchell Lee raised his hands high and wide and called for calm and silence but was ignored by one and all. Most folks

153

knew what the likely topic of discussion was going to be, but no one had any clear understanding of the seriousness and legitimate danger the whole town was facing. Rumors and grossly exaggerated speculations and "*facts*" were being bandied about recklessly, as is typical of any situation involving the prospect of danger. People were shouting over one another in an effort to be heard, and to shout down anyone in disagreement. It was painfully obvious, both to the preacher and to Sheriff Avery, that getting this crowd under control was going to be more difficult than initially anticipated. He was holding his left hand over his stomach, which showed obvious signs of pain and discomfort. After a few more attempts by Preacher Mitchell Lee to calm and quiet the crowd, the sheriff lost his patience and pulled his Remington .45 and fired two shots into the church ceiling. The deafening echo of the two blasts was enough to cause more than a few shrieks from the crowd, both male and female, but it did bring about the desired effect. Silence.

Preacher Lee turned from his position behind the pulpit, which was raised about three feet above the floor, allowing him to look down at Sheriff Avery with eyes blazing. "SHERIFF!" he shouted, with more volume than he had ever used in a sermon. "Was that necessary?" scolded the preacher in as scornful a voice as he could deliver. "You just put two holes in the church ceiling."

The sheriff, still holding his left hand over his stomach, ignored the preacher's admonishment and forced his gun back into its holster with obvious anger and frustration. "Sorry, Preacher. Lost my head there for a minute. Besides, it hardly ever rains this time of year anyway."

The preacher just raised his eyes to the heavens as if asking for patience and forgiveness. His gaze then returned to the sheriff

154

and invited him to speak. "Sheriff, I believe you have something of vital importance to say to the people of our fine community. Please step up and address your friends and neighbors."

Sheriff Avery just waved his left hand, side to side, as if he was swatting away a fly. "I'll say what I've got to say from where I'm standin' Preacher," he said in a calm but firm voice. Placing both hands on his hips, he widened his stance and began. "Folks, we've got some serious trouble likely headin' our way and you all got a right to know about it and what we can do about it—"

Before Sheriff Avery could continue, he was interrupted by a familiar voice. "We all know who's responsible for what we're facin' here, Sheriff," called Amos Lubic, the man Jake had met briefly in the street the day he arrived in Delgado Station. He still had a bandage of sorts across his face covering the broken nose Jake had given him. The bandage was a mass of blood, sweat, snot and dirt and was likely doing more harm now than good. His clothes were also unchanged, as was his attitude. "It was Jake Benteen that brought all this trouble on us!"

The collective voice of the assemblage was a mixture of opinions regarding Jake's responsibility for the current state of affairs. Most were not inclined to blame Jake directly for the current state of affairs. He did save Juneann from a fate no one wanted to even consider, especially once word reached the majority that it was Orin and Buck Wheatly that were responsible.

"Amos, shut yer trap!" yelled the sheriff from the front of the church. "If it weren't fer Jake, Juneann would be dead too. Or worse... and we all know it." The tide of opinion shifted back in the sheriff's favor now, forcing the remaining few that might have shared Amos' opinion to take a more honest look at what might have truly become of Juneann had Jake not intervened.

Amos wouldn't hear of it. "Says you!" countered Amos, who was showing no signs of backing down. "Just 'cuz he's a friend of yorn don't make him all you claim. I still say we don't know what really happened out there. How do we know it wasn't Orin and Buck who came upon Benteen when he was robbin' Ben and taking his pleasure with Juneann? Huh? Answer me that?"

Walking through the church doors was Doc Gibbons just as Amos was tossing out his own twisted theory of the events in question. The doctor held his position in the doorway until Amos was finished, then couldn't hold back his opinion and called out, "Amos, I swear to Christ you've had your head buried so far up your ass for so long, the smell of your own shit has rotted what little brain you had to start with." The assemblage in the church pews released a collective laugh at Doc Gibbon's colorful description of Amos' limited mental capacity. The doctor continued. "Just so you folks know, I've been treating Juneann since she was brought her in and I can tell you, every word Mr. Benteen said as to what happened is true."

A woman, seated on the aisle to the doctor's left asked, sincerely, "But I heard she couldn't talk, Doc?"

Doc Gibbons looked down at the woman, assessed her sincerity and looked to the rest of the people in the church. "She is, only now, able to talk some about what happened and, although a lot of what she's sayin' is pretty mixed up at times, she did say that two men tried to stop Ben's wagon, but he bolted, trying to make a run for it. Some shooting started and she said Ben got shot in the head and fell from the wagon. That's about all she said that made any sense. She has no memory of Mr. Benteen at all. Medically speaking, it's what we call shock. You could say the brain shuts down when it can't handle what's happening and buries horrible things. I've seen it a lot with some

156

of our war veterans. Sometimes, the memories never return. But what they do remember, they don't invent."

"You're sure on that, Doc?" asked another voice in the crowd, but the doctor couldn't determine who it was.

Doc Gibbons paused, wanting to be careful about his answer. "You folks have known me for some time now. I've treated the lot of you for one thing or another and kept your secrets too. I'd like to think, after all the years of delivering a good portion of you, treatin' your kin and making their last days as comfortable as I could, and stitching everything from farm accidents to bar fights and even a few knife and gunshot wounds, that you'd trust my judgment when it comes to assessing a man's worth. Whatever Mr. Benteen's life has been up to now, I can't say. But the look in his eyes when he brought Juneann and Ben in spoke to me of a man with a solid moral character. He cared about Juneann and told me he felt bad he didn't get there soon enough to help save old Ben. That's what he told me, and by God, I believe him. His moral character is not in question with me."

"Moral character?" hollered Amos. "MORAL CHARACTER?" He shouted his doubt with extra emphasis the second time just in case anyone doubted him. "You gotta be kiddin'! You know how many men he's killed, Doc? He's a cold-blooded killer!"

The sound of boots marking a steady stride down the center aisle of the church caused the congregation to collectively turn their heads to see Jake Benteen slowly make his way to Amos' side. He was carrying his famous Winchester, model 86, cradled in the crook of his left arm. Jake stopped, shoulder to shoulder with Amos and looked him eye to eye.

"Sit," said Jake, with in a solemn voice that was laced with doom. Amos looked like a man about ready to toss the considerable lunch he had packed down earlier. Jake leaned in closer to Amos but kept the same level of volume when he reiterated his previous suggestion, albeit with a bit more detail. "I've never killed an unarmed man, or a man that didn't leave me any choice, but I just may make an exception in your case. So, unless you have plans to add to my legacy, I strongly suggest you sit. NOW!" Amos sat, obediently, placing both hands on his lap, like a schoolboy being punished for not doing his homework.

There wasn't so much as a creak of wood, or the rustle of wind to be heard in the chapel, despite every available seat being taken. It seemed as if everyone had inhaled all of the air in the room until their lungs were about to burst.

Finally, the preacher spoke. "I would appreciate it if you wouldn't spill blood in our church, Mr. Benteen," he said, with a mild air of sarcasm.

"Yeah," added the sheriff. "Take him outside first." It was like a pin popping a balloon, with everyone exhaling laughter all at once. Everyone except Amos, of course.

Now that the tension was greatly reduced, Jake continued down the aisle and stepped up onto the raised altar, placing himself between his friend, Val, and the preacher. Val gave Jake a rueful smile and folded his arms across his chest.

"Preacher, I'd be obliged if I could have a word with these folks," asked Jake softly. "If it wouldn't be sacrilegious for a man like me to speak from here?"

The preacher looked at Val for some guidance, even if it was just a nod, or a shaking of his head. The sheriff looked back as if to say, "What are you lookin' at me for? It's your church," but he never uttered a word.

The preacher took a deep breath and even flipped open his pulpit Bible, fumbling through some pages before he spoke. It was as if he was asking for permission from on high to miraculously find a passage that said it was all right for a known killer of men to address the congregation. Nothing popped out. Finally, he said, "Given the importance of what you have to say, I think the good Lord would understand." With that, he stepped down and took his position on the other side of the pulpit, allowing Jake to step into his place.

Reluctantly, Jake stepped up behind the pulpit, still holding his Winchester. The imagery was not lost on the assemblage, where more than a few gasps and whispers could be heard. Val cleared his throat and got Jake's attention. He then gave his friend a knowing nod, hinting strongly that Jake needed to put down the rifle. Jake caught the gist of Val's body language and handed his rifle to his friend, while turning to the people in the room and saying, "My apologies, folks. I'm not accustomed to being in a church. Fact is, I can't remember the last time I was. It would be fair to say that God and I have had something of a strained relationship over the years."

"That's bound to happen if you keep killin' people," mumbled a voice that was all too familiar, and was followed by nervous chatter from every corner of the sanctuary.

Another voice, a late arrival to the gathering, caught Jake's attention as soon the first words broke the brief silence. "Amos, you're a horse's ass and always have been. If Mr. Benteen doesn't shoot you, I will! So, do us all a favor and shut the hell up!" More laughter broke the tension again. Everyone knew who that voice belonged to, even Jake. It was Gracie McCall. She was standing at the back of the room, with her arms folded across her chest and her legs crossed at the ankles. Her scattergun was leaning against the wall by her side. "Go ahead, Mr. Benteen. Let's hear what you have to say."

Jake couldn't help but smile, even shaking his head a little at the bold audacity of the young woman. Damn, she was growing more and more fetching every time he saw her. "Well, come on, out with it!" she called out to Jake. "We ain't got all day. Some of us have work to do."

Even from the back of the room, Jake could see Gracie's smile, telling him she was just giving him a gentle ribbing. "Why, thank you, ma'am," answered Jake, with a smile of his own, directed exclusively at Gracie "I'll try and be brief." Jake took a deep breath and laid out his thoughts as plainly and as logically as he could. He described what he saw happening to Juneann and Ben and that he just couldn't turn away, knowing what fate lay in store for the tortured young woman.

"It's true that I've done a lot of things I'm not proud of and wish I could take back," he said, after allowing his description of the aforementioned events to sink into the crowd. "Show me someone who says they haven't, and I'll show you a liar." More than a few people nodded in agreement. "But I knew that if I turned a blind eye to what I was witnessing and rode away, it would haunt me the rest of my days. And I've got enough nightmares to fight off as it is." The gunfighter paused and placed both hands on the edge of the pulpit as if to support himself. He continued. "Now, here's the thing you folks have got to know. If I had known who those men were and the hornet's nest my taking them down would have caused this town… well… I still would have done the same thing. And that's because I knew I could stop them. Most of you here probably couldn't. You're farmers, merchants, cowhands and so on. You haven't spent your lives with the smell of gunpowder forever burned into your nostrils. It's fair enough to say I have and I really don't know any other way of life and that's the damnable part of it. But what's done is done and there's no taking it back. What I do know for certain is that those men would have destroyed that young girl in ways you don't want to think about. So, ask yourself this; if that was a child of yours, what would you have had me do? What would you have done? Assuming you could have done anything and not get yourself killed." The crowd fell silent again, even Amos. Jake watched the people hang their heads in shame. "That's what I thought."

"But can't you just send word to Wolf and his men that it was you and only you that took down his two men and then... ride on?" This question was the one that was on the minds of everyone in the room. It came from Dan MacNeil, the banker and it was an honest, even logical question that had now been voiced publicly. As soon as he asked it, there was more than an abundance of agreement in the room.

Sheriff Avery felt the need to speak up at this point. "That's a fair enough question, Dan. Fair enough. But we already got word that Wolf and his men are looking for an excuse, any reason they can come up with to make one last big score. A killing if you want the truth of it. Then, they plan on splitting up and making a run for it. To do that, they need cash and provisions. That's why they plan on hittin' us with everything they got. Like I said, they're just looking for an excuse. They know times are changing, especially for men the likes of them. I heard that some of them are callin' it their last hurrah."

"How many men are we talking about, Sheriff?" continued Dan MacNeil. "Can't we get the Rangers or the Army to just come in and clean them out?"

"I already thought of that, Dan, and it looks like they thought of that too," replied the sheriff, reluctantly. "The telegraph lines have been cut up and down the line, so we can't get the word out."

The news that the telegraph line had been cut brought an immediate groan from the congregation, as well as a few cries.

The banker continued. "But can't we fix the lines somehow?"

Pete Adams stood up to address that question. "We don't know exactly where the lines are cut. It wasn't in just one or two places, so connecting them isn't the hard part, exactly. But sending men out to try and fix them, assuming we could find the cuts, might get someone killed. We don't know if they have men watching to make sure we don't try."

The sheriff added his own blunt conclusion to the issue of the telegraph wires. "The fact is, we're stuck with this on our own and we've got to decide how we're going to handle it."

"Can't we negotiate with Wolf and offer to give him and his men what they need?" asked a new voice in the debate. It was Howard Lyndh, the dry goods store owner. "Maybe they'll just take what we give them and run."

The room broke out in a mixture of agreements and doubts as people began to debate the idea. The sheriff interrupted the multiple conversations before they got out of hand. "Hold on, now! Listen up!" The sheriff waited for the room to settle again before he continued. "I can tell you for certain that Wolf is not the kind of man who negotiates with anyone," he said. "Truth is, from what we know, he is just plain crazy. He sees what happened to his men as a breaking of our unofficial truce."

Before anyone could argue that it was Wolf's men who broke the truce, the sheriff raised his hands to signal continued quiet in the room. "Yes, we all know that it was his men that broke the truce first, but he doesn't see it that way. Like I said, he's just looking for an excuse, any excuse, even some phony, made-up revenge."

"But that's just... insane!" cried out a woman sitting in the front pew.

"Yes, ma'am, it surely is," answered Jake. "And that's the main thing you have all got to come to grips with. From everything we've heard about Wolf, he is full-blown crazy and there is no reasoning with him. There's no one coming to our rescue either, at least not in time. So, if you want to hold on to what's yours, your lives mainly, then you are all going to have to fight to keep it... or die trying."

"But this is all your fault!" hollered Amos, who somehow managed to even jump to his feet when he made his charge. This time, there were more than a few townspeople who agreed.

Doc Gibbons spoke up again. "So, you would have had him do nothing, which is likely just what you'd have done, and let Orin and Buck get away with killing Ben and defiling and likely murdering Juneann? We can't keep going over this. It's done!" Doc Gibbons had to pause and catch his breath. He was boiling mad and his face was showing every ounce of blood he had in his body, ready to burst. He calmed his voice as best he could and tried to finish his thoughts. "I would ask what kind of man you are, Amos, but I think we already know the answer to that. The question is, how many more of you here think like Amos?" The doctor paused and surveyed the room. Many heads dipped in shame and embarrassment. "Now this is *our* town, by God, and it's up to us to keep it!" Turning back to Amos, he said, "If you're not man enough, Amos, then gather what's left of your dignity and get out. We sure as hell don't want you or need you!"

Amos looked longingly about the room, hoping for some show of support, but Doc's words carried more weight than anything he could try to say in his defense. Lowering his head,

Amos made for the door as the room fell deathly quiet. Only the sound of his shuffling feet broke the silence as he picked up the pace and made for the door.

Once Amos had fully left the building, Doc Gibbons couldn't resist making a personal observation. "Hmm, it smells better in her already." More agreeable laughter followed his comment.

Then, Jake surprised everyone when he said, "Like it or not, folks, I have to agree with what Amos said," offered Jake, "in part, anyway." His statement was a sort of apology for the mess he had unintentionally gotten himself and everyone else into. The room turned in unison, many stunned by his remark. "But... I've got a plan, of sorts, that may make this a little easier on everyone."

The sheriff looked up at his friend with an instinct that told him he had a pretty good idea of what Jake was about to say, or at least where his thinking was headed. "I don't think I like what you're thinking, Jake," whispered the sheriff.

Jake smiled at his old friend and replied softly, "It's really the best way, Val. You and I both know it."

From the back of the room, Gracie McCall spoke. "You thinking of taking them all on by yourself, Mr. Benteen?" There was genuine concern in her voice and no small amount of amazement.

Jake looked at the mixture of fear and confusion on the faces of the people sitting before him. "Not if I can help it, Miss McCall. But there is something of a code with outlaws of this sort. They fall behind the strongest and most threatening voice of the bunch. Take him out and you cut the head off the snake, as it were."

People began to nod to one another in agreement. They

164

certainly liked the sound of that more than the idea of banding together with guns and fighting off a gang of outlaws. An elderly woman sitting off to the far corner of the left front row pew pounded her cane to get attention. Her name was Mariba Wright and she was the oldest person in town, by far, and was thought to be one of the town's first residents back during the Indian wars. She was widely respected and her advice was often sought for anything from marriage woes to how to handle droughts, dust storms, floods and disease; she had seen them all. When she spoke, people often shut up to listen.

"I got somethin' to say," barked Mariba, in a raspy voice that caught everyone's attention. The room immediately fell silent. With the help of a young man seated next to her, she got to her feet. "I don't know much about this man," she said, pointing her finger at Jake, "cept what rumors you all been spreadin' fast and furious ever since he brought that poor girl back home. It seems to me he put his life out there fer the good Lord to take iffin it tweren't worth savin'. Now he is willin' to put it on the line again fer a town and folks that ain't even his. So, it seems to me we ought to willin' to do the same fer our own, should he fail. It's been a good number of years since I held a gun in defense of what's mine, but I can tell ya fer certain, I'm ready, able and more than willin' to do it again, should it come to that!" The fierce old woman then turned her eyes to Jake. "Mr. Benteen, I am ninety-two years on this earth and have fought and scraped fer everything I got. Lost my dear William in the process. I ain't about to turn it over to a bunch a lazy-ass outlaws fer the takin'. No sir, I ain't! So, when and if the time comes, you tell me what you need me to do and I'll do it!"

If an election were held at that moment for town mayor, which they didn't even have, Mariba would have won an all-hands vote right then and there. The entire room burst into thunderous applause. The tide had turned, almost solely on the words and emotions of a woman who seldom spoke more than a few words of greetings to those who passed her by.

"Ma'am, I don't know who you are, or anything about you either," said Jake, with a slight catch in his throat. "But if this town has any more folks as feisty and brave as you, then Wolf and his gang don't stand a chance." More applause followed, though not quite as bold and defiant as the congregation delivered for Mariba Wright's speech. Jake continued. "But I would like to see if I can stop any fight from coming to your town, or at least improve the odds some. I figure I owe you all at least that much."

"And you think if you can take out Wolf, the rest won't follow?" reasoned the sheriff. "That's your plan, Jake?"

"Basically, yes," answered Jake. "It will likely cut out a big chunk of his men and make them rethink having an entire town against them. Without Wolf, I think much of their courage will disappear, for most of them anyway. There will still likely be a few that won't see any other way for them to go. But it won't be the thirty-odd men Wolf was counting on."

A young man of about twenty-five stood up at the back. His name was Tom O'Leary, a recent addition to the town from back east, near the town of Pittsburgh, Pennsylvania. He had struck out for the West, Horace Greely style, but got stalled in Delgado Station when he met a pretty, young woman named Tammy who just stole his heart. She was sitting next to him and he had placed his hand on her shoulder when he stood up to speak.

"Folks, I came to this town two years ago, just meaning to pass on through." Looking down at Tammy, he finished his thought. "But I found something worth staying around for." Looking back up at the gathering he said, "If that means I have

166

to fight for it, then you can count me in. What can I do to help, Sheriff? Mr. Benteen?"

Jake and Val both looked at each other at the same moment and gave an equal look of disbelief. The sheriff took his position as the legal authority in town to lay out the ground rules, but also to express his admiration for what he saw and heard. "Folks, I can honestly say, I have never been more proud to be your sheriff than I am right now." He took a moment to swallow his emotions. "But... it looks like Jake and I have a plan that I think we should try first. If that fails, well, then... it may well be up to you folks to take it from there."

Jake could tell by the looks on the faces of the crowd that they needed more clarity. "What you *can* do in the meantime, is get yourselves ready, in whatever way you are capable of. Get what guns and ammunition you have and gather together and share with those who don't have much or anything at all. If fighting isn't in your makeup, you can still help those who may need caring for once the shooting starts."

The sheriff suddenly felt the need to add some advice and direction to the group. "If you just don't think you can make a stand of any sort, be of any help with a gun or doctoring, then the best thing you can do is either hide out and stay out of the way, or just high-tail it out of here altogether. Head north to the high country, or straight on to Tucson or Taos. Once the telegraph lines are back up, you can wire in to see if you have a town left to come back to." He looked at Jake and then to the preacher and decided that all that needed saying had been said. "That's about it, folks. Head on back to your homes and make your decision about stayin' or goin'."

"Now, hold on a minute!" declared the preacher. "This is still a house of God and I will not have us leaving his shelter without a word of prayer, asking for his guidance and care." Although the crowd had begun their exit, everyone paused, turning forward, facing the altar and collectively bowed their heads. The preacher looked directly at Jake and Val with some admonishment, both for not responding to his call for prayer, as well as not removing their hats once it was called for. Both men grinned at the other, but Val was the first to just tip his hat and walk out the back door behind the altar. Jake immediately followed, first tipping his hat as well.

Once outside, standing in the alley next to the church, the sheriff looked at Jake with eyes that showed reason and agreement with the basics of the plan, whether he liked it or not. "So, where do we go from here?" he asked. "We ain't got much time, Jake. Word is they're coming here by daybreak tomorrow."

"That's where you come in, Val." Jake gave his friend a remorseful look. "I need someone to go into Tres Mesa and make a challenge to Wolf in front of his men. Throw down the gauntlet, so to speak. Think you could do that, Val, in your official capacity?"

"I sure don't think there is anybody else dumb enough, Jake," said Val, with a nervous laugh.

The two men stood quietly for a brief moment. A gentle breeze blew through the alley by the church. "You realize, of course, you might not come back?" said Jake, bluntly.

Val shrugged his shoulders and answered, "Well, if I don't come back with a direct answer from Wolf, that'll be your answer that the whole damn gang is comin'. That sound about right, Jake?"

"I'd say, so, Val."

The look that both men exchanged at that point told what the stakes were. Jake knew that Val only had a few months to live anyway, so it was a toss-up for him. If Wolf let Val ride back into Delgado Station with word he had accepted Jake's challenge, there was a good chance the odds would turn to the town's favor, presuming Jake could take out Wolf and cut the head off the snake. If Jake failed, Val would at least be in town to lead the people in their own defense. At least Val would likely go down in the streets of Delgado Station, fighting for his town. Either way was acceptable to Val Avery.

If, on the other hand, the sheriff was gunned down trying to deliver Jake's challenge to Wolf, he might be able to take a few of the gang members with him, maybe even Wolf. That was Val's logic and reasoning and Jake reluctantly agreed.

"I'll leave a couple of hours after sunrise, after some coffee and a biscuit. Probably around ten," said Val. "But right now, I'd love one good, last meal and a shot of the best whiskey we have in this town."

"Mind if I join you?" asked Jake.

"I wouldn't have it any other way," replied Val. Jake draped his left arm over his friend's right shoulder as both men walked over to the hotel for what would, very likely be, the last time either man saw the other alive.

Chapter Fourteen

"Mr. Wolf, sir?" asked his portly manservant, Potch. "Will I be goin' along on the… um… raid over to Delgado Station?" It was obvious he was extremely nervous as he was in constant motion, bouncing up and down on his tiny feet. Before his boss could answer, he began to plead his case for why his skills would be put to better use by staying behind and looking after, well, anything that needed looking after. "See, Mr. Wolf, sir, I was thinking that maybe I could stay here and, um, you know, keep an eye on things for you 'til you get back." As he spoke, he began bouncing on his feet faster and matching it with a squeal and giggle, bounce for bounce.

Wolf was stabbing violently at a very rare steak that was bigger than the plate it was served on. A once full bottle of tequila, now half full, was the only other item on the table, with the exception of a few dozen flies buzzing around Wolf's steak, which didn't seem to bother him in the least. His mind was on other things, like killing Jake Benteen and anybody else who got in his way. Ignoring Potch, he took another large bite of steak and spat it out.

"SALT!" screamed Wolf, to no one in particular. He didn't care who brought it to him, just so long as some arrived, and soon. A young, Mexican woman came running from the kitchen area and dutifully placed a bowl of salt on the table in front of him. She never spoke a word and ran as fast as she could get her legs to go back in the direction she came from. Wolf grabbed a handful of salt and dumped it in clumps across the meat. As he resumed the dissection of his steak, he spoke in a mumbled, muffled garble of words that were fighting their way through a mouthful of meat. Potch thought it had something to do with the question he had raised about his participation in the coming raid, but he wasn't exactly sure what Wolf said.

"Um... I'm sorry, Mr. Wolf, sir," Potch begged meekly. "I didn't quite catch that. Am I goin' with you... or... um... stayin' here?"

Wolf spat out a mouthful of half-chewed meat, hitting Potch square in the face, followed by a crystal-clear declaration that answered Potch's question. "You're goin', ya little piece of useless shit!" screamed Wolf, loud enough for everyone within a hundred yards to hear. "Everyone's goin'!" He grabbed the half-full bottle of tequila in his right hand and, with his left, swept it across the table, clearing away the plate of half-eaten steak and the bowl of salt, hurtling them across the room until they slammed against the wall. "Any man who stays behind is a DEAD man! Ya hear me?" Even though there was no one else in the room except Potch, Wolf roared his threat loud enough for the message to make the rounds to every man in Tres Mesa. Just to be sure there was no misunderstanding, Wolf added, "I will cut the heart out of any man that tries to back out! I will cut his heart out and eat it raw!" Wolf gave Potch a push aside with just enough force to knock him down, then stormed outside.

Potch had seen many examples of Wolf's temper over the few years he had been serving him, but this latest eruption was in a class all by itself. Each flare of his temper seemed to surpass the last one. This latest one was so terrifying that Potch was shocked to realize he had actually pissed himself. Tears rolled down his chubby cheeks, but he didn't even try to wipe them away. Deep sobs began to bubble up from within him until they grew into a full body-shaking throb. He had never been more terrified than he was at this moment, feeling like a tortured animal locked in a cage. How he had managed to survive among a group of men that probably averaged at least a half-dozen cold-blooded murders each was a testament to his instinct for survival, as well as his resourcefulness. Although he despised Wolf and every man in his outfit, he also knew how to play the innocent, comical buffoon when it served his interests. The physical and emotional abuse he endured over the past five years would be hard for anyone to believe, let alone understand, but he tolerated unspeakable cruelty for the simple need to survive. What choice did he have? The times when he was ready to explode with rage and strike out at any, and all, of his tormentors were always suppressed, swallowed hard just to stay alive for one more day. Once again, he felt helpless and alone. There was no place to run, no place to hide. Or was there?

As he scrambled to his feet, a thought, an idea that just might save his hide and bring him freedom from the hell of his daily existence came rushing into his addled and terrified little brain. For a brief moment, Potch panicked and looked around the room as if there was somebody there that might be able to read his mind; he was still that scared. But no, he was alone. And in that blink of mental clarity, he had made his decision. Make a run for it! It was now or never. That was his only way out. He slapped his hands together, rubbing them briskly. Yes, his decision had been made. As he started to make for the door, he paused, mid-step. How was he going to slip away without getting caught and having his heart cut out by Wolf and eaten? To some, Wolf's threat might have seemed absurdly hyperbolic, but Potch had seen too many examples of just how twisted Wolf's mind could

172

get. If he got caught trying to escape, he was certain Wolf really would cut his heart out and eat it. So, although just how he was going to escape hadn't fully materialized, all he knew for certain was that he would never survive the war that Wolf was about to start. If he was incredibly lucky, and why not have some luck turn his way for once, Wolf would be the one to get himself killed and Potch would be far enough away for his never-ending nightmare to be of no concern to anyone. He knew that, for a raid like this, his role was insignificant and would largely go unnoticed.

Up to now, Potch had never technically, factually done anything illegal. He was always a spectator of sorts, a clean-up man. He counted the spoils of the various raids, keeping the books, more or less and dutifully waited on Wolf's every demand, no matter how sick, cruel and twisted they may be, and there were many of those. But an all-out war with another town was an entirely different matter. He had already heard several of the men talking about where they were going to run to once the raid on Delgado Station was over, assuming they survived it. A few of the men seemed to be oddly excited about taking on an entire town, not really assessing the risks, acting instead as if it was going to be "easy pickin's" as many had expressed. They would deal with the aftermath later. Others, however, seemed resigned to the fact that a raid like this, the carnage and the national outrage it would bring, would change life in this part of the West for good. Yes, these were changing times and Potch needed to think about his own future. There would be no place left to hide for him if he was involved, much less the lives for the likes of men who made their living by taking from others.

But Potch was not like any of these men. Not really. Although never seen as a threat to anyone, he had learned to survive by allowing himself to be the freak, the curiosity. He was far more intelligent than anyone gave him credit for, however, partly because he intentionally hid his true intellect. It was easier, safer even, to just let people think his diminutive size equaled his intelligence, not realizing he was far cleverer and industrious than anyone really knew. Indeed, his survival instincts were his greatest asset and he had decided that it was time to exercise them.

The first step in his plan to escape was also the most dangerous. First, he needed to gather what piddling possessions he had, saddle up his mule, Sugar Pie, and hope his absence wouldn't be noticed until the gang was well on its way to Delgado Station. Initially, Potch had given thought to escaping across the border into Mexico. He quickly erased that thought because he knew that many of the men had already planned on heading south as well. He would be easily recognized there. How could he not be? There was no one else like him anywhere. So, Delgado Station was his only real hope of survival, assuming he was able to convince the town's people that he was on their side. If he could make it there before the fighting started, he thought, he just might make it through this nightmare alive.

Potch leaned his ear against the door that led outside. Wolf was heard barking orders to one and all, telling them to finish packing their gear, to make sure they had plenty of ammunition, that their knives were sharpened and to be ready for one, last and glorious raid. He was afraid to look out any of the windows for fear he would be seen and told to join the entire gang for Wolf's pep talk. From what he could tell, however, all of the men were hanging on Wolf's every word. Most had already gotten their respective rigs together, so if he was going to make his move, it had to be now. If anyone saw him gathering his meager supplies and weapons, they would likely assume he was getting ready to join the group, as ordered. No one paid much mind to him anyway, except to tease and ridicule him, but even that mistreatment had its limits, as everyone knew he was Wolf's pet, his "little helper."

There was a back door that led to the privy that Potch managed to sneak out of without being seen. The stable where he kept Sugar Pie was really only a shed, set away from the general stable the rest of the men used for their horses. They didn't want his mule stabled with their mounts. He managed to slip into the hovel of a room he had to himself, which was cobbled together out of whatever scraps of wood he managed to find and was next to Sugar Pie's bedding area. His room was nothing more than a storage shed, about four feet by five, but that was more than enough for him. His bed was just a blanket on a pile of hay, with two old crates he kept his belongings in, which consisted of a gold pocket watch that didn't work and never had since he robbed a dead man of it, one more shirt that was worse than the one he was wearing, some spare socks and a few trinkets of cheap jewelry he had managed to squirrel away. What no one knew, however, was that Potch had managed to save over three thousand dollars in gold and silver coins, as well as about two hundred dollars in paper currency. Some of his cash was his meager cut from the various raids and robberies the gang had committed over the years. While most of the men who came, went or died in the group over the years spent their cut on women, gambling and just day-to-day expenses, Potch managed to squirrel away his cut by stuffing it in his stall, where no one would ever think to look... or want to. Plus, he was also smart enough to slip a few extra coins into his share without anyone being the wiser. He was always careful not to overdo it, never being seen as an extravagant spender. Women avoided him, and gambling was never something that appealed to him, as fights and killings over claims of cheating were an all too common occurrence. No, he would keep his money where he could keep an eye on it.

His well-earned stash would finance his escape. If any of the men, especially Wolf, knew he had that much money hidden away, any one of them would have slit his throat for it. It was everything he possessed and his only way out.

As he heaved his satchel of gold and silver over Sugar Pie's neck, hooking in on the saddle horn, he also grabbed the only weapon Wolf allowed him to carry. It was a sawed-off, double-barreled twelve-gauge shotgun, with a blunt handle. Potch never used it against anything but the occasional rabbit, prairie dog or rattlesnake. Nothing human.

"Where do you think you're goin' little man?" came a sneering, low-pitched voice from behind him. Potch jumped and squealed and turned around. Thankfully, the voice asking the question didn't belong to Wolf. It belonged to Jack Holden, a man Potch disliked more than any of the others because he seemed to enjoy picking on him more than anyone else. "You planning on cuttin' and runnin'?" The man stepped forward and slapped his hand rough and hard against Sugar Pie's rump, causing her to kick up her hind legs. The sound of jingling coins made Jack Holden throw a curious glare at the satchel Potch had just hooked over the saddle horn.

"Well, what do we have here?" he said, as he stepped forward and patted the side of the satchel again, causing it to make a more distinct jingling sound. Potch stepped between Jack and his satchel, pushing him back a little. That's when Jack noticed the mini-shotgun Potch was holding. The man burst into

176

mocking laughter. "And just what do you expect to do with that, ya little freak?" he roared, slapping his thighs with both hands.

Something snapped inside Potch's emotionally scarred soul that seemed to take over his judgment faster than he could stop it. "This!" said Potch, with a glint in his eyes as he pulled the triggers on both barrels. The double blast lifted Potch's tormentor off his feet like a circus clown slipping on a banana peel. Jack Holden landed flat on his back, dead. Potch stood still, his feet frozen to the ground. He had never taken a man's life before, although he had seen many taken by others and the sight never seemed to bother him. This time, it was done by his own hand and, at first, it didn't bother him this time either. In fact, he felt something of a release, absorbing the recoil of the shotgun and seeing the man's puzzled expression as his guts exploded into the air around him.

The sound of men's voices roused Potch from his momentary trance. He knew he had to think fast about how to explain what they were about to see. First, he threw a small saddle blanket over Sugar Pie's back to cover the satchel bag filled with his bounty, just as a group of four men came scrambling around the corner of the shed with guns drawn. Another group of six was catching up, also with guns drawn. Wolf was forcing his way through the gathering crowd standing before Potch. The realization of what had taken place made every man hold their position, letting the picture sink in; Potch, holding a shotgun over one of their own, with his insides spread out on the ground. No one spoke, waiting instead for Wolf to make his way to the front of the pack. Potch never moved but held his now empty shotgun in front of him, smoke curling upward in gentle whisps from both barrels. It was an odd scene for these men to behold and hardly a vision they would associate with the little man they had always assumed to be a harmless little freak.

Pushing men aside and breaking through into the clearing, Wolf stopped dead in his tracks as he examined the scene. "Well, well, well, my little clown," he said, calmly, but with genuine curiosity. "Looks to me like you and Jack here had a serious disagreement."

Potch had just enough time to put together a story that he hoped would pass muster, not just with Wolf, but with the rest of the gang as well. "You said we was ALL goin' on the raid, Mr. Wolf. No one was stayin' behind."

Wolf folded his arms across his chest and slumped on to his left hip as he looked down at the man that was once Jack Holden. With some suspicion, he looked back at Potch and said, "And you're tellin' me that Jack was planning on high-tailin' it outta here?"

"Yes, sir, Mr. Wolf," said Potch, in a very straight-forward, matter-of-fact way. "He said he didn't wanna get killed over the likes of Orin and Buck and was plannin' on breakin' free, first chance he got once we got on the road. He even asked if I wanted to join him. Tried to convince me that it was for my own good, that I would likely get myself killed if I went along. I said no and that I was goin'. He laughed and called me a fool and said if I said anything to you or any of the others, he was gonna slit my throat right here and now." Potch held his voice firm, never wavering or allowing it to shake and give away any of his lie.

Spud Pierson stepped forward to offer his perspective. "Well, it kinda makes sense, Wolf," he said. "Jack never liked either of them boys and I could tell he wasn't too keen on possibly gettin' shot up or killed over 'em neither. Looks to me like, Potch here took it upon himself to make an example of Jack just like you wanted." Spud looked at the rest of the assembled group and then back to Wolf, adding, "That's my take on it, anyways."

178

Slowly, each man with a gun drawn began to holster their weapon. Wolf looked to his left, then to his right, reading the eyes of each man. He liked what he saw and judged that, although he was now down a man, it was probably for the best. So, killing Jack Holden was probably a good thing in the end. It sent the desired message, although he would have liked to have done the killing himself, which was precisely the point he was about to make to Potch.

"Come 'ere, little man," Wolf teased with a voice that was dripping with menace and devilish charm. Potch stepped forward, with timid, tiny steps. He was still holding his shotgun, though now empty and useless. He didn't speak but still tried to show courage and strength. Wolf crouched down on his haunches until he was eye to eye with Potch. "You got more spunk and guts than I ever gave ya credit for, Potch." He patted him on the head in a way that brought laughter from the rest of the men. Right then, Potch couldn't shake the feeling and the wish that his shotgun was fully loaded so he could unleash both barrels into Wolf's face. Oh, how he wished his gun was loaded. "But next time, little man, you come to me first, ya hear?" He reached up and pinched Potch's cheeks with both hands. "You denied me the pleasure of cutting his heart out and eating it for dinner." There were mixtures of laughs and groans as Wolf raised up to his full height and stretched his back. "You killed him, little man, so it's up to you to bury this piece of shit!" he ordered. Turning to the rest of the men he added, "Potch has first dibs on Jack's rig. Now, all of ya get back to packin' your own! We ride at high noon! I want to make Delgado Station when the sun and Black Moon are hanging side by side!" With that decree, the men dispersed, leaving Potch to bury his first kill, which would also give him time to decide his next step.

Chapter Fifteen

He had started the morning with a few cups of strong, black coffee. The night before, he spent with his friend, Val Avery, discussing old times, people they both knew, many now dead and gone, mistakes they had both made too obvious to deny, and the fact that the West was changing, and their way of life would soon be a thing of the past.

At first, both men did their best to avoid any talk of Wolf and of Val's decision to ride out alone in advance to make the offer, or to "throw down the gauntlet" as Jake put it, for Wolf to meet Jake, one on one, man to man, to settle this and hopefully avoid a bloodbath. It was a long shot, but it was agreed that it was one worth taking. The exact number of men Wolf had in his raiding party was unknown. Rough estimates from those who were brave enough to travel back and forth delivering supplies was that it seemed to average around twenty men, with spikes in population more often related to those men hiding out to avoid capture for crimes committed in other areas of the country. Those drifters seldom stayed on to consider themselves "Wolf's men," so the actual number of combatants the town might face was most likely in the fifteen to twenty range. The hope was that a number of those men, as well as a few of Wolf's men had already deserted, wishing to avoid a war with an entire town, however small. Additionally, they hoped that, upon hearing Val present Jake's challenge, Wolf's remaining army would insist he accept, if for no other reason than to prove his leadership to them that he was as tough as they thought. The additional, unspoken hope was that if Jake could take down Wolf, it would rid them all, not just of his presence, but the unpredictable mania that came along with him. Most wanted a strong leader to make decisions and keep some sense or order within the group. They just would prefer it to be somebody who wasn't full-on crazy. All of those hopes and expectations added up to a long shot, but it was better than no hope at all.

Under normal circumstances, if there even was such a thing in this case, Jake knew Val would never have volunteered to be his delivery man, nor would Jake have even allowed it. Val Avery was a brave and honorable man, but he wasn't one to carry a death wish... until now. But since Jake knew that Val's time was limited, doing this one last honorable thing for the people of his town was something he would not be denied.

"I got nothin' to lose, really," Val said with his characteristic bluntness. "The pain of whatever in hell this is is gettin' worse and worse every day. Doc gave me some laudanum for when things get too bad to handle. I mostly take it so's I can get a decent night's sleep. If I take it during the day, it makes my head a little too dipsy and too hard to focus my eyes."

"How are you feeling right now?" Jake asked. There was obvious concern in his voice, as he needed to assess his friend's mental and physical abilities to determine whether he would be able to accomplish what would likely be his last duty as sheriff.

Val looked at his glass of whiskey, one that Jake had just refilled, and tossed it down in one swallow. "My nerves have got me a little rattled, I don't mind sayin' and that's making things pain me more than usual. But if I drink much more of this, it won't matter," he finished with a laugh.

"Then maybe you should call it a night?" offered Jake. "Me

too if I was to be honest with myself. The truth is, tomorrow could well be the last day on this earth for both of us." He finished his own freshly refilled glass with one swallow just as Val had. "So, if we want to stand any chance of making it through—"

Val cut him off. "And of reducing the odds in the town's favor?" he added with a wink.

Jake leaned back in his chair and looked his friend straight in the eyes. "Yeah, that too." After an awkward pause that just needed to end, Jake asked, "So... what exactly is your plan, Val?"

The question was not unexpected but providing Jake with an answer was something Val couldn't do without first looking away and out the windows to his right. "Let's face it, if he says no, just as we discussed, then what's to stop him from shooting me down right then and there?"

"True enough." Jake crossed his arms over his chest. "Just as you said at the church, if you don't come back, that will be his answer."

"Yup," was Val's simple reply.

"So, I take it if things look like they're heading south, you plan on taking out Wolf and as many of his men as you can before they cut you down?" Val nodded his acceptance of Jake's prediction.

"I'll be goin' out on my terms, Jake," Val said with a firm, no-nonsense attitude. "Besides, like I said, this is my town and what happens here is my responsibility. You can't deny me that."

"Nor would I, Val," Jake said, reluctantly. "The truth is, it makes sense... in a weird, fatalistic sort of way."

"I've got one more favor to ask of you, Jake, if you wouldn't mind?" Val reached into his inside vest pocket and pulled out a letter, sealed in an envelope. "This is my last will and testament, such as it is." He slid the letter across the table. "It sure ain't much, but it's all I got in this world."

Jake just stared down at the letter, never making a move to pick it up. He felt like his entire body had gone numb and wouldn't move. "What do you want me to do with it?"

"Just read it out loud to the folks at the church, or maybe give it to the preacher if you don't want to." Val snickered a nervous giggle. "Hell, you might not be alive yourself to read it."

Jake couldn't help but see the logic of his friend's reasoning. "That could well be the case." Both men laughed softly. "Hell, maybe I should write up my own last will and testament. Not that I have anything of value to pass on, except some money in a bank in Kansas City and my guns."

"What about your horse, Teacher?" asked Val.

"I already told M.B. she could have her if I died before I could pay my bill," recalled Jake. "If she wanted to stay, that is. Teacher goes her own way. Always has. But maybe I should put all of this in writing, just in case."

"Might not be a bad idea, Jake." There was, yet another awkward pause between the two old friends. They seemed to be having a lot of those lately. "The letter is just my way of saying thanks to the people here. They've been good to me. They gave me a chance to be somebody decent, which is something I never thought I could be. As far as my belongings, well, fact is, I ain't got shit 'cept my horse and saddle, my guns and such and a few books."

"Books?" Jake couldn't hold back his surprise.

"Yeah, BOOKS!" laughed the sheriff. "Why are you so surprised? I told you, I like to read that Shakespeare stuff. I like the poetry. I got his entire collection of plays and poems. Sonnets, he calls them." With uncharacteristic boldness, the sheriff launches into a famous soliloquy from *Henry V*. "Once more unto the breach, dear friends, once more! Or close the wall up with our English dead. In peace there's nothing so becomes a man as modest stillness and humility."

Jake sat dumbstruck for a brief moment, then offered some sincere applause. "Bravo!" He continued clapping his hands. "Bravo!" Both men sat in silence. "That's twice you've quoted Shakespeare to me. I never would have expected you to know any Shakespeare, much less quote something from *Henry V*."

Val was immediately impressed himself and was surprised that Jake knew which play his little performance was from. "I see you know some of the Bard yourself."

Jake smiled at the compliment. "I've seen a few performances of some of his plays. I saw Edwin Booth once in New York City. He did that play, *The Merchant of Venice* and *Hamlet* too. Quite a performer."

"Yeah, too bad his brother was such a crazy bastard," said the sheriff. "Set the whole acting profession back for a time." Another awkward pause passed between the two men that just begged to be filled. "Anyway, believe it or not, I did manage to save myself a few dollars, which Dan MacNeil has over at the bank. I left instructions for what I want done with it. It's all written down there in the letter."

"I'll see to it that your wishes are followed, Val. You can rest assured on that score."

"I know I can, Jake. That's why I'm leavin' it with you. So, don't go and get yourself killed."

With blatant sarcasm Jake said, "I'll do my best."

Val smiled in a manner that seemed to relieve him of a great burden. He patted both hands on the table in something of a drum beat, one, two, three, four, then finished by slapping both hands down at the same time. There was nothing more to say, except farewell. Pushing his chair back, Sheriff Val Avery stood, extending his right hand to Jake, who immediately stood, accepting his friend's firm grip. "What does a man say to an old friend at a moment like this?"

Jake felt a catch in his throat. The two men, both alike in so many ways yet also so very different, shared a look that spoke more than words ever could. All Jake could say was, "It's been an honor."

"Likewise," was all Val Avery could manage before his voice cracked with emotion.

As the sheriff turned to walk away, Gracie McCall came into the room. The sheriff tipped his hat, saying, "Miss McCall, you take good care of Jake's horse now," he said, with a charming smile as he continued out the door. The young woman's expression showed surprise, not just at being treated in such a courteous manner by the sheriff or at being asked to do something she would do for any of the horses in her charge, but at the expressions on the faces of both men. She knew she had interrupted something special between them. There was a feeling of sadness in the room that was potent.

"I'm sorry, Mr. Benteen," she said in an uncharacteristic, apologetic tone. "I didn't mean to interrupt your meeting with the sheriff. I imagine you're both laying out some sort of plan for when the shooting starts."

"Something like that, Miss McCall," Jake said. "And please call me, Jake. Mr. Benteen seems a bit out of keeping with the situation."

Gracie smiled. "Only if you stop calling me, Miss McCall," she said, with just the slightest giggle. "I thought we settled that. Makes me feel like an old maid. Like I told you before, my friends call me Gracie and I'd be obliged if you would do the same."

"Does that mean we're friends now, Gracie?" There was just the slightest tease in Jake's question.

Gracie shuffled her feet from side to side and didn't seem to know what to do with her hands. "I've done a lot of thinking, Mr. Ben... I mean, Jake. A lot of folks in town have. Everyone keeps saying how times are changing and I guess that's true enough. We're really a pretty good bunch once you get to know us. I think the sheriff would agree with that. We think we have a damn fine town here and it's one worth saving. The fact is most of us agree we've been living on borrowed time with that gang down in Tres Mesa. Speaking for myself, I can't believe we haven't had a more serious run-in with them before now." Gracie paused and took a step forward and gazed longingly out the window. "Many of us have talked about how, sooner or later, those men were going to get restless and decided to make a move. A 'last hurrah' as some folks have been calling it. What happened to Juneann and Ben just made that possibility a reality. The truth is, if it hadn't been them, it would have been someone or something else. It was bound to happen sooner or later. Maybe this is that time." Gracie McCall took a deep breath and blew it out with a whoosh. "Well... howdy-do! That was a lot more than I was planning on saying. Sorry for babbling on like that."

"No reason for apologizing, Gracie. It was obviously something you felt needed saying. I'm grateful you did and that you felt you could share those thoughts with me." Jake took his own long look out the side window. The main street was a buzz of activity, with people rushing from one place to the next. Horses were noticeably absent. "Mind if I ask what's going on out there?"

"Folks are getting ready to defend their town, Jake," she said with obvious pride. "Just like you said. We're not gunfighters with knowledge of guns or fighting tactics like you and Sheriff Avery, but we can damn sure fight for what's ours and that's what we plan to do." Gracie blushed with pride at the end of her declaration.

The pride in this young woman's face and the way her chest swelled when she spoke made her more attractive to Jake than ever, and he thought she was pretty fetching before. "And that's what will catch Wolf and his men off guard," Jake said. "Chances are they have never had to face more than a few men at a time when it came to taking what they wanted. They always relied on the strength of their numbers. I'm betting that facing a whole town, or at least a good number of citizens with guns is not something they have ever had to face before. Just knowing that fact might be enough to scare off a few of them."

Gracie liked the sound of that reasoning. "Let's hope so, Jake," she offered cautiously. After another pause, she took another step forward, closer to Jake. "I don't mind telling you, we're all pretty scared, Jake. But, like I said, most of us have decided to put up a fight. We just wanted you to know we're prepared to do what needs doing. We were also hoping you'd be able to... I don't know... talk to us a little about what to expect. Lay out some sort of strategy for us. Is there any sort of plan other than the sheriff going out alone to try and talk to them, change the odds, if possible and then you, maybe, doing the same thing out in the middle of the street? Honestly, if that's your whole plan, I gotta say, it ain't much."

The woman standing before him was making Jake lose his concentration on the task at hand. He needed to get back on track. "How many guns do we have, Gracie? And more to the point, how many folks do we have that know how to use them?" Jake was still scanning the street outside, assessing who was who and what was what, such as he was able.

Gracie crossed to stand next to Jake. "All totaled, men and women, I counted thirteen, including me."

Jake turned a sour frown to Gracie "Thirteen?" He paused and blew out a breath of exasperation. "Not that I'm superstitious, mind you, but I'd sure like to round that out with one more."

Gracie looked at Jake with a quizzical eye. "But you make it fourteen, Jake. If you plan on standing with us once you take down Wolf, that is."

Jake laughed at himself for failing to do the proper math, given the circumstances. "Ha! Well, math was never my strong suit, Gracie. And yes, I sure plan on standing with everyone else. So, fourteen it is."

"I didn't count the sheriff for reasons I think you already know," offered Gracie "I spoke with him earlier this morning and he explained his part of the plan pretty clearly. Can't say I like it much, but I also know what else he has figured into his plan if Wolf declines your challenge."

"Oh?" Jake was surprised.

"Look, Jake, I've been tending animals ever since I was old enough to care for something other than myself. My folks both died on the way out here of a fever that took most of the wagon train. That was some twenty-odd years ago, when I was just six years old. The wagon train couldn't take me any further, so I was dropped off at the livery stable owned by Russ Oechsle and his wife Janet. Good, solid folks. They lost their only two boys in the war, splitting up and fighting for both sides, if you can believe that. So they took me in. I was the lucky one. When they died, they left me the stable. I've been caring for horses and other sick animals ever since. Sick humans aren't much different. So, I've known for some time now that the sheriff has been dealing with something serious. I've seen his face turn sour and watched him grab his stomach in ways that don't look like it's just a belly ache from bad food. He's been going to see Doc Gibbons at least two or three times a week for the past few months, so it doesn't take a genius to know something's wrong. It also doesn't take a military mind to know what he's planning on doing, one way or another, when he rides out to meet that Wolf and his gang." Gracie gave Jake a cold, hard stare. "Am I wrong?"

It seemed to Jake that every time this woman spoke her mind, she not only made sense, but her honesty made her more appealing than any woman he had ever met. Oh, he had met prettier ones, here and there… maybe. But none of them had that combination of spunk, charm and physical attraction all rolled into one. Jake shook his head.

"I'm going to go out on a limb here, Gracie, and ask you a question I'm hoping you'll give me an honest answer to, not that I think you wouldn't." Jake took his hat off and fumbled it in his hands.

Gracie's expression indicated she had no idea what that question was going to be, but she sure was interested. "Well?" she said. "You got something to say, you best spit it out."

Jake's smile grew even bigger. He didn't think it was possible, but he was liking her even more. Gracie's total lack of pretense set Jake at ease. He raised his eyes to hers and said, "Would I be out of line, Miss McCall, and I'm addressing you as, Miss McCall because of the formality of my request so… if I were to call on you once this whole situation is over? Assuming we both come out alive, that is?"

Gracie's eyes flew open wide and a welcome smile filled out her face. Not wanting to give her reaction away too much, she waited a few seconds more than her true emotions really wanted. Finally, she said, "Would that 'call' be one of a romantic nature, Mr. Benteen?" This time, it was she who folded her arms across her chest, tipping to one side and settling into her right hip, presenting something of a sassy pose. She wore a smile that was even bigger than before.

"Well, it sure wouldn't be to ask you to tend my horse," replied Jake. "You're already doing a fine job of that so, yes, my intentions would be of a romantic nature and entirely honorable… mostly." Now he was smiling.

Gracie unfolded her arms and slipped both hands into her back pockets as she rocked her hips back and forth. "Well… then I guess you better not get yourself killed, Mr. Benteen," she said, with her customary bluntness. She turned and walked over to the front door, stopped and turned back around to face Jake. "Just so you know, I've had more than my fair share of… offers, Jake. Life's too short out here and too damn tough to sit alone every night when there's someone out there I think might be worth the time."

There was a hint of history in her voice when she said, "with someone worth the time." He was confident enough in his interpretation of her statement to take it she meant she wasn't a virgin. That possibility was not an issue with him. In fact, he couldn't have cared less. It hardly seemed fair to pass judgment on a woman's romantic attachments, be they fleeting or of an intended long-term arrangement. His own past was hardly unblemished when it came to the women in his life. He could rationalize that he led a dangerous, nomadic existence that led to many a passing romantic fling, but that wouldn't be entirely fair or honest. The truth was Jake took advantage of his wandering lust for the female sex whenever it suited him. If he was to be entirely honest with himself, he also took advantage of his fame and reputation with the ladies, as many made sexual advances toward him just for the bragging rights to say they bedded the infamous Jake Benteen. Both parties knew what the game was and was willing to play. But that was then, and this was now... and now he was tired of that life. The callousness of it all left him empty. Sex was easy to find. Love was something he always avoided. He had toyed with the thought of settling down somewhere, if that were even possible, given his reputation. Finding a woman, and a town that didn't know who he was, had proven an impossibility. Perhaps that was why he kept traveling to more distant parts of the country, hoping his name and deeds wouldn't travel with him, or if they did, at least to people who wouldn't care, or judge him on his past alone. Was Delgado Station that town? Was Gracie McCall a woman who could look beyond his past?

Jake's expression turned serious. "Am *I* worth the time, Miss McCall?" Jakes wasn't being coy, and his question was sincere, with no judgment attached.

Gracie McCall could tell there was something more behind Jake's question than asking for a simple date. "I don't give myself freely, Jake, but I'm no wallflower either. If I take a man to my bed, all I ask for is honesty."

Something happened at that moment that sent a signal, a shockwave even, to both of these lonely souls. They were suddenly drawn together simultaneously. Both met in the middle of the room in a passionate embrace that was a combination of sexual explosion and emotional release. As their lips met, Jake lifted Gracie off the floor, spinning her around, trying to find a solid surface until he pressed her body against the wall by the door. Gracie wrapped her legs around Jake's waist as they held their kiss until their lips were rubbed raw and they needed to come up for air.

Jake placed both hands on either side of Gracie's face and broke their kiss so he could ask, "I'm not interested in a one-night romp in the sheets. I want more. A lot more. Is that honest enough for you, Miss McCall? Gracie?"

"For the time being, Mr. Benteen," she answered, catching her breath as she untangled her legs from Jake's waist and planted her feet on the floor. "But you damn well better not die after riling my blood like that. I expect you to finish what you started."

"Fair enough." Jake adjusted his clothing, as did Gracie, given that both sets of hands had just been exploring the other's body parts in a fever of sexual curiosity and desire. "Now, would you do me a favor and gather the townsfolk along both sides of the street? I need to talk to them about what to expect and how best to protect themselves."

"You need to make it clear that killing will be a part of this too, Jake," added Gracie. "I don't think most of them realize just what that means and that they may be taking someone's life in this fight."

"They'll be doing it to save their own," answered Jake. "That's the main thing they need to let take hold. This is life-or-death."

Gracie swallowed hard. The realization of what was at stake just hit home with her at that moment. She had never taken a life before either. A human life. She had been forced to put down the occasional sick or injured horse in her time, and certainly hunt for food, but taking a man's life, no matter how deserving or necessary, just seemed, well, different.

"I'll gather the folks," she said, then turned to leave, but spun back around, rising up on her toes and gave Jake a kiss on his left cheek and repeated, "You damn well better not die, Jake Benteen." With that declaration, Gracie McCall turned with a hop in her step and ran out the door.

Chapter Sixteen

As Sheriff Val Avery rode his horse along the dusty trail to Tres Mesa, the personal realization that his life was fast coming to a close was an unavoidable fact he was forced to come to grips with as he and his horse plodded along. He wasn't in a hurry. Doc Gibbons had already delivered the sobering news a few months back that the pain he was experiencing, a pain that seemed to cramp his entire abdomen, sometimes causing him to buckle over, was likely the result of some form of cancer. Specifically, what Doc Gibbons couldn't say. Without further testing, something the doctor was unequipped to offer, he couldn't be sure if it was his colon, or maybe his liver or his pancreas, but the doctor said his best hunch was that it was the latter of the speculations. Regardless, whatever it was, surgery was not an option and it was getting worse. His time was limited. All things considered, going out this way suited him just fine.

He had managed to last fifty-seven years in a profession not known for a long lifespan and even survived his stint in the Civil War, coming home without a scratch. In all that time, and in all of the scraps and skirmishes he encountered, he had only taken four bullets in the course of his life as a hired gun. Oddly enough, he never got shot until he took the job legally as town sheriff for Delgado Station.

Bullet number one came from a woman who shot first and asked, "Who's there?" later. She had fired a single bullet through the front door of her farmhouse from a .22 caliber rifle her late husband used to shoot rodents, rabbits, snakes and anything else that was considered edible and close enough to be killed while never leaving the front porch. She felt truly horrible for shooting the sheriff but scolded him for not announcing himself first, even going so far as to insist that it was his own fault. Fortunately, the bullet only creased his left side, removing about an inch of fat the sheriff admitted he could have done without anyway. He was also too embarrassed to admit who had shot him and how, preferring to swear Doc Gibbons to secrecy, since he had only been on the job less than a week. His intent was to go around to all of the outlying farms and ranches in his jurisdiction and introduce himself. Getting shot in the first place he stopped was not a good way to start.

The second bullet came from a ruckus he was walking toward in the hopes he could break it up before someone got hurt. It seems an argument had arisen between three drunken prospectors over a disputed claim. It was never clear which of the three men fired the shot that hit him, since all three were firing their pistols rather indiscriminately, hitting anything and everything they weren't intentionally aiming at. What or who they were aiming at was, presumably, each other, more or less. Fortunately for them, they were all poor shots, drunk or sober. Unfortunately for the sheriff, one of them managed to hit him in the right calf muscle, the bullet passing through his boot, but missing the bone. He still managed to arrest the drunkards without further incident, each professing their sincere apologies for shooting him, but blaming each other for it. In this case, the sheriff managed to convince the prospectors to accept the blame equally and to pay for all damages. Each collected an equal amount of gold dust from their claims, worth about three hundred dollars in total to cover the damages, which actually only came to less than one-hundred-and-fifty dollars. The sheriff took what was left, to cover some considerable pain and suffering on his part and to buy himself a new pair of boots. If truth be told, he needed new boots anyway, so taking a bullet through one of them justified his purchase even more.

Two more bullets came at the same time, from one man named Ryan Gates who remembered the sheriff from a time long ago, roughly ten years. While passing through town on his way to no place in particular, he stopped into the local saloon, The Dancing Dollar, for a drink and casually asked, "Who is the law in this town?" It was always wise for saddle tramps and wandering cowboys to know who was behind the badge in any town they passed through just in case they had a wanted poster out on them for some petty crime or worse. When he heard the name Val Avery, he slammed his shot glass down on the bar and hollered, "Avery? Your sheriff is Val Avery? Where is that son of a bitch?"

Not waiting for an answer, Gates spun on his heels and headed out the bat-wing doors and across the street. He had seen the sign when he first rode in, indicating the sheriff's office and was making a beeline straight for it. When he reached the office, Gates stopped in the middle of the street and called out for the sheriff.

"Val Avery! You in there?" Gates had a full grip on his Remington .45, which he had sitting in a reverse position in his holster, that hung off his right hip. Some men preferred to ride with the handle facing in while riding, rather than down the side. It made it easier to reach across for the draw while sitting on a horse. How effective it was for a street showdown was debatable. "You comin' on out, Avery, or am I comin' in?" screamed Gates.

The sheriff pulled the office curtain to one side and looked out onto the street. He didn't recognize the man demanding his presence and chose to call out from inside. "Who's askin'?" he said, as he reached for his gun and holster, which were hanging on a peg just inside the front door. The anger in the man's voice told him he might want to consider taking a scattergun too, especially since he had no idea if there were others outside waiting for him to open the door.

Cautiously, and very slowly, the sheriff opened the office door but stood against the doorframe to the left of the knob. He had already been shot through a door once and got off lucky, so he was not about to make the same mistake again.

Seeing the empty doorway made Gates even angrier than he was before. "What's the matter, SHERIFF?" He seemed to spit out that last word as if the sound of it was poison. "Afraid to face me... man to man?"

It was clear the man knew who he was, but the sheriff still didn't have a clue as to who was making the threats, or why he seemed so bent on killing him. "Mind if I ask yer name, friend?" asked the sheriff.

"Well, I sure as hell ain't any friend of yours!" came the reply.

"Just the same, would it be askin' too much if you told me just who you are and what this is all about?" The sheriff was trying to remain calm and stall for time. He was hoping some form of recognition would pop into his head as to who this man might be and why talking out the problem was out of the question. Given his past, there could be any number of possibilities of men who wanted him dead. He didn't have anywhere near the legacy of Jake Benteen, but he had left enough graves behind to make it more than probable someone was out for revenge.

"Ryan Gates!" hollered the man. "That name mean anything to you?"

After a brief moment to ponder the name, which did not ring any bells, the sheriff replied, "Sorry. Should it?"

"You slept with my sister and took her innocence," claimed the brother. "Then you left her carrying your child!"

This news scrambled Val Avery's brain more than tequila and mezcal combined. Yes, he had had his way with many a young woman back in his youth. A few old ones too, for that matter. Just how far back and in what town was where the memories got a little foggy. His next statement needed to be delicately phrased. "Umm… I sure don't mean any disrespect to your sister, but could you be a little more specific?" he asked, tentatively. "About how far back are we talkin'? Where was this? And you still haven't told me your sister's name?"

"You don't even KNOW?" screamed the revenge-minded brother of the jilted young women from a time and place Val Avery couldn't recall.

"Sorry, friend," came the sheriff's rather meek reply. "Like I said, I'm not tryin' to be disrespectful here, but I've been to a lot of places and covered a lot of territory in my time, so you're going to have to be more forthcoming with a name, time and place."

"It was back in eighty-one, ya sick, son of a bitch! You deflowered by baby sister, Sarah Mae!" A single gunshot sent a bullet through the office window, shattering the glass and fluttering the flower-patterned curtains the Ladies Beautification League were kind enough to decorate his office with.

"Woah, woah! Just hold your fire there before somebody gets hurt! I am tellin' you honest and true, I do not remember anyone by that name," claimed the sheriff. "I swear to you, if I

198

had known, I would have done right by your sister and her child, boy or girl. Honest and truly, I would have, had I known."

After the first shot was fired, the street began to fill with curious spectators. Most onlookers came from the saloon, but a few were just citizens heading home, or taking care of last-minute shopping or walking the cool evening air.

The distraught brother would not hear any of the sheriff's excuses. "My sister died of infection three months after giving birth to your bastard son! Did you even know that… or CARE?"

Hearing the terrible news of the woman's death and the discovery that he had a son, possibly, was a punch to the gut Val Avery never expected to hear in his life. He was trying to sort out the when, where and who of it all again, then remembered the year the man had said. He was desperately trying to piece together his history during that time but could only recall that he was in the Wyoming Territory then, helping settle a small range war over water rights and some minor rustling. The Indian wars were still going on as well, so there was a lot of movement in multiple directions. "Wait! You said it was back in eighty-one?"

"That's right!" screamed Gates.

"I was working in the Wyoming Territory back then, for most of two years!" Are you sure it was me that… um… had… I mean took… I mean…?" That was not a question that should have been asked at that time.

"WHAT ARE YOU SAYIN'?" The brother's rage had escalated far beyond reason at this point. "Are you callin' my sister a whore?"

Three more gunshots, fired in rapid succession, ripped through the door frame, sending shards of wood into the room. The sheriff caught a few splinters in the face as he pulled his head back away from the casing just in time. That was all the negotiation he was prepared to tolerate. The scattergun was the logical choice at this point, so the sheriff stepped boldly into the center of the open door. His only mistake was allowing a momentary pause to clearly identify his target. But Gates was prepared and fired again, emptying his gun. Two bullets found their mark, one parting the sheriff's hair just above his left ear. A fraction more inside and he would have taken a bullet from a .45 straight through his left eye. The other hit the sheriff in the left shoulder, just under the clavicle. That shot likely would have been fatal as well had the sheriff not been twisted in a half-circle from the impact of the shot that grazed his face. The bullet to the shoulder passed through and into the room, lodging in the wall by the stove. Everything happened in such a blur of gunfire that, despite his injuries, the sheriff was able to maintain his balance, right himself and pull the trigger on both barrels of the scattergun. It was more than enough. His close proximity to Gates sent a tight spread of buckshot that did epic damage, hitting him flush in the groin, severing the femoral arteries of both legs and obliterating everything in between. As he lay dying, he told the sheriff his full name and begged him to "do right" by his sister's boy. But before the sheriff could get any more information, Ryan Gates died in his arms, having bled out in a matter of minutes.

Of all the men taken down by Val Avery, justified or not, this one haunted him the most because he was left with too many unanswered questions. The funeral was paid for by the sheriff, with him also being the only witness at the graveside. A very young Preacher Lee presided over the man's remains. It was his first duty as pastor upon arriving in Delgado Station.

The sheriff made more than a dozen requests by wire trying to get additional information on Gates and any family he might have, especially the son he may or may not have fathered, notifying them of their kin's demise and ultimate burial. Nothing came back that was of any help. The thought of a son growing up without a father, without even knowing who he was, was something he had never considered in his wild youth. As a child, he was fortunate enough to have the love of both parents until both were taken by a cholera epidemic in Homer, New York, in 1854, when he was thirteen years old. He often wondered what course his life would have taken had they lived and he stayed on to finish school. As it was, he joined the Army at the start of the American Civil War in 1862 and the course of his life was set.

As the sheriff rode along on what he believed could be his final journey, he was struck by how much of his life came flooding back. He tried to recall more fond memories, if possible, but was disheartened to discover none were forthcoming. The only memory he could reflect on with any sense of pride was the day he agreed to take the job of sheriff for Delgado Station. The previous man behind the badge was Don Berg from Tupelo, Mississippi. The town was just starting to get civilized and Don was the only one wearing a gun and knew how to use it, more or less. As a young man, he had been a farm hand, working for various spreads throughout New Mexico and had learned to use a firearm when necessary. He wasn't wild and reckless with it, or his life in general, and folks in the region respected his work ethic and honesty.

As the town grew, members gathered to discuss the need for someone to uphold law and order. No one stepped forward. Don was unemployed at that point, just getting by doing odd jobs here and there, and the town, up to that point anyway, seemed relatively quiet. So, he raised his hand and was hired on the spot.

Initially, Don Berg had a pretty easy time of it, only needing to settle the occasional bar fight, or drag the regular overachievers in alcohol consumption off to jail to sleep it off. Then, one night, he made the fateful mistake of assuming a man to be unarmed, letting down his guard.

The man, known as J.D. Walsh, was your basic, common card sharp, or to some, a card shark, as he was believed to be cheating by double-dealing, or dealing off the bottom of the deck. One of his early victims had alerted the sheriff of his suspicions and asked him to intervene and to "check this feller out." Hoping to prevent any gunplay, the sheriff came into the saloon just as Walsh was pulling in a hefty pot and asked him to stand and empty his pockets and remove his coat so that he could check for extra cards or other gaffing mechanics. Walsh stood slowly, without indicating any intentions, then raised his right hand and pointed straight at the sheriff's head just as a .45 caliber Remington, double-barreled Derringer slid down his arm from his sleeve, resting in his hand. Without uttering a single word, Walsh pulled the trigger, firing a single ball into the sheriff's head, just above his right eye, killing him instantly.

All spectators and fellow gamblers just backed away as Walsh resumed collecting his "winnings." He made it known that his Derringer still had one more bullet left, and he was ready to use it on anyone who tried to stop him. Val Avery, who was across the room making time with one of the barmaids, pushed her to the side for safety and stepped into the path of Walsh as he tried to make his escape, telling him to drop the gun. Why Val did this has always perplexed him as it was not his habit to interfere in the disputes of others, no matter how foul the offense. But for some unknown reason, he did this time. Walsh seemed equally perplexed by Val's actions.

"By my reckoning, you've got one shot left in that coward's piece," said Val. "So, the question you have to ask yourself is can you beat me, then make it out the door before everyone in this town tears the flesh from your bones?"

A desperate man often does foolish things, and this man was no different. Although his hands were filled with paper and coin, he still tried to raise his gun hand just enough to indicate to Val that he was going all in. Val drew as fast as he ever had, drilling three shots dead center into the card player's chest in a grouping no bigger than a silver dollar. Walsh stood motionless for a few seconds, as if he wasn't sure his life was over. Money began slipping from his fingers, floating or clinking onto the floor while the dying gambler watched helplessly. Val knew the man was dead, but his body hadn't gotten the message from his brain just yet. When both of Walsh's hands dropped, limp by his sides, he fell forward, face first, slamming into the floor. His body came to rest next to Sheriff Berg, whose eyes were still open, fixed on the ceiling.

What happened next was what made folks realize Val Avery was a man they could trust and the man best suited to take over from Sheriff Berg. As more than a few people in the room began to drop to their knees and collect the table winnings, Val ordered them all to drop their stolen or reclaimed treasure and step back. He told the bartender to collect all of the money and stuff it in the sheriff's hat. He told others to get a doctor, if the town had one, or the undertaker and to remove both bodies and to collect their belongings. He then asked if the town had a telegraph office so he could send a wire to the nearest marshal's office detailing what took place. In short, Val Avery was reestablishing law and order. He even went so far as to handle all of the legal communications himself, as well as locking the money away in the bank vault as evidence, until a judge could fairly determine how it was to be distributed.

He found himself sitting in Sheriff Berg's office over the next few days, "taking care of business" in a town he was only planning on staying in for a few days. Those few days had come and gone. Ultimately, what amounted to a town board gathered in the sheriff's office and offered him the job.

"From what we've been told, it was you who stopped that killer cold and took control of the situation," observed Dan MacNeil, the banker where the gambling money was locked away. "The circuit judge and a Federal Marshal will both be arriving tomorrow to put this whole tragedy to rest, thanks in no small part, to you."

Pete Adams stepped forward, or more accurately, was pushed forward by members of the group. "I did some investigating on you, Mr. Avery, sir," said Pete. "I knew I recognized your name, so I sent out some inquiries about you."

Val was sitting behind the desk in Sheriff Berg's office and folded his hands behind his head. "And?" was all he said.

"Well, sir," began Pete. "You got something of a reputation back east a bit, and some up north too. Word is you're a hired gun."

Val's expression remained unchanged, still holding his hands, fingers laced behind his head. "It's true I have been hired for my skills with a gun. What's your point?"

"Well, sir," stammered Pete Adams, "from what information I got, all the places where you... um... worked, the folks gave you high praise for being honest and fair."

Val leaned forward, placing both hands, with fingers still laced together, in front of him. "I'd like to think I am," he replied. "Again, what's your point?"

"The point is, Mr. Avery, you're not a gunfighter... exactly," answered the biggest man he had ever seen, standing behind the group. "My name's Bonawitz. Eric. I've been to a few places and seen some gunhands and gunfighters and such, but you're… you're different. From what folks said that were there that night, you could have taken all the money and then some and walked right out the door and nobody would have done a thing to stop you."

"But you didn't," added Pete. "Folks said you restored order and we all know what you did since. That means something to this town. We all liked Sheriff Berg, a lot. He was a good man, and you did right by him."

"You did right by this town too, Mr. Avery," said the banker. "That's why we would like to offer you the job of sheriff of the town of Delgado Station. And we're hoping you'll accept."

With that offer now laid on the table, the three men who spoke, as well as two more who stood in the back but remained silent, choosing to let the others do the talking, all looked to one another and each offered some form of verbal expression of agreement. Val remained silent.

"Well?" asked the banker. "What do you say?"

A rueful smile crossed Val's face as he recalled that fateful day. It was a little more than a decade ago, but the memory was still fresh. That was, indeed, a good memory and one that he cherished. The day that changed his life from a wandering gun for hire to a respected town marshal. Maybe his life wasn't all for naught after all, he wondered. Maybe he did do some good that will leave a mark worth remembering.

The heat of the late morning was beginning to turn into the blistering heat of noon and was also beginning to take its toll and brought the sheriff out of his trip down memory lane. It was only a little after eleven in the morning and it was already hot enough to fry an egg on a rock. Val stopped his horse and pulled his

205

canteen for himself and took a healthy drag of warm water. With some grunts and groans, he climbed down off the saddle and pulled down a water pouch and filled his hat for his horse, which gratefully lapped up his own warm liquid. Val scanned the road ahead of him and noticed a plume of dust in the distance. By the size of the dust cloud, he figured it was kicked up by at least a dozen or more horses. "Wolf!" he thought. It had to be. There wouldn't be that many riders coming from that direction that weren't somehow affiliated with Wolf's gang. Val felt a churning in his stomach and it didn't have anything to do with the disease that would kill him if Wolf or one of his men didn't take him down first.

He pulled his hat away from his horse and poured the remaining water over his head and took some of the spill to wipe it across his horse's snout and neck. Although judging distance in the desert can be tricky, he was reasonably certain he would come face-to-face with the approaching riders in about an hour, probably less. Nothing else to do but wait and let them come to him. No sense tiring himself or his horse in this heat. No sense rushing to his own death any earlier than necessary either. Nothing to do but try and find some shade and wait. Val stepped off the trail and crossed to a tall, desert ironwood tree where he tied off his horse and sat down on the shady side to await his fate.

Chapter Seventeen

"Folks! Thanks for coming out," Jake hollered as loud as he could. He wanted to make sure he got everyone's attention. "You can all stay up on the sidewalks, under the roofs and out of this heat if you like. I just need you to be able to hear me clearly."

"Are they comin'?" asked an anxious citizen from in front of the bank. Jake couldn't tell who it was, but it was likely the main question all were thinking.

"Not that I know of!" Jake yelled. "It could be a few hours yet, so that gives us some time to get ready."

The banker, Dan MacNeil, stepped down off the wooden sidewalk in front of his bank and into the oppressive heat. He shaded his yes from the sun and asked, "Is it true that Sheriff Avery rode out there alone to try and talk sense into that bunch?"

"I'm not sure how much sense he or anyone else can talk into them, sir, but yes, Sheriff Avery did ride out earlier to try and meet with them first," answered Jake.

"I heard he was going to take them on all by himself," a woman called out from across the street.

"Why ain't you with him, Benteen?" came another voice. "You're the one started this!" Everyone knew who belonged to the repeated charge, hollered from a coward's seclusion.

"We don't see you ridin' out to back the sheriff, Amos!" came the booming voice of Eric Bonawitz.

Jake raised both hands in an attempt at quieting the crowd. "We don't have time for this! Sheriff Avery is his own man and he made this decision on his own, thinking it was the best way to protect this town. HIS town! I'm following his orders. So, if you're here to fight, to protect your family and your town, then there are some things you need to know to be ready."

"You expectin' us to do some killin', Benteen? That's your line of work, not ours!" Once again, it was Amos who just couldn't resist the chance to open his big mouth one last time. "Why should we listen to you? You're gonna get us all killed!"

Eric Bonawitz put an end to any more babbling nonsense from Amos. "Nobody's expecting you to do anything, Amos," he said. "You've always talked big, but when it comes to puttin' your actions where your big mouth is, your just pure chicken shit. So, do us all a favor and go run and hide under the rock you crawled out from under. This talk don't concern you!"

He stepped into the street and addressed the crowd. In his hand was his old Springfield .54 he brought back from the war. Tucked into his waist were two mismatched pistols, one a Colt .45 and the other a .36 Army Colt. He even had a twelve-inch Bowie knife strapped to his left leg. This man was loaded for bear... or Wolf. Now that he had the crowd's attention, he continued. "I been doin' some serious thinkin' on this and, well, I never thought I'd say this, but I gotta side with Mr. Benteen here." Eric extended his hand to Jake, who immediately responded, grasping it, adding a nod of appreciation. Eric then turned to address the crowd again. "I was born here in Delgado Station. Doc up there brought me into this world." Doc Gibbons was standing on the second-floor landing of his office, looking down at the town's people. Eric gave him a wave of thanks and appreciation, which the doctor immediately returned. Eric continued. "My mam and pap are both buried here, right up on that hill over yonder, along with a lot of your folk's family. They built this town. Some of them even died for it. It's time we did too, if that's what it takes."

The street was silent. Only the sound of a slow, heated wind filled with dust whispered down the street. Eric still had more to say. "Now, I heard a story that may or may not be true. Don't really care. But I heard it said that back at the Alamo, Colonel Travis drew a line in the sand with his sword and asked each man to decide whether they was gonna cut and run... or stay." Eric lowered the barrel of his Springfield and dragged a line across dirt that ran from one side of the main street to the other, leaving himself and Jake on one side and all of the town's citizens on the other. "What we gotta decide here and now is just that. Who's stayin' and who's goin'?" The big man then stepped to his right and took his place by Jake Benteen's side and waited.

The first to move was Gracie McCall who had all she could do to stop herself from running to stand at Jake's side. Next to step into the street was the barbershop owner, Lou Hudson. He was carrying an old squirrel rifle of some undetermined manufacture and caliber. The weapon's functionality was in serious doubt as well, but he stepped over the line just the same. Pete Adams handed his pencil and note pad to Amanda Hudson, Lou's wife, and stepped into the street. He was unarmed. Much to everyone's surprise, even banker, Dan MacNeil stepped into the street, meeting Pete Adams at the halfway point and joining him to walk the rest of the way.

Two more men, known only as Kerby and Frank, were standing together assessing the situation. Both men looked to the other and shrugged their shoulders in unison and then shook hands. Both men had guns strapped to their hips, but no one could ever recall if they had been known to use them. As far as anyone in town knew they lived together on their own small ranch and kept to themselves. They were always friendly and minded their own business. Seeing them now, together and standing with the town surprised everyone when they stepped into the street and across the line.

After a lull in the action where no one else appeared ready or willing to move, much less cross that line. Then, a powerful voice boomed from the far end of the street. "MOVE!" Everyone turned to see ninety-two-year-old Mariba Wright making her way down the street, scattering the undecided, left and right. She had her walking cane in her right hand and a shotgun that was probably as old as she was resting on her left shoulder. It took a few minutes for the old girl to cover the distance, but no one dared move until she crossed the line and took her place with the others. She looked up at Jake. "Ready when you are, Mr. Benteen," she said loud enough for all to hear.

Maybe it was inspiration, or maybe it was guilt, but one by one, the people of Delgado Station all stepped into the street. Everyone, that is, except Amos. He had stepped out of the shadows to witness the spectacle of unity in a town he never really considered his own. Amos could feel the eyes of everyone in town burning a hole into his soul. He hung his head and turned away, trying his best to hide his shame and walked into a blind alley, never to be seen or heard from again.

As Amos slinked away in shame, two young boys stepped into the street. One was Pete MacDougal, the kid who was one of the first to see Jake Benteen and witness what he could do with a rifle. Next to him was Jeff Van Patten, the young punk who could have easily died by Jake's hand, twice, but was spared instead. Both his hands were still bandaged, making them look like they were wrapped in winter mittens. Behind both boys were two men who Jake had not seen or heard from since he came into

210

town. They were the boy's fathers, Arthur MacDougal and Douglas Van Patten. The foursome continued marching steadily down the street until they made it to the line in the dirt. Douglas Van Patten spoke first.

"You could have killed my boy twice, Mr. Benteen, and likely had enough reason both times." Jeff's father was having a difficult time controlling his emotions but cleared his throat enough to continue. "I gave Jeff those guns because I thought he was ready and man enough, smart enough to handle them. Since his maw died, I've tried my best to teach him right, but I guess I failed." The weary and troubled father filled his chest with air and courage. "Now, we're here to do what's right."

Arthur MacDougal stepped forward, stopping next to his son, Pete. "Us too, Mr. Benteen. We don't know much about shooting guns, or killing men if we have to, but Doug and me and both of our boys will do whatever you think we can to help. To do our share."

Jake was feeling a bit overwhelmed by what he was hearing and witnessing and didn't know what to say. Before he could answer, Jeff Van Patten, the kid with no thumbs, held both hands up and said, "I can still use my fingers some, so maybe Pete and I can help Doc Gibbons, or some of the others by passing out ammunition. Whatever you need."

Most of the folks didn't have a weapon of any kind, but eventually they all crossed the line, if not to fight, then to show they were all united; wives, children and neighbors all banded together. One man, Michael Charles, seemed to intentionally hold back so he could be the last to step over the line. He stopped in the center of the street, just ahead of the line in the dirt, or what was left of it and walked back and forth along the row of would-be fighters and shook his head in dismay.

211

"You are, without a doubt, the sorriest-looking bunch of gunfighters in all the West." Michael Charles with the town's gunsmith and owner of the only such shop within fifty miles. His work saw him on the road so often that most of the people in town tended to forget about him unless they needed his skills to repair their rifles or pistols, or to buy new ones. He was always something of a quiet man, never attending church services, weddings or funerals, always choosing instead to keep to himself unless spoken to. It was unusual for him to go out of his way to speak to people on his own and certainly to address a crowd in this manner. Before anyone could speak, he continued.

"From the looks of some of those firearms, I have serious doubts they won't blow up in your faces." His comment caught the assemblage completely off guard. They wondered if he was mocking them for their pathetic excuse of defensive weaponry, which he was. But once again, before anyone could speak, he added, looking only at Jake, "Why don't I open my shop and properly equip this army, Mr. Benteen, seeing as how they're all bound and determined to put up a fight." With a grin, he added, "Might as well make it a fair one." With that, Michael Charles turned and with a wave of his hand said, "Those of you wanting or needing a proper weapon… and that's most of you… come with me." He tipped his hat to Jake and headed back down the street to his store.

"Well, I'll be," said Gracie as she watched about a dozen citizens follow Michael Charles down to his store. "That man hasn't spoken more than ten words in one sentence to anybody in this town the whole time I've known him. Least, not that I know of." She looked up at Jake. "In fact, I'm not sure I ever heard the sound of his voice 'til now."

"Courage is a funny thing," pondered Jake. He was looking

off into the distance, not really focusing on anything specific. "Some people rise to the occasion in ways even they never expected. Others, those that always thought of themselves as brave or unafraid to face a challenge or take on difficulty or hardship, suddenly fall back." Looking down at Gracie he concluded, "I guess we don't know how strong we really are until we're put to the test."

Eric Bonawitz turned to Jake. "I figure you've probably already been asked this but have you got any sort of... you know... plan for fightin' these men, Mr. Benteen?"

"Just call me Jake, if you don't mind," he replied. "And to answer your question, yes, I do have a plan, although I'm not sure how well it's going to sit with some of these folks. Most of them, more than likely."

"You mean to kill them first before they get a chance at killin' any of us," opined the big man. "That about the size of it?"

"That's about right," answered Jake.

Eric looked over at Preacher Mitchell Lee standing in the shade under the roof overhang of Howard Lyndh's dry goods store. "Think maybe we should gather those willin' to fight back at the church one more time so's you can explain the reality of the situation a bit more?" he said to Jake. "Only a few of us have ever done some killin'," he said, as if just reminding himself of the fact filled him with sadness. "I thought, after the war, that my killin' days were over." He looked down at Jake and Gracie and added, "I guess not," then gave a gentle pat on Jake's left shoulder, then nodded to Gracie, and headed for the preacher.

As Eric was about halfway to his destination, a tiny woman only about half Eric's size came marching down the middle of the street, heading straight for him. The young woman was his wife, Mariah, and by the look on her face, she was in a very determined frame of mind.

"Mariah! Damn it, woman, what are you doin' here?" barked the big man. "I thought I told you to stay home where it's safe." He wasn't so much angry as he was startled at seeing his diminutive wife carrying a double-barreled, twelve-gauge shotgun in both hands. She also seemed to be carrying a bag of extra shells tied around her waist. "And what in tarnation are you planin' on doing with that?" he asked with a look that was both bewildered and amused.

"You think I'm gonna let my man get his big ass shot off without me?" Mariah's smile was mixed with fierce eyes that told Eric she was not going to be deterred. Her mind was made up. "We got babies to make and I plan on makin' them with you! No one else! Ya hear me?" As tough as she was sounding, it was clear by the tears welling up in her eyes that she was scared. She took as deep a breath as her body could hold and held it for a brief pause, then said. "'Til death do us part, remember? We're in this together. You, me and the rest of this town. So, by your side is where I belong and where I aim to stay 'til this is over and we ain't discussin' it no further." Her voice quivered a little at the end, but she managed to speak her piece.

Her husband's eyes filled with tears of pride and overflowing love for his partner. There were a few spectators that couldn't help but overhear Mariah's pronouncement and it had a moving effect on them as well.

Eric looked back at Jake and Gracie. and said, "Ain't she somethin'?" Shifting his rifle to his left hand, he wrapped his right arm around his wife and lifted her off the ground in a one-armed bear hug, kissing her hard and long. He put her down and turned to Preacher Lee and said, "Preacher, as soon as folks get themselves set up over at Mr. Charles' store, Mr. Benteen... I mean, Jake… wants us to meet one more time at the church so's he can tell us his plan and what to expect." Looking back at Jake, he asked, "That about right, Jake?"

"That would be fine, Eric. Thanks." Jake tipped his hat. Although he was not looking directly at Gracie, he couldn't help but express his admiration for the events he had just witnessed. "If you had told me three days ago that these folks, this town, would have said and done what I just saw, I'd have sworn you had lost your mind."

Gracie, bursting with pride, couldn't disagree. "Trust me, Jake. I'm as gobsmacked as you are," she said, then added, "But I am more damn proud of my town right now than I ever thought possible." She hooked her left arm through Jake's, at the elbow, looked up at him and smiled. "Let's go to church," she said with a wink, as they both walked down Main Street at high noon, heading for a church sermon unlike anything anyone had ever heard before.

Chapter Eighteen

When they left Tres Mesa, Wolf had twenty-two, well-armed and experienced fighters and killers behind him. After about forty minutes on the road, two of them had drifted back to the rear until they felt it was safe enough to make a run for it south, across the border. Those men were Bo Dillingham and Nate Hudson. They were never in the same league or vicious caliber as the rest of the group but were too cautious to say anything about their objections to Wolf's outrageous plan. They had each agreed they would cut out together as soon as they reached enough distance at the rear of the group and were sufficiently hidden in the cloud of dust kicked up by those ahead of them. The two riders a few yard in front of them, also hugging the rear, suspected the two men were planning on making their move as soon as opportunity struck, but agreed to remain silent. When one of the forward riders, Carl Moses turned his head to cough out a mouth full of dirt, he noticed the two deserters were more than a half-mile gone. He debated, briefly, whether to yell up to Wolf and alert him of the two men but once again chose to keep it to himself. Instead, he took off his hat and slapped the shoulder of the rider to his left, Alex McCumbie, and indicated for him to look back. Alex shifted in his saddle enough to look behind him, then nodded his awareness of the two men riding in the opposite direction. He just winked and whispered, "More for us."

Carl Moses offered a broad smile and replied, "Sounds good to me."

Wolf pulled up sharp and hard on the reins of his horse, causing it to snort and snap its head side to side in protest at the sudden jerking of its neck. "Everybody listen up! Water your horses and take somethin' fer yourselves. This'll be your last chance before we get to Delgado Station."

As each man and horse halted, the dust cloud began to settle quickly. There was no wind to push it around, which allowed each rider to temporarily dust themselves off and grab for their water bags or canteens. Many had brought along bottles of whiskey as well and chose to take a hefty swallow of that instead, thinking it would help cut the choking dust at the back of their throats.

Wolf stood up on his stirrups to do a head count. That's when he noticed he was down two men from when they started. It was already hot enough to boil a man's blood but realizing that two of his men had made for the border made his temper flare and his blood boil even more. Since everyone was covered with enough dirt and dust to make them all look like statues carved in dirt, it was not immediately clear just who ran off.

"We're down two men!" he snarled, then spit out some dust. "Who'd we lose?" All of the men began examining each other to see who, was whom, although most were easy enough to identify despite the layer of crud that covered them from head to toe.

Potch, who had missed his opportunity to make his own escape earlier, was riding next to Wolf on his mule, Sugar Pie. He pulled away from the horses behind him and circled around to his left side to walk down the rows of men, lined up, riding two by two.

"Looks to me like Bo and Nate, Mr. Wolf," reported Potch. "I don't see them here in the group."

Wolf snarled again and swung his horse around to walk

down the line of riders himself, glaring at each man as he passed. "Anybody see when they cut out?" His question seemed as much a threat as a genuine need to know when two of his men left the group. "Answer me, damn you! Did anyone see them leave?"

Carl Moses spoke up first, since it seemed to him that Wolf directed his threatening question more at him than anyone else. He and Alex were at the back of the pack, after all. "I noticed it just after we stopped, Wolf. It's so dusty out here, I couldn't tell they were gone until then." He slapped his hat against his body to release more dust, which he hoped helped make his point a bit stronger.

"Same here, Wolf," replied Alex. "I was half-asleep in the saddle from this heat. They could have left a half hour back for all we know."

"So you let them get away!" screamed Wolf. "After I warned you all what would happen if anyone ran scared!"

"I'm sorry, Wolf," came Carl's sheepish defense. "I didn't realize it was our responsibility to keep watch over them like they was prisoners or something." His fatal mistake was laughing at his own statement.

Alex made an equal error in judgment by adding his own laugh at Carl's comment and added, "Besides, don't that mean there's more for the rest of us after this raid is over?" He looked at Carl for agreement, but before their combined laugh's passed their lips, Wolf drew his gun and shot both Carl and Alex dead, putting a single bullet into the head of each man. Carl fell first, rolling back off his saddle, dropping to the ground next to his horse, who jumped and kicked at both the gunshots and the impact of Carl's body at his feet.

Although Alex's horse jumped at the gunshots, he remained upright in his saddle for a moment, his eyes rolling up, showing only the white. His hands were still locked around the reins as he slipped to his right and fell sideways off his saddle.

Every horse instinctively backed away from the carnage, with each rider trying to regain control over themselves and their horse. They were all accustomed to seeing Wolf do some truly crazy and unpredictable things, but even this was an unexpected display of insanity.

"Damn it, Wolf, we were already down two men," Spud Pierson said from the front of the group. "Now you just made it four. If you keep this up there won't be enough of us left to raid a whore house, much less a whole town." No one dared laugh at Spud's comment, although all of them agreed with the reasoning behind it.

Wolf ignored Spud's protest. "That'll make it crystal-clear to each and every one of you that I mean what I say! Nobody cuts and runs in my outfit. NOBODY!" Wolf made eye contact with every man left, still sitting in the saddle. "Take their guns and whatever else they got that's worth takin' and tie up their horses to some scrub brush. We'll pick 'em up on our way back." Wolf was strangely calm when he spoke, showing no signs of his murderous vengeance that claimed two more lives just moments before.

"What do we do with our boys, Mr. Wolf?" asked Potch. His voice quivered when he spoke.

"Leave 'em," answered Wolf without emotion. "Let the buzzards have 'em." Wolf replaced the two spent shells in his pistol, snapped the chamber shut, but held it high enough for all the men to see. "Anyone else got somethin' to say?" He looked straight at Spud Pierson when he asked but noticed that Spud had his hand on his own pistol. It irked him sorely that every time there was a dispute or a debate over his handling of the outfit,

Spud was the man to speak his piece. That insolence needed to stop. But taking him on now could be a foolish and dangerous mistake, deadly even. Besides, Spud was a good gun hand and might be needed in town. There was no way of telling what they might face there and having him do his share was more important than killing him here and now, much as the thought appealed to him. He would settle their score later, preferably when Spud's back was turned. "Then let's clear this shit off the road, tend to their horses, divide their rig and rest up fer ten minutes. Then we ride!"

Chapter Nineteen

Sound carries in the desert, but just as judging distance can be tricky, so can judging the direction of sound. Sheriff Avery heard the two shots fired close together, which was puzzling. Was there a shootout, with each man firing once at the other? Was there a victor? Whatever the reason for the gun fire, the sound was enough to make Val jump to his feet. Since there was only one road and the earlier dust cloud in the distance indicated some riders of significant numbers, Val reasoned that the gunshots he heard could only have come from them, the presumed gang, led by Wolf.

It seemed obvious the gang wasn't shooting at him since they were still too far away for any bullet to reach him, whether fired from a pistol or rifle. Plus, he was sitting on the ground under a tree, so it was unlikely they would have seen him or even known who it was they were shooting at. Target practice didn't make sense either. Hunting, perhaps? Since he heard only two shots, Val settled on the reasoning that it must have been a skirmish between Wolf's men and not some raid by Federal Marshals or Rangers. That was some possibly good news. It may mean some internal strife or disagreement. Anything to better the odds for himself and the people back in Delgado Station.

Val noticed that the dust cloud had diminished, indicating to him that Wolf and his men may have stopped to rest their horses during or after the shots were fired. Given the distance of the dust, as well as the sound of the gun fire, Val guessed Wolf and his men were still about twenty minutes away, assuming he stayed under the ironwood tree and waited for them to arrive. The pain in his stomach was getting worse, almost intolerable. If he took a healthy swig of laudanum now, it might make him too drowsy to function and be of any good should Wolf turn down Jake's challenge, which he expected anyway. In truth, he was hoping Wolf refused. He was confident the men were coming regardless, so if he could take Wolf, a longshot to be sure, and maybe one or two more, that would substantially shift the odds in Jake's and the town's favor. It might also be enough to deter the rest of the men from continuing with their plans to raid the town.

He took another large swig of water and untied his horse from the ironwood tree, then poured the rest of his water into his hat again so his horse could take one last drink before setting out on the road to meet the oncoming raiding party and his likely end.

As he scanned the road ahead, he could tell the dust cloud had resumed and seemed to be growing in volume. That indicated to him that the advancing riders had picked up the pace and were at a modest canter now. Both sides would be within clear eyesight of the other in a matter of minutes. Val pulled his Colt to check what he already knew was a full load and placed it back in the holster. He then reached down and pulled out his Winchester. It wasn't the beauty Jake's rifle was, and wasn't tricked out with a large ring, or set for rapid firing, but it was a deadly enough weapon for what Val needed. His plan, such as it was, was to meet the men with his rifle set across his saddle. At the sign of any threat, he could easily get at least one shot off, preferably at Wolf. Anything after that would be a bonus he could easily take to his grave with a smile.

Val took a deep, easy breath. He was calm. His stomach had

settled a bit and hadn't given him a twinge of pain since he saddled up back at the ironwood tree. Is this what knowing you are going to die feels like, he thought. It was oddly comforting, knowing one's death was imminent, especially when he considered what lay in store for him should he wait for the cancer to eat away at his insides. He would much rather go out in style, doing something righteous and decent for a town that had been so good to him. It gave him time to think, probably more clearly than he had in a long, long time. He had already replayed his past and was now resigned to his future and he was okay with what he saw.

Although he had never seen Wolf directly, not up close and personal, he could tell with reasonable certainty that the rider at the head of the pack was him. He had heard of the little man, Potch, that was riding at this side, but had never seen him either, not even once. It was a peculiar sight, one a rather tall and imposing figure with a shock of long black hair and a wide-brimmed black hat, the other about half the size, both man and mule. Behind them were about a dozen men, as well as he could make out. The gang remained in line, two men to a row behind Wolf and his curious companion. When both sides reached a distance of about thirty yards, Wolf raised his right hand to signal everyone to stop. Val rode on for another ten yards, then gave a gentle pull up on the reins and stopped.

"Afternoon gents," said Val in a voice that was calm and cheerful. "I have a message for you all, but one specifically for" – he looked directly at Wolf – "I'm guessing is you… provided you are the man they call Wolf."

Wolf cocked his head to one side in a perplexed manner, suggesting he was not prepared for someone to address him so formerly and showing no sign of fear. He adjusted himself in his saddle, then placed both hands on the horn. "I'm Wolf," he replied, sternly, trying to show some menace. "Who the hell are you?"

Val pulled back his vest to reveal his sheriff's badge. "Name's Val Avery. I'm the sheriff over in Delgado Station." He let go of his vest and resumed his grip on the Winchester with both hands. "Word is you men plan on comin' into my town and causing a lot of pain and suffering for folks that done you no harm."

There were a few snickers and outright laughs from the assemblage. "So," answered Wolf.

"So… I'm afraid I can't allow that," replied Val, in kind.

More laughs and snickers followed, but Val needed to make his challenge known to Wolf and his men before things got out of hand, which seemed imminent. "But first, I have a message for you, Wolf, from Jake Benteen."

There were noticeable gasps from the gang members, with even a few oohs and aahs as well. Wolf cocked his head to the other side this time. He was genuinely confused. This man sitting astride a horse in front of him was not showing signs of any fear and that made him nervous. "Why isn't he here delivering this message himself?" he asked.

"Funny you should ask," replied the sheriff. "He wanted to come out here on his own, but I told him it was my job to try and talk some reason into you and your men first." More laughter followed and the sheriff waited until it subsided before he continued. "But I can see that ain't likely." More laughter. "So, Jake said he would meet you just outside of town, or in the middle of the street if you like. Your call. Just so long as it's you and him. No one else." Val paused just long enough to let the challenge sink in. "He has thrown down the gauntlet, Wolf. To you and just you."

"Gauntlet?" asked Potch. "What's a gauntlet, Mr. Wolf?"

Before Wolf could answer, Spud Pierson chimed in, which was a good thing for Wolf because he didn't really know what it was either. "It's a glove, you pint-sized buffoon. Like what the nights wore back in England hundreds of years ago. They would throw it at the feet of someone they wanted to fight. Kind of an honor thing. Like a private fight nobody else was allowed to stick their noses into." Spud leaned forward in his saddle to make direct eye contact with Wolf. "It looks like Jake Benteen has challenged you to a duel, Wolf," Spud said, with a broad grin.

Wolf roared with laughter. "Ya hear that, boys? Jake Benteen wants to take me on, man to man!" He laughed again, louder than before, but it seemed to Spud and a few of the others that it didn't have a great deal of confidence behind it.

"What are you gonna do, Mr. Wolf, sir?" asked Potch. He actually liked the sound of that challenge. If Jake Benteen managed to take down Wolf, his worries would be over. He could leave the gang free and clear. No one would care if he stayed or left. The question was, would Wolf accept the challenge?

Wolf hesitated. He knew his men were curious and anxiously awaiting an answer from him. He shifted in his saddle. "Why should I waste my time fightin' Benteen in the street when we're just gonna pick your town clean and then burn it to the ground anyway?" replied Wolf.

"Well then, I would say that it sounds to me like you're afraid to face him, Wolf," came Val's reply, as he strengthened his grip on his Winchester. He could feel something in the air, like how it feels just before a thunderstorm is about to strike. Electricity was in the air. Every man behind Wolf could feel it too. "So, what do I tell him?"

225

This time, Wolf didn't so much as shift his body in the saddle as squirm. His pathetic excuse for honor, not to mention his courage, was being questioned in front of his men. "If I accept Benteen's challenge, what happens if I win?"

"Then your feud is satisfied and you ride on back to Tres Mesa and leave my town alone." The sheriff leaned forward to add one thing more. "*BUT*... the same thing applies if Jake wins. The feud is over and everyone rides away. That's the deal."

Wolf snapped back his reply. "That ain't no kind of deal!" he hollered. "What's to stop my men from stripping your town to the bone and then burnin' what's left to the ground?

"I'm afraid it won't be that easy, Wolf," came Val's measured reply. "Jake feels that since your main beef is with him for taking out the likes of Orin and Buck, then your killing him should settle it. The rest of the town ain't to blame, so there's no cause for bringing pain to them. Besides, we sent riders out to fix the telegraph lines; one to Taos and another to Tucson for the Federal Marshals." None of this was true, as no one knew how to fix the telegraph lines, or even where they were cut. They only knew no messages were coming in and there were no responses to calls for help going out. The town couldn't spare any men to ride for help either, so this was nothing more than a bluff. Still, Val continued playing the cards he was dealt. "It'll take a few days for them to get there and back, I admit, but you can bet the Army, Rangers, Marshalls and anybody else they can get will be comin' after every last one of you." He could tell by the look on the men's faces that this last threat of them being ridden down by every arm of the law was something none of them wanted, although they had considered it a possibility. The sheriff's threat just made it a more realistic possibility. For some, it was enough to give them serious second thoughts. For others, it was something they knew was an eventual reality they would have to face. The question for each was which side of their own line in the sand they were prepared to cross.

Wolf could tell by the grunts, groans and chatter he was hearing from behind him that he needed to do something definitive and do it now. The primitive instinct Wolf had relied on for most of his life was a vital part of why he had survived for as long as he had. He had always trusted it, even when logic dictated otherwise. Catching his opponent off guard was always his best defense. Looking first over his right shoulder, then slowly back over his left, Wolf thought his actions would relax Sheriff Avery just enough to give the drop on him. He was wrong. Val Avery hadn't survived as a gun hand and a sheriff for this long without seeing every trick in the book.

When Wolf turned his head back to center, he pulled his Remington from his waist and fired. But Val was already anticipating such a move and shifted his weight to his right, raising his Winchester to center it on Wolf's chest. Both men fired simultaneously. Wolf's bullet missed Val's head by a fraction, but enough to feel the air move as it whistled passed his ear. Val's bullet, if it had been six inches more to the right, would have struck Wolf square in the chest. As it was, however, the hot lead passed just under Wolf's right armpit, tearing some leather from his vest, but striking one of Wolf's men, Orville Bennett in the throat.

Orville grabbed at his throat, choking and spitting, but was dead before he hit the ground. Val was off balance now and couldn't recover in time to get off another shot before Wolf fired two more times, hitting him with both slugs. Val slumped to his right side and rolled off the saddle and on to the ground in a slow-motion death dive.

Some of the men were focused on Orville, although there was nothing they could do except grab the reins of his horse to keep it from bolting. A few of the others had instinctively drawn their own pistols, but soon realized there was no cause for concern. As far as they could tell, Sheriff Val Avery was dead.

As the sound and actions of the gunfire subsided, Wolf hollered in triumph. "Hoo yaaa! I took down my first lawman!" He held his gun-filled hand high and proud. "I want that man's badge!" He looked down at the sheriff's body and spoke through a grin, saying, "I'm gonna wear it to town when I kill Jake Benteen!" He looked around for someone to retrieve his trophy. "Spud! Get me his sheriff's badge!"

"Get it yourself!" defied Spud in a tone that was definitive. "I ain't your damn servant!"

Blood lust was in the air. Wolf turned his glaring, fire-red eyes at Spud but immediately realized he was one of the men who had instinctively drawn his gun when the shots were fired. He also noticed an odd smile crossing Spud's face that suggested he was ready, able and willing to settle their contentious differences here and now, so he quickly changed his mental course to pick on his tried and true servant, Potch.

"Potch!" The shout caused Potch to jump and squeal in fear. "Git yer little fat ass down off that mule and get me my badge! NOW!"

As usual, Potch obliged Wolf's every demand and climbed down off Sugar Pie and scurried over to the sheriff's body, which was lying face down in the dirt. The Winchester had fallen to his side just in front of Wolf's horse. When Potch approached the sheriff's body, Wolf leaned down and picked up the Winchester. It was too valuable a firearm to leave behind. As Potch leaned down to turn the sheriff's body over to retrieve the badge, Val rolled himself over on his back, with his pistol in hand and fired one wild shot that wasn't aimed at anyone in particular but was just fired in a blind hope that it would hit someone, anyone. It did. Although the bullet missed Potch, it did hit Deek Olson in the left ear and came out the top of his head. Like Orville Bennett, he was dead before he hit the ground. Before Val could pull the hammer back for another final attempt, Wolf fired three shots from Val's own Winchester. Val took all three shots directly in the chest, with the third one hitting his badge, dead center.

"Well, I'll be a son of a bitch!" cried Wolf with genuine shock and surprise once the dust settled. "That old fool was playin' possum." Knowing the sheriff was now most certainly dead, Wolf began to laugh in disbelief. "Can you believe that? He'd liked to have blown my head off!" More disbelieving laughter followed. Some of his men also couldn't help but release some nervous laughter of their own. Anyone of them could have taken that last bullet that took down Deek Olson.

Potch scrambled as fast as his legs could carry him, back up on Sugar Pie's back. His heart was pounding so fast and hard that he was sure it would burst.

"Where are you goin', ya little chicken shit?" Wolf was laughing at how panicked and terrified Potch looked. "Git your ass back down there and get me my badge! I plan on wearing it into town when I face Benteen." Potch hesitated. "Go on! Git!"

With great reluctance, Potch climbed down off Sugar Pie and retrieved the sheriff's battered badge and handed it to Wolf. "Here you go, Mr. Wolf," he said as he passed the badge up to his boss. "It's a little dented, but I think it will still pin on okay."

Wolf took the badge from Potch and began to examine it when Spud Pierson asked, "Was it worth it, Wolf? We're down four more men now, six if you count Bo and Nate that we lost a ways back." He kept his pistol at the ready but stood up in his stirrups to do a head count. "We're down to fourteen men now," he said, just after finishing the count. "I don't like those odds."

"So, are you sayin' you ain't got the stomach for this raid now, Spud?" Wolf was holding the Winchester along his right side now, loosely aiming at Spud's midsection, but not making an obvious threat with it. "Besides, what was I supposed to do, let him shoot me first?"

"That's not what I'm saying, Wolf," replied Spud cautiously. He could see where Wolf had repositioned his newly acquired rifle. "Just pointing out the obvious," he said, as he lowered his pistol in a non-threatening way but still managed to hold it in a like position, pointing it at Wolf. Both men seemed to acknowledge the standoff. "If we want to come out of this raid alive and in one piece, we have got to stop killing our own, or getting them killed by being careless. That's all I'm saying." The tension seemed to ease up at that point. Just then, Spud brought everyone's thoughts back to the sheriff's initial message. "But I do gotta ask, are you planning on taking Benteen's challenge or not?"

"What difference would that make, Spud?" replied Wolf. "We're still gonna take that town for everything it's worth, no matter if I fight Benteen or not. Are you questioning my courage?" He raised the Winchester in a more obvious, threatening position. "'Cuz we can settle that right now if you have any doubts!"

Spud smiled and relaxed in his saddle, making an obvious display of slipping his pistol back into its holster. "What, and be down another man, possibly even two? No thank you. Just wanted to know your intentions."

Wolf looked about, trying to get a sense of the mood of the

remaining members of the gang. He didn't like what he saw. There was something in the air again and he read the collective emotions as doubt.

"I'll tell you what," he said, with a hint of challenge in his voice. "When we get to town, I'll call out Jake Benteen to meet me in the middle of the street like he asked. Just him and me. If I win—"

"Oh, you'll beat him fer sure, Mr. Wolf," offered Potch, in an effort to goad him on. "Fer sure! Benteen don't stand a chance! No, sir, no chance at all!" In truth, he was hoping Benteen would kill him, although he wished he had the courage to do it himself.

"Shut up, ya gutless little shit!" barked Wolf. "This ain't yer fight and none of yer business either." Looking at the rest of the men, he added, "If I win, we take the town, same as before. If Benteen takes me, you can still take that town for all its worth and go back to Tres Mesa and clean out my stash too. So, either way, you win!" The men all let out a collective cheer.

Even Spud Pierson liked the sound of that and roared his approval.

"Now let's stop jabbering!" he snapped. "I got a man to kill and we got a town to rob!" Wolf turned to address the rest of the men. "Strip what's worth keepin' from these boys and tie their horses to a tree. We'll pick 'em up with the others on the way back." Wolf polished the dented sheriff's badge against his leather vest and pinned it on his left flap. He liked what he saw and smiled with pride. "Now let's *RIDE*!"

Chapter Twenty

Unlike the previous church gathering which was a deafening chaos of angry and confused citizens, where some were unsure of why the meeting was even called, the purpose of this one was clear. They were going to get details on what it means to be asked to put their lives on the line for themselves and each other. The collective realization that they had no other choice but to stand and fight for what was theirs seemed to bring many of them a sense of calm, an acceptance that they had made the right decision. The question many of them still had, however, was what that all meant once the shooting started.

Michael Charles, the town's usually quiet gunsmith, had equipped everyone with the best weaponry he had available, which was considerable. To many, a gun is a gun. Not so in a modern gunfight of the magnitude this one was predicted to be. First, Charles had stripped anyone who possessed a pistol or rifle that fired black powder. Those weapons, although many still technically functional, would be of little tactical value in a skirmish where accuracy and rapid firing were paramount. The black, acrid smoke the older weapons kicked up would have made it difficult for the inexperienced to see what was happening and how to deal with it. They also needed the ability to reload quickly, which the newer models were designed for.

Still, the reality of *why* they were firing a gun had not entirely sunk in. That was about to be Jake's contribution to the cause as he took his place in the front pew, where he sat quietly, hat in hand. Gracie sat next to him.

The somber atmosphere was reminiscent of a funeral. Preacher Lee stepped to his pulpit and raised both hands, signaling quiet, which was largely unnecessary this time. "Folks, this is a solemn day for all of us here in Delgado Station," he said. His voice lacked the traditional volume he used to deliver his Sunday sermons. "Today, we have been asked to put our faith in God and in each other to protect our homes, our businesses and, most importantly, our lives and the lives of those we love."

A few "Amens" were heard, scattered through the congregation.

"Now... I can't pretend to tell you that I know what this means and to understand what you're going through. I've never had to take action to defend myself or anyone else. My life has always been about traveling the path of the Lord, preaching peace and love. But today, we face a crossroads. Do we fight? Or do we run? What I saw out in the street told me that all of you here have decided to stand and fight, and probably to kill. If you are struggling to find an answer in God's words, I invite you to turn to Psalm 144:1 where David says, 'Praise the Lord, who is my rock. He trains my hands for war and gives my fingers skill for battle.'"

Another round of "Amens" was heard. Preacher Lee then surprised everyone by raising a pistol that had been sitting on the Bible in front of him at the pulpit, out of view to the congregation. He held the pistol as if it were some strange, alien object he had never seen before. "I have never fired a gun in my life," he said. "I've never even hunted for food. Never had to. I've always relied on others to do the hunting and gathering for me. But hunting and ultimately killing for food is one thing. Having to kill a fellow human being, well that's something else altogether."

He gently placed the pistol back down on the Bible in front of him. "Today, my friends, I can't let you fight this battle alone. You are my flock, but you are also my friends and this is my town too. In all honesty, I'm not sure I can take another man's life. But if it comes to making a choice between one of them, or one of you, I trust that the Lord will guide me in making the right decision." He paused, taking a moment to let his words sink in, not just to his flock, but also to himself. Then he turned to Jake and said, "Mr. Benteen, I think these folks could do with some guidance on your part. If you would, please." The preacher stepped away from the pulpit and indicated to Jake that he should take his place.

As Jake stood, he gave his hat to Gracie. and slowly stepped up behind the pulpit, a very strange and unexpected place for him to be for the first time, he thought. He never thought he would find himself standing there again. Looking out over the silent gathering of people, it seemed as if they were all holding their breath, nervous with anticipation of what he was about to say.

"Thanks, Preacher," he said, with a nod to Preacher Lee. It took Jake a few deep breaths and a swallow of nerves before he could continue. "Um… folks, this isn't an easy thing for me to say, but… what you are about to… embark on… is something I'm sure none of you ever expected you would have to do… and that is kill someone. But make no mistake, killing is what will be required if you want to protect yourselves and save your town."

"But are you for certain that we have to kill them, Mr. Benteen?" asked a woman sitting in the front pew, almost directly in front of him. Her voice was filled with anguish and wonder. "If the sheriff managed to tell them how many of us are willin' to fight, won't they decide to ride?"

"Let's hope so, ma'am," Jake said quietly. "But just having

them *think* we will put up a fight means nothing if we aren't really prepared to deliver one. I've spent my life fighting men like Wolf and his gang. They are used to taking whatever they want, from anyone who stands in their way. Killing you to get it is just a part of who they are."

"But I thought the sheriff rode out to ask this Wolf fellow to meet you, man to man?" This question came from Lou Hudson, the barber, who was standing in the back by the door. "If you kill him, won't they ride on? That was the deal, wasn't it?" A few mumbles of agreement echoed about the room. "I mean, you're Jake Benteen after all," he added, in earnest. "Surely you can take him."

Jake smiled and ran his fingers through his hair. "Thank you for the vote of confidence, Mr. Hudson," he said, "but gun fights are unpredictable things. Despite what you may have heard or read about me, killing is not something I relish. Believe it or not, I've walked away from more fights than I've ever fought." Jake let that fact sink in for a moment. "Besides, what if *he* kills *me*?" he asked. "Do you ever consider that possibility?" The room fell silent again. "Look, folks, even if I do manage to kill Wolf, there is still no guarantee the rest of his men won't try and take this town for everything it's got. They know times are changing for men like them and they see this as their last hurrah."

"But I still don't see why we have to kill to protect what's ours," pleaded a man sitting in the middle of the chapel. His name was Carter Innskeep. He was the owner of Innskeep's Grain & Feed store situated at the end of town, directly across the street of Gracie's Livery Stable. He was a stern businessman, but fair. If he knew you to be hard working and honest, he would extend credit if needed. If he thought you were lazy and didn't follow The Good Book to his liking, he would just as easily turn you out.

"May I ask who you are, sir, and what you do?" Jake's question was polite. "I don't believe we've met."

Carter Innskeep cleared his throat before he answered. "I'm the owner of Innskeep's Grain & Feed. My store sits across the street from Gracie's Livery. Why do you ask?"

Jake furrowed his brow and asked, "If one or more of Wolf's men stormed into your store and demanded that you turn over all your money, and anything else they wanted,… will you give it to them, Mr. Innskeep?" asked Jake. It was a simple question asked in a non-threatening way, but it still made the store owner nervous.

Hearing his name called out by a gunfighter, a known killer of men, but also the only man the town could rely on in this most desperate of times, caused him to sit up, ramrod straight. "Well… I'm… I'm not sure. It's hard to say. Like many of the folks here, I've never killed a man before," the store owner said. If it was possible, he even sat up straighter than he was before.

"I understand, sir, and it would be my hope that you and everyone else in this town who has never had to cross that line could go to your graves making that same claim," said Jake. He noticed a woman sitting next to the store owner that hugged his right arm when Jake asked his question. "Mr. Innskeep, is that your wife sitting next to you?" Innskeep and his wife exchanged worried looks before Jake got his answer. "Why, yes, it is. This is my Emma. Why do you ask?"

If people thought Jake was blunt and painfully honest before, they were about to get a jolt of reality they had never considered. "Well, your Emma is a fine-looking woman, sir, if I may say. So, if any of these men decided to take liberties with your wife, or any of the other women in this town – and when I say 'liberties'

236

I mean to rape and likely kill them just for sport – would you let them?"

Innskeep and virtually everyone else in the congregation were dumbstruck. The store owner jumped to his feet. "No, *SIR!* I would *NOT!*" he shouted, his anger showing in his red-flushed face. The room burst into applause and cheers.

The gunfighter raised his hands to silence the congregation. As the supportive enthusiasm died away, Jake said, "Then you'll have to kill them to protect her." The room fell silent, yet again.

Eric Bonawitz was seated on the other side of the room with his wife, Mariah by his side. He stood during the renewed silence and offered his own observation as he turned to the store owner. "None of us want to kill, Mr. Innskeep. I did enough of that back in Virginia during the war. But I'll be damned if I'll let anyone lay a hand on my wife or anyone else in this town." His wife, Mariah stood and buried her head against his chest.

More cheers and applause erupted, although it was decidedly less enthusiastic than before. The stark reality of what they were all facing was beginning to sink in.

To press the point a little further, Jake looked down at the woman seated in the front row that had asked the first question and said, "Ma'am, you asked if it was necessary to have to kill these men. I wish the answer was no but I cannot honestly say that some of you won't have to do some killing today. And I'm as sorry as I can be about that. The truth is, I've never killed a man that wasn't set on killing me first. Think of it as kill or be killed. Wolf is the leader of a band of outlaws that don't follow the laws of government or the laws of human civilization. They follow their own laws. Their plan is to hit this town hard and fast and then likely split up and head for the border or further west, or maybe up north to spread law enforcement as thin as possible.

If you all put up a fight, one that stings and reduces their numbers, the rest might just be persuaded to cut and run. You have all been asking if there was a plan. Well, there it is, plain and simple. They are expecting you to be weak and afraid. You need to show them that you are not." That last comment seemed to give the crowd a jolt of inspiration. Jake pressed on. "There is an old military principle that says a strong offensive action will throw your enemy off guard and hinder their ability to stick to their initial plan. Our advantage is that they won't be expecting more than a few guns turned against them. So, if we can throw everything we've got, and I mean *everything* at them, they just may decide this town isn't worth dying for."

"So, what are you proposing, Mr. Benteen?" asked Pete Adams, the newspaper editor. "How do we defend ourselves, specifically, against a bunch of men on horseback?"

"That's a good question, Mr. Adams," answered Jake, "and I'm glad we are getting down to those specifics you mentioned." Referring to the gunsmith, he added, "Thanks to Mr. Charles over there we have some of the best firearms money can buy. But they won't be of any use if the people holding them don't know how to use them. So, I want everyone who has a rifle and thinks they can hit what they're aiming at to position themselves along the rooftops, covering both sides of the street. You'll be aiming at a downward angle, so there's less chance of hitting one of your own in a crossfire. You'll also be hidden from view when they ride in. We're fortunate that some of the roof tops have some facia and signage you can gain some cover behind."

Lou Hudson spoke up again. "I'm not much of a long-range marksman, Mr. Benteen, but I think I can hit something up close with a pistol if need be. Where should I be?"

"You stay in your barber shop and cover yourself along the

238

edge of your door frame. The wood is thicker there and can take a bullet," advised Jake. "That's what I'd like the rest of you to do to protect yourselves and your businesses. Stay inside and don't shoot unless they kick your door down. Let them come to you and then, let 'em have it with all you've got."

"Where are you going to be, Mr. Benteen?" asked Carter Innskeep.

"Standing right out there in the middle of the street," he answered, as he gestured out the door. "We haven't seen or heard anything from Sheriff Avery so I'm thinking he's not coming back." There was a sudden collective gasp as if all the air was sucked out of the room. "It was his call, folks. He was a dying man anyway, as some of you may have already known." Quick glances were exchanged from person to person, each wondering if the other knew something they didn't. "This town meant a lot to him and everyone in it. You gave him a sense of belonging that he cherished. So, he wanted to do whatever it took to protect you while he still could. He said this town was worth dying for."

"He was a good man, Mr. Benteen, I mean, Jake," remarked Eric Bonawitz. "We'll make sure he didn't give his life for nothing."

"Val would expect nothing less," replied Jake, his voice cracking a little. "My hope is that Wolf will accept my challenge and meet me out in the street first. If I can take him out, I will then ask that his men turn around and leave, with no more killing. It's a long shot, I admit, but if I see any hesitation on their part, I may have time to ask that each of you with a gun, man, woman and even child if necessary, show yourself briefly with your gun at the ready. That may be enough to tip the scales and make a few of them decide to leave." Jake paused. "But don't bet on it. These are desperate men used to getting their way. So, listen to me when

I say if I go down, you need to open up on every rider you can see."

"You mean, just cut 'em down?" asked the same woman in the front row.

"Yes, ma'am, that is precisely what I mean," replied Jake.

"No mercy?" asked a meek voice buried somewhere in the middle of the room. It was the voice of Carter Innskeep's wife, Emma.

"That's right, ma'am. No mercy!" said Jake in agreement. "Believe me when I say they won't be showing you any, so hesitating, even a little bit, could be what costs you your life or someone else's. I know that's harsh, and if there was a better way, we'd do it. But there just isn't."

As the life-or-death reality of their situation hit the members of the congregation, a young boy of about ten years of age, Declan Hudson, son of Lou and Amanda, burst into the chapel.

"They're comin'!" he shouted as loud as he could, running over to his parents and wrapping his arms around his mother's waist.

"How far back are they, son?" asked Jake in a calm, soothing voice.

"My sister Ava and me, and my cousin Kennedy Ann were waiting up on the high mound along the riverbank and we could see the dust from their horses." He looked up at his parents and assured them all were safe. "I sent Ava and Kennedy Ann back home and I hightailed it here like you asked me, Pa."

The crowd began to show signs of restlessness and uncertainty at the news of the approaching army, so Jake knew he had to calm their fears immediately before their emotions got out of control and panic set in.

"That's very helpful, son," offered Jake. Asking no one

specific, he said, "Anyone know about how far out that is and how much time it gives us?"

Eric Bonawitz called over to the young boy, Declan. "Hey, Dex, could you actually see their horses, or was it just their dust?"

"Just the dust, sir," answered the boy.

Eric looked back at Jake and offered his assessment. "They wouldn't be riding at a full gallop that far out, Jake, especially in this heat. So my guess is that they are still a good three miles out." He pondered the situation a little further and added, "They'll likely be holding their horses back and then kick them into a full gallop just at the edge of town. My guess is we have about twenty minutes. Maybe more."

"That gives us plenty of time to get ready, then," Jake replied to Eric's assessment. Calling out to everyone in the room, he said, "Folks, the time for talking is over. It's time for action. Lock your doors if you're staying inside. Have your guns loaded and extra ammunition at the ready. Ladies, if you aren't planning on firing a weapon, I'm going to ask that you boil up some water and prepare some clean bandages in case we need any. If you are taking your position up on the roof, go there now, but be sure to put the sun *behind* you as best you can! Let them look up into the sun and try to see where the shots are coming from. Everyone else, if you can't fight, go to safer ground. The fewer people in harm's way the better." The room was silent as if everyone had decided to take the same breath and hold it. Jake shouted from the pulpit in a booming voice that any preacher would envy, "GO!"

The room burst into a frenzy of activity as people rushed to get ready in whatever manner Jake had prescribed for them. Gracie stood and walked to the front and met Jake as he stepped down from the pulpit. To Jake's surprise, she embraced him with

241

her left arm around his waist. She still held her rifle in her right hand and didn't speak, or seemed to not even want to, as if finding the right words to say was too difficult. Jake returned her embrace and squeezed her tight against him.

"You okay?" he asked, knowing she wasn't. With the slightest tease in his voice, he said, "You seem a tad apprehensive," and gave her another squeeze.

Throwing back a little sarcasm of her own, Gracie replied, "Gee, you think so, cowboy?"

Jake leaned down and kissed her on the top of her head and even nestled his face in her hair. "You'll be fine if you stay inside your barn and take cover behind one of the stalls."

Gracie looked up at him, revealing tears that were flowing down her cheeks. She wasn't crying, exactly, just allowing her emotions to show only in her eyes. Her voice was strong and showed no emotion when she said, "I'm not scared for me, you horse's ass! I can take care of myself. At least I'll be behind some cover. It's you I'm worried about, standing out there in the middle of the street." Jake let out a laugh that he followed with another gentle squeeze and another kiss on the top of her head. "It's not funny, damn you!" She pushed back and turned her head away.

Jake stepped up behind her and placed both hands on her shoulders. "I'm not laughing at you, Gracie, I promise. It's just that… well, I've never had anyone show signs that they cared what happened to me." He turned Gracie around to face him, but she kept her head down and her eyes closed. Jake lifted her head up by the chin until both sets of eyes met. "For the first time in my life, I think that even *I* care what happens to me."

Although Gracie's eyes were swollen with tears, her voice remained strong when she asked, "Does that mean you're not gonna do anything stupid like get yourself killed?"

Jake smiled again, realizing that, for the first time in his life, his heart was filled with a love he had never allowed himself to feel. "Miss Gracie McCall, I swear to you that I will do everything in my power to walk away from this day and into your arms, if you promise to do the same."

The emotional damn that Gracie McCall had been holding back suddenly burst, releasing a shed of tears and sobs that surprised her. Part of her, the stoic part, was embarrassed to be seen crying, for any reason, let alone over a man. The other part, the human part that knows no gender, was relieved she had that level of love and emotion to set free. She cleared her throat and tried her best to collect her emotions while she fidgeted with her hair and fussed with her clothes. She even gently bounced the butt of her rifle on the floor a few times before she spoke. "It's a deal," she said when she felt she could get the words out without choking back more tears. She even extended her right hand to offer to Jake to seal the agreement.

Jake cocked his head to one side at seeing Gracie offer the handshake. This woman was full of surprises, he thought, and he liked every one of them. He ignored her offer of a handshake and, instead, reached under both her arms and lifted her off the floor, holding her in front of him, eye to eye. "I swear, you are the damnedest woman I have ever met in my life," he said, pulling her to him. He pressed his lips as tightly to hers as he could without crushing her. His passion was met with equal thirst as both held on tight until their breath was spent. As he gently set her down, he said, "Now, go get ready."

Gracie turned and ran up the center aisle of the church and out the front door. There were a few stragglers left that were standing at the door discussing their own individual plans when they witnessed what passed between Jake and Gracie McCall. In a strange sort of emotional exchange, the spectators couldn't help but feel a sense of hope as they watched two unlikely lovers commit to making it through this fight together. If *they* can, they thought, then maybe we can too. Each witness passed their own handshake to the other and then set about making themselves ready to save their town.

Preacher Lee waited a respectable amount of time before he came up alongside Jake and stood, silent, waiting for the right moment to speak. It was Jake who spoke first, sensing that the preacher had something he wanted to say or ask.

"What's on your mind, Preacher?" asked Jake, without ever taking his eyes off the front door to the church where Gracie made her exit. "Time is running short."

"I don't know Miss McCall well, Jake, but I'd like to think I'm a good judge of character," said the preacher. "I could say the same about you, from what little I've learned. But seeing you two together... well, it just fits. I get the sense you need each other, and I pray to the Lord you both survive this day so I can hold the service that brings you together in his name."

Jake still kept his eyes glued to the front door and replied, "Me too, Preacher. Me too."

Chapter Twenty-One

Riding on horseback in the direct heat of the noon-day New Mexico sun was a physically draining exercise. Each man riding behind Wolf was fighting the scorching blast of hot air and dust that every horse's step kicked back at them. Those who didn't bring along enough water to keep themselves hydrated but chose to bring a few bottles of whiskey instead were suffering the most. Excessive heat and cheap alcohol were a bad combination. It was clear that many of these men thought taking on the town of Delgado Station was going to be easy. Their foolish assumption and lack of preparation could soon prove their downfall.

Wolf raised his right hand to signal a stop. In the distance, they could see the town beginning to take shape. In the waving haze of heat, the town looked more like a mirage than a collection of actual buildings. Wolf reached for his canteen, released the stopper and pulled it to his lips. It was empty.

"Potch! Give me some water!" Wolf never took his eyes off the horizon when he barked his order, but just extended his left hand expecting Potch to fill it immediately with whatever he desired. After a beat, he looked down at Potch and made his demand louder, as if Potch never heard it clearly the first time. "POTCH! Give me some damn water!"

Potch was searching his own water supply but was devastated to discover that all canteens and water flasks were empty. He didn't even bring any whiskey to supplement his own store of liquid. He looked up at Wolf with terrified eyes and sheepishly replied, "I'm sorry, Mr. Wolf, sir, but we're all out of water." As soon as he gave Wolf the bad news, he ducked his head as if expecting to be hit.

Spud Pierson may well have saved Potch a beating, or at least a slap across the top of his head, when he offered Wolf some water of his own. "Here!" he said, with an outreached hand holding a canteen. "You can finish off mine. We'll be filling our pockets and canteens soon enough, once we get to town."

Wolf turned a cautious eye toward Spud. Why was this man, perhaps his most dangerous ally in the gang, offering him his own water? Was this a peace offering of some sort? "Why are you giving me your water, Spud?" asked Wolf, not even attempting to hide his suspicion. "Is there something wrong with it?" Wolf turned with a wink to the other men. Many of them laughed, but many were equally curious about Spud's strange gesture of kindness. They all knew there was no love lost between the two men.

"Suit yerself," Spud said, taking the offer back and pouring a mouthful without ever letting the edge of the canteen touch his lips. He even poured what was left onto his face and made a big show of how good it felt.

If they hadn't been so close to their final destination, Spud's strange offer and insulting actions would have been the final straw. The two antagonists exchanged looks that acknowledged an equal understanding of just where they stood in the other's estimation. Both also knew that, when this raid was over, provided both survived, they were going to have it out, once and for all. The exchanged glances between the rest of the men showed that they all knew it too.

"Forget it!" said Wolf with a snarl. "I ain't drinkin' your piss! I'll wait 'til we get to town." He turned around in his saddle to address the rest of the men. "Clear your heads and check your guns. That sheriff may have been full of shit about the people in this town puttin' up a fight, but we can't be sure a few of them won't, so pay attention." Turning back around to face the town, he pulled his hat to better shade his eyes as he tried to cut the glare of the sun and the haze on the horizon. "I'd say we're less than a quarter mile from the edge of town." He replaced his hat and raised his newly acquired Winchester from his lap and opened the breach to blow out any dust that may have collected along the way. He did the same with his pistols. Once he was confident his weaponry was fit and ready for battle, he said, "Let's ride."

Back in town, Jake was standing in the middle of the street, inspecting the positioning of each man up on the roofs of the surrounding buildings. He also took a quick look at all of the storefronts for the same reason.

"Everybody, listen up!" he shouted, his voice carrying a peculiar echo as it bounced off the buildings. "They're less than a half-mile out and coming in, slow and easy. Either they're being real cautious, or they're feeling especially cocky. I'm banking on cocky. I want to let them ride straight into town and right up to me. That's when I'll make my challenge to Wolf. Whatever you do, DON'T get trigger-happy and start shooting until I give the signal. And *DON'T* show yourselves! Surprise is on our side. We want them to ride in together as a group and not split up and start riding through town, up and down the side streets. We need to keep them bunched in here where we can see them and control them." Jake took a stroll back and forth and up and down, inspecting his surroundings, but always remained in the center of the street. "Take a moment to calm yourself as best you can, but remember one thing, no matter what happens to me, this is *your* town. Don't let them take it from you."

Jake's nerves were a mixed-up jumble of emotions that, heretofore, were unknown to him. In all of the gunfights and shootouts he had been through in his long career, the only person whose health and safety he ever had to consider was his own. Now, he had an entire town to think of, and one special woman he hoped he hadn't found too late. As he finished the inspection of his fighters, he stopped his eyes at Gracie who was standing just outside the doors of her stable at the far end of the street. She was standing, feet firmly planted, set at shoulder width, with her shotgun held at the ready in front of her. If Gracie was afraid, she showed no sign of it. She raised her right hand and gave a thumb's up signal to Jake, then stepped back inside the stable, just behind the edge of the sliding stable door.

Knowing she was safe, it was back to business for Jake. "Remember, I want everyone to stay out of sight!" he ordered. "But… if I go down, I want those of you who are hiding outside to step out and open up on them with everything you've got. Don't hesitate. We don't want any of them to have a chance to escape. The more of them you take down, the better chance we have of making the others run for their lives." Jake turned back around to face the southeastern end of the street.

Jake could just make out the figures of men on horseback slowly making their way into town. He pulled his Colt one more time, probably the tenth time, at least, to check the load, which was the same as it had been the other times. It suddenly occurred to him that he didn't think to bring his Winchester, which was still in the boot hanging with his saddle and rig back at the stable. His Winchester was, by far, his most deadly and accurate weapon of choice when it came to fighting more than one man at a time, especially at a distance. His only thought had been facing Wolf

248

up close, but he neglected to consider what would happen if he brought him down first, then only had five other shots left to fend off the other gang members that were likely several yards away. As he spun on his heels to run back to the stable to retrieve his rifle, he almost ran head-first into Gracie who was standing behind him, holding his valued Winchester at arms-length, offering it to Jake.

"Thought you might need this, cowboy," she said. Her eyes were open as wide as they could go and there was the faintest hint of a smile. "I checked it and made sure it was fully loaded and ready to go. I gotta get back to my position." Jake didn't know whether to just take the gun or grab Gracie and kiss her first. "Well, go on, take it." Gracie tossed Jake's rifle the remaining distance, about three feet, which Jake snatched out of the air.

"Thanks," was all Jake could manage to say.

"See you when this is all over," Gracie said with as much confidence as she could muster. She then took a quick glance over Jake's shoulder. "You got about five minutes," she said, then turned on her heels and sprinted back to her position in the stable.

Normally, Jake would have not taken the word of anyone regarding the readiness of any of his guns and given his rifle a once-over himself. But knowing Gracie for the type of woman he felt he knew, even in such a short time, told him he was good to go.

Each of the town's citizens that had stayed to fight had gone through their own individual and unique ritual of sorts to get themselves as ready as they possibly could. For many, it was like preparing for another dust storm so common during the summer months, or even one of those spring floods that seemed to take on biblical proportions when the heavy mountain snows melted faster than ever before. Basically, they were readying themselves for the worst possible outcome imaginable. What was coming was, indeed, a storm of sorts, but it was not something one could hide from, hoping it would pass them by. With each advancing minute, they knew death was coming. How it would play out for the town would depend on how they faced it as individuals.

Lou Hudson repeatedly hugged his wife, Amanda, as they expressed their love for each other. Carter Innskeep did the same with his wife, Emma, as did Eric and Mariah Bonawitz. They were as ready as they could be. Ready for killing, if necessary. Ready to die for one another too.

Doc Gibbons had prepared a makeshift triage area in the only saloon in town, The Dancing Dollar, using the bar as an operating table, which was long enough to accommodate up to three bodies, if necessary. The saloon also had the largest supply of alcohol on hand, although not the type best suited for treating gunshot wounds. But rot-gut whiskey was certainly better than nothing at all for killing germs and cleansing bullet holes.

The girl at the heart of this entire nightmare, Juneann, whom Jake had rescued less than a week ago, had been moved to a small ranch outside of town. Physically, she was almost fully recovered, with only the cut below her right breast inflicted by Orin still bandaged but beginning to heal nicely. Her mental recovery, however, was still a long way off. It would take considerably longer for trauma of that magnitude to heal. If ever. The important thing was that she was removed from immediate danger. If the town could survive the next hour, maybe Juneann would have the time to make a full recovery and go on to enjoy the life she deserved, thanks to Jake.

Michael Charles, the gunsmith who had generously supplied

the townspeople with better armaments, had set aside a few surprises of his own, should any of Wolf's men make it down to his part of town. He and Gracie had buried two sticks of dynamite in the middle of the street, between his shop and the stable. The gunsmith was something of an unknown asset to the town, having already surprised everyone with the generosity of his stock of guns and ammunition. What they didn't know was that he was also a crack shot with a rifle, in this case, a lever action long gun Marlin Model 1894, Carbine. If more than one man got within one hundred feet of either his store or Gracie's stable, he would fire into the staked-out posts and obliterate anything within a fifty-foot radius. Initially, Gracie objected to the very realistic probability of killing defenseless animals along with any of Wolf's men. But given the possibility of just one of those men killing her and anyone else in town made her reluctantly accept the reality of the situation. To protect the stock under her care, however, she had already moved all the horses to the outskirts of town.

When she tried to move Teacher, however, her efforts proved futile. Jake's horse simply would not budge. It seemed to Gracie that Teacher just knew Jake was in danger and was not about to desert him now. Knowing it would be a waste of time and delay her from removing the rest of her stock to safety, she decided to leave Teacher alone, untethered, in her stall. Gracie had even left the stall door open, hoping Teacher would follow a typical horse's instinct and run at the sound of gunfire, especially if it was not holding a rider. Still, when she opened the gate, all Teacher did was walk out of the stall and stop at the barn door of the stable and look down the street at Jake, who was still standing in the middle of town, waiting for Wolf. Teacher let out an explosion of air that struck Gracie as an almost human-like sound

251

of exasperation.

"I agree," she said, as if replying to something Teacher said. She patted the mare on the neck. "I'm not too happy about his decision either." Teacher turned her head and looked Gracie directly in the eyes and let out a grumbling sound and followed it with a head shake, then resumed her observation of Jake.

Chapter Twenty-Two

Spud Pierson had worked his horse up alongside Wolf's but still had his right hand on his Colt. Wolf shot him a quick glance, wondering why he had made a move like this, especially as they were approaching the edge of town.

"You got somethin' more to say, Spud?" asked Wolf. "Or are you hoping I'll protect you once the shootin' starts?"

Spud gave a hearty laugh and said, "I don't need any help from you, Wolf. I can fend for myself just fine."

"Then what are you doin' ridin' so close to me?" he said. "Aren't you afraid you'll get hit by a stray bullet aimed at me?" Wolf looked back at his men and added, "Or are you plannin' on shootin' me in the back, first chance you get?" A few of the men offered mild laughter.

"The difference between you and me, Wolf, is that I'm not a back-shooter," he replied, looking back at the men in the same manner Wolf did. His comment got more laughter than Wolf's. Spud continued, "If I wanted you dead, I'd do it myself. I just wanted a ring-side seat if you decide to pick up Jake Benteen's gauntlet."

Wolf could feel his influence with the rest of the gang slipping away. He never did answer if he would accept Benteen's challenge or try and find some tactful way out of it and still keep face with his men. His ego was easily bruised and Spud's constant prodding to face Jake Benteen, man to man, was beginning to have some effect on him and the rest of the men.

"That's important to you, ain't it, Spud?" asked Wolf. "You think I can't take Benteen?"

Spud removed his hat and ran his fingers through his sweat-soaked hair. "Well, I've seen you fight, Wolf, and I know what you're capable of." He replaced his hat and continued. "But I've only heard stories of Benteen. They say he's one of the best there is with a pistol or that rifle he's known for. So, as a gambling man, I confess to being a might curious to see just which one of you is the better man." Spud turned his eyes to Wolf and he waited until his stare was returned before he finished. "That's all I'm saying. Call it professional curiosity." Spud winked at Wolf and then turned his eyes straight ahead and pulled up easy on his reins to hold his horse back a few paces.

Spud's comments, heard by all, were equal to Benteen's own challenge, essentially being one and the same. Wolf knew he had to answer it here and now and jammed his spurs into his horse's haunches, causing the animal to lurch forward for a few short gallops until both rider and animal were about ten yards in front. Wolf then gave the reins a sharp yank to his left, spinning his horse around until both rider and horse were facing Spud and the rest of the man. They were only about fifty yards from the edge of town.

"Is that what the rest of you men think?" hollered Wolf. "You think I ain't got the stones to face Benteen on my own?" Wolf waited for an answer but nothing came as the men just either shrugged or looked down at the dirt. "Well! Do ya?"

Spud stood up in his stirrups and lifted his hat to shade his eyes. "Well, I'll be!" he said, with some genuine surprise. "I think that's Benteen standing right square in the middle of the street, just like that sheriff said he would." Spud looked back at the men and then at Wolf. "Looks to me like he's ready. Question is, Wolf... are you?"

Wolf spun his horse around again to face the front to witness for himself the man who stood between him and the command of his men, as well as his own pride. At that moment, Wolf knew he had only one choice. Without turning back to face his men he said, "When I cut Benteen down, I will tear out his heart and hold it up for you all to see. That will be your signal to burn this town to the ground and take it for everything you can carry." He turned to Spud. "Is that good enough for you, Spud?" He then turned back to the rest of the men, adding, "Is that good enough for all you boys?"

No one offered a single word of praise or encouragement, which seemed to surprise Wolf and even take some of the wind out of his emotional sails. He had expected a few shouts of support, but total silence tugged at his confidence. Still, he had no choice now but to follow through with his boast. Wolf gave his horse another jab of his spurs, just enough to nudge it forward into a sort of quick step. Jake heard Wolf's boastful claim, the likes of which he had heard many times before from others. They were typical, hyperbolic, "whistling in the dark through a cemetery," boasts that were a sure indication that the individual making the claim was more scared and unsure of himself than he was letting on.

One gunfighter from Jake's past, a loudmouth named Johnny Beasley, who longed to build his own reputation on the back of Jake's, shouted to the assembled crowd of thrill seekers that he was going to "empty my gun into your belly and then piss in your guts!" Jake shot him once in the center of his chest. The man was dead before his body hit the ground, his gun still frozen in his hand, although he did manage to get off a single shot of his own, which hit the dirt less than a foot in front of his own boots.

Given Jake's history of hearing such bravado, whether it was from Wolf or anyone else, didn't faze him in the least. He had learned a long time ago to just let threats and taunts roll off him like water off a duck's back. His only response was to spin his Winchester in one motion, with his right hand, chambering a load. Then, with his left hand, he rested the rifle on his left hip, freeing his right hand, which hovered over his Colt. Left hand or right, he was ready.

Wolf continued his forward movement, allowing his horse to walk at an even pace, not pushing it faster or slower. Everyone in town that could catch a view of the street without giving away their own position waited with baited breath.

Eric Bonawitz had positioned himself atop the bank, just behind the sign. He had a clear angle of the street, as well as the riders, who held their position, sitting patiently just outside of town. Hearing Wolf's threat and seeing Jake's response made him shake his head in awe. He was speaking more to himself, when he said, "Jake Benteen, you are one brave son of a bitch. I'll give you that."

"Or, just plain crazy," added Tom O'Leary, a fellow rancher, who was positioned at the other edge of the sign.

"That too," answered Eric. "That too."

On the other side of the street and up on the roof, hiding behind the signs of the dry goods store and the ladies' fashion shop were two more men with rifles, John Hartsock and Dan Hayes from neighboring farms less than five miles out of town. John Hartsock raised sheep and Dan Hayes raised pigs. Both ranches did well and were growing. Neither man had ever fired a gun at a human being before, only animals and purely for hunting food for their families. Both heard Wolf's boast as it echoed down the street and were far more concerned about their survival than either man wanted to admit.

"That Wolf fellow is as mad as a hatter, don't ya think, Dan?" John kept his eyes glued on the specter of Wolf as he and his horse crept closer with each step.

"It don't matter to me, one way or t'other," Dan Hayes replied. "Just as long as Benteen drops him in the dirt. If he does that, I'm thinkin' a few of those men will back off and head back to Tres Mesa, or just skedaddle. Fewer men fer us to deal with."

"And if Wolf takes Benteen instead?" asked John, his voice showing concern.

"Well then," Dan answered, with equal caution, "It looks like you and me will be doin' some shootin' of our own."

John took a deep breath, then said, "Yup. Looks like. Never thought I'd be actually trying to kill a man though. Even knowing we got to… well, it just don't seem right." He paused and took another deep breath. "Still…?"

"Just pretend you're shootin' a mountain lion that's attacking your stock, or one of your kids," reasoned Dan. "That's what I'll be doin'." He took a deep breath of his own and almost whispered, "Otherwise, I think I'll puke."

Both men looked at the other with a shyness that told them all they needed to know about how the other felt, but also seemed to give them both the confidence to know they weren't alone in their fears, but would still do what was necessary.

As Wolf crept closer to what could be his final destination, newspaper publisher Pete Adams mumbled to himself, "By the prickling in my thumbs, something wicked this way comes."

Banker Dan MacNeil, who was standing next to him, turned and said, "Enter Macbeth." He then winked at the newspaperman and added, "I've always been partial to Shakespeare too."

"Ya don't say," answered Pete Adams. "The sheriff and I

used to trade some of his plays back and forth. Macbeth seemed an appropriate reference, under the circumstances."

The banker nodded in agreement. "You can say that again."

Horse and rider continued a few more feet, then stopped directly in front of Jake, about ten yards apart. Jake never flinched or moved a muscle. His eyes were clear and sharply focused on Wolf.

"Well, well, you must be the great gunfighter Jake Benteen everyone is so scared of?" asked Wolf snidely. "You don't look so tough."

"And you must be that sick animal they call Wolf," answered Jake. "You're a lot smaller than I expected." Jake's insult was meant to sting since Val Avery had told him that Wolf took great pride in his size and often used it to intimidate his opponents, which usually worked. Jake could tell his insult did, in fact, sting, although Wolf tried his best to hide it. But a squint in his eyes gave it away.

"I hear you offered me a challenge, Benteen." Wolf did his best to sound gruff and unafraid. "Leastwise, that's what that sheriff you sent out said… just before I shot him."

Jake paused at the confirmation that his old friend was dead. He already suspected it, of course, but hearing it definitively struck him with a sharp jab in his chest but remained stoic and calm, showing no reaction at all. "I take it Val isn't coming back then?" asked Jake in a monotone that was intended to show no emotion or concern, even though he could feel his stomach churn at the thought of his friend lying dead in the road. He needed to stay focused and sharp.

"No, 'fraid not," said Wolf, with a sick smirk on his face. "I left him on the side of the road a few miles back. I'm pretty sure that with all the bullet holes I put in him, he's dead, but you never know. I gotta give the old coot credit for balls though. He took out two of my men before I cut him down. Took this off him though," he said as he lifted his vest to reveal the sheriff's badge he had pinned to it. "Looks good, don't ya think? Think I'll keep it." Wolf held up Val's Winchester. "I took this off him too! It's not as nice as yours, but I like it well enough. It's kind of like a trophy." He rested the rifle on his right thigh and hunched forward to take a closer look at Jake's own Winchester, then raised his eyes to look at the sun and moon resting side by side on the horizon. "You ever hear of a Black Moon, Benteen?"

Although not a superstitious man by nature, Jake knew enough about old myths and legends to have heard of the theories and paganistic beliefs associated with a Black Moon. "Nothing more than an extra moon in a cycle," Jake answered in a deadpan way to indicate he thought it was meaningless and that he didn't care, regardless. "Some believe it to be an omen, good or bad, depending on which side of the belief you're on. Why?"

The stunned look on Wolf's face was nothing short of disappointment. He was hoping to be able to explain his interpretation of its meaning and that it would intimidate Jake. The fact that Jake knew something about it and also seemed unimpressed took Wolf by surprise. He tried to recover some of his bluster when he said, "Well... yeah... you got that right. It is an omen for sure. It means bad luck fer sure. It means someone's gonna die today."

Before Wolf could continue his prediction, Jake said, "And yet, knowing you were going to die today, you still came? I'm impressed."

Wolf was completely thrown off guard. "What? *ME*? No! No, I'm not the one who's going to die today, Benteen. It's you! The Black Moon rising today is the sign of *your* death, not mine!"

259

Jake just shrugged and smiled. "Well, if telling yourself that makes you feel better, you go right ahead."

Wolf tried his best to regain his composure, but it was clear to anyone within hearing distance that his confidence was clearly shaken. He shifted nervously in his saddle and tried to change the subject.

"I hear you're the best there is with a Winchester, Benteen. That true?" Before Jake could answer, Wolf added a little boast of his own. "I prefer a Colt myself. With a pistol, I ain't never been beat. I like it up close and personal, if you know what I mean."

"I can kill you with either," Jake replied. "Your call." Again, the monotone in Jake's voice was smooth and even, showing no signs of fear. "Why don't you step down and we'll see just how this plays out."

Wolf arched his back in the saddle and looked over his right shoulder. His men had crept in a little closer but did not actually cross the line that designated the edge of town. It appeared they were more interested in getting a closer view of the impending action than exposing themselves to risk.

"Are you in that much of a hurry to die, Benteen?"

There was something new in Wolf's voice that belied his question. Fear. Jake noticed his voice had gone up an octave and gave the slightest crack on the word "die" as if he were thinking more about his own demise than Jake's.

"Not particularly," said Jake. "But if all you're going to do is shoot your mouth off and make silly-ass threats, then why don't you and your men just turn around and head back to Tres Mesa? These folks have work to do. Honest work. Besides, I just poured myself a nice hot cup of coffee and I hate to drink it cold." This time, Jake made sure his voice carried far enough for all of

Wolf's men to hear.

Spud Pierson turned to the rest of the men and responded to Jake's suggestion. "You have got to admire the man's pluck," he said. There was a hint of suspicion in his voice. "That makes me wonder what he knows that we don't." Spud sat back in his saddle and openly pondered the situation as he tried to scan the town's buildings and rooftops. He had seen many a gunfight in his life and felt he could tell if a man was all talk and no show, or if he was holding something back. He couldn't shake the feeling. "Boys, something just don't sit right."

One of the men saddled just behind Spud said, "The town looks deserted to me, Spud. I only see Benteen standing out, facing Wolf. Looks like the rest of the town either cut out or is in hiding. This could be easy pickin's for us."

"That's what bothers me," replied Spud, shaking his head. He pulled his hat off again and placed it on his saddle horn. This time, with both hands, he massaged his scalp as if trying to clear his mind to think. Finally, he said, "I'm gonna cut a wide path and head around back to the other end of town and take a look see." Spud deftly tugged back on the reins of his horse, making it walk backward until he was behind the rest of the riders. Then, he slumped down over the front of his saddle and slithered off to the side to try and hide his maneuver. Most eyes in town were focused on Jake and Wolf anyway, so Spud was able to make his escape without being seen. Even Wolf's men largely ignored Spud's move, choosing to keep their eyes glued on the two men about to engage in a long-awaited and much-anticipated gunfight.

Wolf had been sitting still, silent after Jake's last comment. His eyes scanned the roof line on either side of the town. He also looked along the storefronts for any signs of life. Something wasn't sitting right with him either. The town appeared empty and quiet. Too empty and too quiet. "You think I'm fool enough to fall for an ambush like this, Benteen?"

"There's no ambush, Wolf," he replied calmly. "Just a few townsfolk willing to fight to keep what's theirs." So far, everyone was doing exactly what Jake had asked, which was to remain hidden until he called them out or they saw him fall. "Right now, this is between you and me. I'm the one that took down two of your boys, Orin and Buck I believe were their names, no one else."

"I don't give two shits about those two!" Wolf barked back. "It's the principle of the thing. You broke our truce."

"I didn't break any truce with you, Wolf, and you know it," Jake snapped back. "I didn't even know these folks or the people those two men attacked. I'd never even been to this town before. So, as far as I'm concerned, it was *they* who broke your so-called truce, not me. And, certainly, none of the folks in this town did. You're just looking for an excuse." For the first time since Wolf entered the town, Jake changed his position and took a slight side-step to his right and about half a step backward. "This is your final warning, Wolf." Jake flexed the fingers of his right hand as they hovered over his Colt.

Wolf's eyes widened. "Or what?" He seemed genuinely confused.

"Or die in the saddle," said Jake. "I'm through talking."

Wolf smirked and even tried to laugh a little, but it was obvious to Jake that it was fake and a classic attempt at a bluff. It was the move of an amateur and one Jake had seen far too many times to be fooled by it now, especially from someone of Wolf's sordid reputation. Wolf tried it earlier on Val Avery and it didn't work on him either. It was only sheer luck that saved him that time. Another part of the bluff is to pretend to look away, as if looking at one's surroundings, or even taking a moment to think before giving an answer to the challenge. Jake anticipated the entire ruse and was charged and ready.

Thinking he had fooled his opponent, even a little, Wolf jerked his head back to center and tried to level his Winchester, all in one quick motion, hoping to distract Jake so that he could pull his own pistol instead. It was, indeed, a quick move, but nowhere near quick enough. Jake was prepared. He had pulled his own fake on Wolf, who assumed Jake was expecting him to go for his own pistol as well, which is why Jake repeatedly flexed his fingers over it. Classic misdirection. All the while, Jake intended to use his own Winchester, which he leveled on Wolf faster than Wolf managed to pull his pistol. In the end, both men tried to fool the other, but it all came down to who did it better and faster.

Jake dove to his right and fired first. His aim was dead-on perfect, except that his bullet struck the side plate of Wolf's newly acquired Winchester. It was a freakish bit of bad luck. The impact of the bullet kicked the rifle barrel back into Wolf's face, splitting his lower lip and slamming the barrel against his nose. The reflex action caused Wolf to fire his rifle harmlessly into the air, while also causing his right hand to instinctively reach for the injury to his face and away from his Colt. Neither man was hurt by the exchange of gunfire.

Despite the number of people who witnessed the two men and their almost simultaneous single gunshots, what each thought they saw greatly depended on precisely where they stood, the angle of sight, how far away they were and what they were looking at exactly. If their focus was on Jake, they saw him fall to his right. If they were looking at Wolf, all they could tell was that he was still sitting on his horse. The assumption made by Wolf's men, who were all positioned behind him, was that he was unharmed and Jake, who was lying on the ground, took a bullet and was likely killed, or at least seriously injured.

One of Wolf's men, who thought Jake was down and dead, screamed, "Wolf did it! He took Jake Benteen! The town's ours! Let's go!" He jabbed his spurs into his horse's rump and sprinted his steed forward, heading for the center of the town. All the other riders responded in kind, adding whoops and cheers as they charged the last fifty yards heading into the heart of Delgado Station.

In those split seconds of action, the human brain tends to take extreme action and the instinct for survival slows everything down to a snail's pace. Jake was unhurt yet was also aware that his perfectly aimed shot freakishly missed its mark. He had seen the sparks fly off the Winchester's side plate and knew Wolf was not critically injured. Just stunned. Jake spotted the oncoming riders and could hear their shouts, but never lost sight of Wolf, who had tossed the damaged Winchester to the ground and recovered his senses enough to still try and drag his Colt across his body to fire at Jake, who had been sitting in the dirt on his right side. With his legs curled under him, Jake twisted up on his knees and leveled his Winchester at Wolf's exposed chest. The sun hit Val's sheriff's badge, giving Jake a perfect target. Wolf's Colt was just coming around the top of his horse's head when Jake fired six shots in rapid succession, each one hitting the disgraced badge of his friend, effectively obliterating it, driving the shattered pieces of metal deep into Wolf's heart.

Jake knew for certain that his aim and all six bullets had hit their mark, yet Wolf still sat upright in his saddle, frozen, with a look of shocked surprise and disbelief. There was still enough life left in him to look down at the mark of death on his chest, then back up to see Jake, now standing with his rifle ready to deliver more lead.

Wolf choked out, "What?" then fell backward, dropping his Colt as he slid off the back of his horse. As his body hit the dirt, his horse skittishly lurched forward and trotted further down the street, stopping about twenty yards away. Wolf's men were in various positions and angles as they were storming into town and most didn't see the final scene play out that would have shown them their leader was flat on his back with a hole in his chest big enough to bury a man's fist in.

As the riders got closer to the tableau of death still holding center stage in the middle of the street, the riders began to peel off, left and right. Jake held his position and fired a warning shot into the air. Seeing Jake clearly now, alive and well, and Wolf lying dead in the dirt made the lead rider, Wert Moody, hold his hand up high and holler, "Hold up!" signaling the rest of the men, now numbering less than a dozen, to stop.

"Wolf's dead!" called out Jake, loud enough for everyone to hear. "So, unless you want to join him, I suggest you all turn around and make tracks back to Tres Mesa or for the border. This raid is over!"

Wert Moody, now the titular head of this band of misfits, took a brief moment to evaluate the situation. Seeing Wolf lying dead just a few yards from his horse's feet had the opposite effect Jake was hoping for. Instead of fear, or at least giving Wert Moody and the rest of the men second thoughts about continuing their plan to raid the town, the sight of Wolf's corpse seemed to invigorate the men instead, giving them a false sense of superiority. After all, they were almost a dozen men standing against only one man. Or so they thought.

"So, you got 'im," stated Wert Moody, with what appeared to be unrestrained delight. "I think I can honestly speak for the rest of the men when I say, THANK YOU!"

"My pleasure," replied Jake. "So, there's not much point in continuing this fight, is there?" Jake stepped sideways about three feet to place himself in a more direct line of the remaining members of Wolf's gang, but more specifically directly in front of Wert Moody. "Like I said, it would be best if you all just turned around and headed for parts unknown."

Wert took his pistol, a Remington .44, which he still held in his right hand, and used it to lift his hat and tip it slightly to one side while scratching the side of his head with the barrel. He gave a few quick glances to the rest of the men, who all seemed to be waiting for orders from their new leader.

"Well now… see… here's the thing," he said. "We had our hearts set on taking this town and loading ourselves up with money, provisions and anything else we felt like takin'… before we headed for the border, or for parts unknown, as you say." His men responded to his comments with a variety of positive verbal agreements.

"That would be a mistake," advised Jake. His manner was cool and carried an almost disinterested attitude. He had placed his Winchester in his left hand and was casually loading replacement shells in the chamber in a very deliberate manner, as if each shell were intended for someone in particular.

Wert Moody looked around, side to side and down the street along the storefronts. All still seemed deserted, with no obvious threats to consider. "Oh, and why would that be?" He paused and leaned forward, resting his left hand on his saddle horn while still holding his Remington. "I don't see anything to make me reconsider my thinking."

Jake leaned side to side to scope out the rest of the gang members and then came back to set his eyes on Wert Moody. "Are you the new leader of this outfit?"

Wert looked about and was surprised to see some of the men offer positive head nods or shrugs of acceptance. "Looks like I was voted in without my even knowin' I was runnin'," he said. "So, yes, sir, I guess I am. Name's, Wert! Wert Moody. And you must be Jake Benteen. That right?"

"I am he. So it looks to me like you have a decision to make, Wert." Jake tossed a look over his left shoulder and then back to the gang's new leader. "Are you going to go ahead with this plan to try and take our town, or turn around and ride on?"

Wert sat back in his saddle, looked at Jake and added, "You managed to take Wolf, one on one and that is an impressive feat, I'll grant you, Mr. Benteen. But the way I see it, there is only one of you that I can see and there's close to a dozen or so of us. Although I ain't done a head count lately, but from where I'm sittin', those are impressive odds that don't favor you. So, the question *you* have to ask yourself is do you think you can take all of us before we cut you down."

"All of you? No," Jake answered quickly and calmly. "But you, absolutely." Then Jake teasingly pointed his freshly reloaded rifle at each of the men sitting astride their horses on either side of Wert Moody, most still with their guns drawn. "And I'm dead certain I can take a goodly portion of you before I hit the ground." Jake could tell the men knew this was no idle threat. He might have decided to stop there and see if it was enough for them to reconsider their next move, but he also had another card to play in this dangerous game and decided now seemed like the perfect time to play it. "And just in case you think I'm bluffing and those odds still favor you enough to go ahead with your intentions, here is something else to consider." Jake called out in his loudest, most commanding voice, "FOLKS! Everyone! I need you to step out into the open just enough to show these men what they're up against!"

The first to stand up and be recognized was Eric Bonawitz, who was pretty hard to miss as he towered over the sign above the bank. Next to him was Tom O'Leary, no small man himself, coming in at six feet, three inches. Both men leveled their rifles on the riders. "I got myself a few choice targets picked out Jake," the big man bellowed. "You just give the word and I'll drop them where they sit."

Tom O'Leary spoke next, saying, "I picked out a few for myself." Adding, "That fella in the back with the flat-brimmed hat with the feather in it, ridin' the gray mare, is as good as dead. So's the one next to him."

Across the street, up on the adjacent roof stood John Hartsock and Dan Hayes, each with their own rifles aimed and ready. John Hartsock spoke up first. "Can't swear to my accuracy, Jake, so I'm planning on just aiming for the center of the bunch and emptying my entire load. Figure I'm bound to kill a couple… or mess 'em up pretty good."

"Whatever he don't cut down, I'll finish off," countered Dan Hayes as he stood up, making his presence known.

Down the street, one by one, the rest of the town's citizens stepped out and into the clear, just enough to be seen, along with their guns. Even the oldest lady in town, Mariba Wright, walked out of the lady's finery store and sat down in a chair under the roof. She rested her shotgun in her lap. She didn't need to say anything.

Carter Innskeep stepped out of his store, holding a rifle he had never used before, but made every effort to like he knew how to handle it.

Lou Hudson, Pete Adams and Dan MacNeil all stepped out of the bank, holding their chosen weaponry, an assortment of pistols and rifles. Lou Hudson had one of each.

Across the street, the two farm hands, Frank and Kerby stepped out of the alley between Howard Lyndh's dry goods store. Howard stood in his doorway, holding a Winchester, which he cocked and held to his shoulder.

Once Jake felt everyone was fairly represented, he turned back to the would-be raiders and asked, "I think you can see that, aside from our own impressive numbers, we've got cover on our side. You're all sitting out here in the open. Now, I don't know how many of you play poker, but I am guessing there are more than a few of you that don't want to play this hand."

Wert Moody didn't have to look to each man behind him to know how they would vote. He raised his left hand slowly as if to signal surrender and with an even more deliberate and especially slow motion slipped the revolver in his right hand back into its holster and then raised the empty hand, equal to his left. His message was clear.

"I ain't no fool, Benteen," he remarked. "I can't speak for the rest of these boys, but I'm willin' to bet they agree." He looked behind him and asked, "Anyone here damn fool enough to want to take a chance on this town now?" One by one, each man with either pistol or rifle surrendered them back to their respective holsters or rifle boot and raised their empty hands. Wert looked back at Jake. "There's your answer, Benteen." After an awkward pause that released some of the tension, Wert asked, "So... where do we go from here?"

"You turn around and head to wherever your heart desires... just as long as it isn't here," answered Jake.

Wert smiled and said, "Sounds reasonable." He looked down and to his far left to notice that Potch and his mule, Sugar Pie had settled far and away from any possible action. Jake had noticed it too, but something about the way Potch had positioned himself and how his eyes looked to him in an almost pleading manner made Jake feel he wasn't a threat. Besides, he had never pulled out the sawed-off shotgun, which Jake saw hanging off to the side against the mule's neck. It was almost as if Jake knew this strange little man didn't want to be there but was dragged along against his will. As Wert turned his horse around he called out to Potch. "You comin', Potch?"

Potch cast his desperate eyes back to Jake and asked, "Would it be all right with you, Mr. Benteen, if I stayed here and took the next stage out of town?"

"You ain't comin' back with us, Potch?" asked Wert with some genuine surprise.

"No sir, Wert, I sure ain't," he replied. "Wolf is dead and I ain't cryin' over it. I'm finally... free. Free to go where I want... and that sure ain't back with you boys. No offense." Potch looked back at Jake and asked again, "If that's all right with Mr. Benteen, here?"

"The next stage won't be for some time," said Jake with a marked warning. "You think you can manage to stay out of trouble until then?"

Potch took a deep breath and released it with an almost joyous escape of air and answered, "Yes sir, I surely do, sir. Thank you, Mr. Benteen, sir. I promise I will be no trouble to you or anybody else here. I promise you that, sir."

It seemed as if Potch was never going to stop expressing his gratitude so Jake cut him off. "All right, all right, I get it. Drop any weapons you've got right there in the dirt and take your mule down to the livery and wait for me there. There's a lady there who'll take care of you. But I warn you, if you cross her… she'll burn you down and send you straight to hell."

"Oh, thank you, Mr. Benteen, sir!" Potch almost let out his familiar squeal of delight but managed to contain it to only a giggle of relief. He pulled his shotgun from its boot and gave it a toss to his side as if it were red hot, then reached into his right boot and pulled a small knife commonly referred to as a "pig sticker" and tossed that into the dirt as well.

"That it?" asked Jake.

"Yes sir, Mr. Benteen, sir! That's all I ever carry." Potch held up both hands. "That's all I got, I swear," he added.

"Hey, Potch!" came the voice of Wert Moody again, but with a suspicious tone. "When you cut Jack Holden in half with that scattergun back in Tres Mesa, was it because HE was plannin' on cuttin' and runnin' or because he caught YOU makin' plans to run?"

Potch knew he had been found out but remained silent, only reaching forward to pat Sugar Pie on the head.

"That's what I thought." Wert Moody smiled and said, "Well, I can't say I blame you. Jack always seemed to enjoy his torments of you when Wolf wasn't lookin'. I'm sure he had long been askin' for it."

Although Jake didn't know the particulars of what Wert was alluding to, he could tell by the expression on both men's faces that it was a private matter that seemed to be settled to each man's satisfaction.

"Potch! That's your name?" Potch just nodded his head. "Head on down to the stable like I told you, with your hands raised the whole way," was Jake's warning.

As Potch nodded his agreement to Jake's warning, Wert

Moody offered a very unexpected farewell to Potch. "You take care there, little man!" Potch only nodded to Wert his acceptance of his salutation. Wert then looked to Jake to offer something of an odd apology for Potch by way of an explanation. "Just so's you know, Potch never really rode with us, Benteen. He was more of a mascot for Wolf. A toy, you might say. He was treated pretty damned awful, if you want to know the truth. I think he would have left a hundred different times if he had the chance. You taking out Wolf, likely as much, set him free. It was good of you to give him a chance at somethin' better."

"You know, times are changing for the likes of men like you and me, Wert," Jake stated plainly. "I think it's plain to see the road ahead doesn't look too promising for either of us."

Wert shrugged and said, "Yeah, well, likely as much I'll end up shot dead somewhere, along with a lot of these boys." None of the other men disputed his prediction but instead nodded to one another in agreement. They were also getting restless and wanted to head back to familiar territory. Wert continued, "My mamma always used to say, 'You make your choices in life boy, so if things turn sour, you have to live them or die by them. So, don't come cryin' to me if things don't turn out right in the end.'"

"Your mamma sounds like a wise woman," offered Jake.

"Yes sir, she sure was that," agreed Wert. "Probably should have listened to her a bit more closely but I think it's probably too late for that now." He tipped his hat and turned his horse around to leave.

"Hey, Wert!" Jake called. The new leader turned his horse back around to Jake. The rest of the men held up, waiting to hear what the two men were discussing. "I've got a favor to ask of you. The sheriff was a friend of mine, named Val Avery. He was also a friend of this town. I'd take it kindly of you if you would see to his body before the buzzards tear him up too much. Cover him over with something, maybe. I'll send out some folks to collect him."

Wert tipped his hat and said, "Sounds reasonable. He died well if that matters to you and this town. I'd be proud to go out that way."

"I appreciate your saying so," answered Jake. "It means a lot to this town."

"Mind if I ask what your plans are for Wolf?" Wert's question was odd and unexpected.

The gunfighter slumped to one side to consider the idea. "I hadn't thought that far ahead, to be honest," answered Jake. "Why? You want to take him back with you?"

Wert roared with laughter. "Ha! Not a chance in hell!" The rest of the men agreed with Wert's sentiments. "You can do whatever you like with him. Although I might suggest you *not* bury him alongside any decent folks in your church plot. They might rise up and leave! Ha!"

Since Jake hadn't gotten around to considering what to do with Wolf's body, the current topic of discussion got him thinking. "What would you suggest, then?"

Wert thought for a brief moment, then surprised Jake by suggesting, "Burn him!"

"Burn him?" Jake was caught off guard at what appeared to be a rather primitive suggestion. "Why?"

Wert lowered his voice as if he were embarrassed to say it out loud. "Well, another thing my mamma used to say was to always respect the things you don't know or understand. It's my feeling that this Black Moon thing Wolf talked about ain't been put to rest just yet. I'm not sayin' I believe in any of that superstitious talk, but" – Wert smiled and shrugged – "why risk it? My suggestion would be to burn his body somewhere outside of town and then scatter his ashes to the winds. It will finish off what soul he had, if any, and maybe free this territory of him fer good. That's my thinkin' on it."

With that, Wert Moody twisted the reins of his horse around again until he was fully facing back the way he and the gang had come into town. "Well, boys, I think we've got enough whiskey and women back as Tres Mesa to keep us occupied for the next few days. What say we head on back and have ourselves a farewell party?" As the men shouted their approval of Wert's invitation and individually split off and began heading back to their own lair, Wert noticed one man missing from the group, Spud Pierson. He pulled up on his reins and spun his horse back around as the rest of the gang continued back down the road out of town. Wert saw Jake still standing in the exact same spot, in the exact same position. "Hey, Benteen!" he shouted. "I forgot, but we had another man with us, name of Spud Pierson. He split off about a mile back saying he was going circle around and come in from the other end of town. Can't say where he is now though. I lost track of him. He's a clever bastard and always does things his own way, so I'd watch out for him. Fair warning."

Jake tipped his hat to Wert in an equal, appreciative gesture and said, "Thanks for the warning."

Wert spun his horse around one last time and jabbed his spurs into the horse's rump and sprinted down the road to catch up with his compadres. Knowing there was an unknown human factor unaccounted for made Jake spin around on his heels and sprint down the street, heading for Gracie's livery stable. Potch had only made it about halfway when he turned to see Jake sprinting past him on a dead run. The street in front of the livery and Michael Charles gun shop looked deserted, showing no sign of Spud Pierson or anyone else. Jake slowed his run and stopped directly in front of one of the sticks of dynamite Michael Charles had planted, not realizing what it was or even noticing the broken-up dirt.

"Gracie!" Jake's call sounded desperate. "Gracie, where are you?"

"What's wrong, Jake?" Gracie was just stepping away from the cover of the barn door and into the clearing. "I saw them turn around and ride out?" she added as she stepped away from the barn and out further into the street. "Is it over?"

Jake took a quick step to his left, intending to run straight into Gracie's arms to pull her back inside. The step to his left saved his life, as a bullet ripped into the back of his right shoulder, spinning him around and causing his Winchester to fly from his hand. As Jake fell to the ground, Gracie bolted away from the barn door and sprinted to his side just as another bullet ripped into Jake's right thigh, just below the hip. Gracie screamed and threw her body over Jake, who was stunned by the impact of both bullets coming in such rapid succession. Not only did he lose his Winchester when the first bullet struck, but the damage to his shoulder made his right arm hang useless so that he couldn't even pull his Colt.

Stepping out from the back corner behind the gun shop came Spud Pierson. He had made his way around to the far end of town just as he had planned but was not fully aware of what had transpired earlier at the other end of the street. He was too far away to clearly see Wolf get burned down by Jake, or to hear what Wert Moody and Jake had settled on. As far as he knew, the town was still ripe for the taking. Seeing Jake hurt and lying on his left side, with his right arm draped limp and motionless made Spud assume he was done for and, therefore, no threat. As he stepped deeper into the street, he noticed Potch and Sugar Pie slowly meandering toward him. Spud reasoned that Potch and the rest of the gang must have taken the town and that, perhaps Jake was actually trying to make a run for it by trying to get to his horse.

"Well, well," said Spud, as he slowly approached Jake and Gracie, who was still covering his body with her own. "What do we have here?"

Potch was just coming up to the trio and stopped about twenty feet away. "Please don't, Mr. Spud," pleaded Potch. "He's hurt enough."

"Shut yer trap, little man!" snapped Spud. He looked back up the street to see it slowly begin to fill with the people of Delgado Station. The sight was peculiar in that he did not see Wolf or any members of the gang. "Where's Wolf?" he asked Potch, as he continued to survey the people in the crowd, looking for a familiar face. "Where's Wert and the rest of the boys? I heard some shootin', but don't see any of 'em."

"They all left, Mr. Spud," answered Potch. "Wolf's dead. Mr. Benteen took him fair and square, with six bullets to the heart."

Spud looked back at Jake, who had managed to lift himself up on his left elbow. Gracie was still covering him, with her left arm holding him against her chest. Spud was not absorbing the full picture but was both impressed and delighted to hear that Wolf was dead. "So, the great Jake Benteen took down Wolf." Spud paused and then let out a raucous laugh. "Ha! I'm sorry I missed that! I'd 've paid good money too." He looked over his left shoulder to see that the townsfolk had all lined up, side by side, covering from one side of the street to the other. All still had their guns at the ready. Perhaps out of habit, or maybe just fear of the unpredictable outcome he was facing, Spud raised his rifle to level it on Jake. He locked eyes with Gracie and said, "Ma'am, I don't generally hold with shooting women, especially unarmed ones, but I'm willing to make the exception if you don't move out of the way." Looking back at the assembled crowd he shouted, "It looks like I may not get what I came here for, but I will for damn sure kill this woman and Jake Benteen unless someone brings me a bag of money, as much as you can fit in a pair of saddlebags! On that, you can be sure!"

"You'll never make it out of this town, or even this territory if you do," responded Eric Bonawitz. "I'll hunt you down myself."

"That may be, big man," said Spud, "but I will promise you this, the only chance these two got of not dying, one on top of the other, is my getting that money. I'll take my own chances after that."

Tom O'Leary had raised his rifle, ready to take down Spud, but Eric didn't want to risk it and pulled O'Leary's rifle slowly down until it was pointing to the dirt. Eric and Tom, along with several other townspeople turned their eyes to the banker, Dan MacNeil, who had already made up his mind.

"I'll get you your damn money!" MacNeil spat out. "Just don't do anything 'til I get back." He turned to Lou Hudson and said, "Give me a hand, Lou." Lou handed his gun to his wife, Amanda, and jogged up next to Dan MacNeil as they headed for the bank.

From behind Spud Pierson came an unexpected voice. "You ever see a man get blown up by dynamite?" It was the owner of the gun shop, Michael Charles. Spud didn't want to take his eyes off his hostages but tried to steal a glance over his shoulder in the direction of the voice. Michael Charles was standing in the doorway of his gun shop, with his rifle aimed at Spud's feet. Spud had to look twice, both at his feet and to see that the gun shop owner was, indeed, aiming at them.

"What the hell are you talking about?" shouted Spud.

"You're standing on a stick of dynamite, mister," answered the gun shop owner. "And I've got my sights trained dead on it." Spud stole another quick glance down at his feet, which was just enough to see the packed pile of dirt and the tip of the dynamite and fuse sticking out. "You burp, sneeze or fart and this town will be scraping your guts off the front of these buildings for a month."

Spud was momentarily speechless, as he needed time to figure out his next move. This latest development was about as unexpected as things could get – and just when he thought he had figured a way out of this mess. Then he decided to put all of his eggs in one basket and call the gun shop owner's bluff. "That don't change a thing! So, go ahead! Shoot!" he challenged. "Just remember… you hit me, and you'll kill these two to boot! I know enough about dynamite to know how far the blast will cover… and I'm willing to bet it will take them out, same as me!"

Hearing of the dynamite made all of the townspeople back away, some even running for cover inside buildings or down alleys.

Seeing the people back up and run made Spud think he had been successful in calling the bluff when out of the barn came Jake's horse, Teacher. Spud's reflexes weren't fast enough to handle the startling image of a blood-red animal charging at him with fire in her eyes. As he tried to raise his rifle to shoot, Teacher drove her right shoulder into Spud's chest, knocking him on his back. At the same time, Gracie pulled Jake to his feet and the two of them, Jake hobbling on one foot and Gracie lifting him, with

278

his left arm over her shoulder, stumbled into the barn. Gracie scrambled to her feet and managed to close the door.

Spud was still on his back but was trying to regain his footing. Teacher had knocked him almost ten feet farther back, away from the first stick of dynamite. Unbeknownst to him, he landed on top of the other one. As he rolled up on his knees and tried to catch his breath, he noticed the second stick of dynamite between his legs and pulled it the rest of the way out of the dirt. Spud had a quizzical look on his face as he stood, still dazed and confused, holding the second explosive. He was slightly hunched over when a single rifle shot rang out, hitting the second stick. Just as Michael Charles had predicted, Spud exploded, sending body parts in every direction. Only his lower torso remained standing, if only for a brief moment before it collapsed into the dirt. Spud's head, arms and chest were unrecognizable and did, in fact, ultimately have to be scraped off the surrounding buildings… which took about a month.

At first, those who were witnesses to the explosion assumed it was the gun shop owner, Michael Charles, who had fired the explosive shot. But at the time of the shot, Spud had his back turned to the gun shop owner and was also too far away from that first stick to make shooting it effective, so Charles had held his fire. When the dust settled, it was Potch who they saw standing in the middle of the street, holding Jake's Winchester that had dropped when he was struck in the shoulder by Spud's first bullet. Spud had noticed that Potch had picked it up but never anticipated the little man would turn it against him, or that he was enough of a marksman to hit the stick clutched against Spud's chest.

The shockwave from the explosion was enough to blow out several windows and was also powerful enough to knock Potch several feet back and on his butt. Sugar Pie was knocked to her knees. Teacher had made it down a side alley, facing away from the explosion and was fully protected from the blast.

Potch dropped Jake's rifle and scrambled to his feet and scurried to his beloved Sugar Pie, cradling her head against his chest. Tears welled up in his eyes as he pleaded, "Don't die, Sugar Pie! Please don't die." Potch rocked the mule in his arms as he wept.

Gracie had managed to get Jake to his feet again and slowly stepped out of the barn. They were met by Doc Gibbons, who took over for Gracie, holding Jake up and directing him to his makeshift hospital in The Dancing Dollar saloon just down the street. "Hold on, Jake," he said. His voice was calm, almost cheerful. "It doesn't look too bad. We'll get you all fixed up." As the two men staggered up the street, the doctor took a closer look at Jake's wounds and said, "Besides, something tells me you've had worse in your time."

Jake laughed and replied, "Once or twice. Maybe even three times if I think on it long enough." Both men chuckled.

Gracie had broken away from Jake and Doc Gibbons once she knew Jake was in good hands and stopped next to Potch and Sugar Pie to examine the animal. She knelt down on the other side from Potch and checked all four limbs and the animal's eyes to see if there was any blood, indicating an internal injury. All seemed clear enough and her diagnosis was that Sugar Pie would recover just fine. "What's her name?" she asked Potch, who was still crying.

"Sugar Pie," he said, choking back tears. "She's all I've got. Please tell me she's going to be okay."

Gracie gave Potch a gentle pat on his shoulder with her left hand as she stroked Sugar Pie's head with the other. "She'll be fine," she said, in a soft, reassuring voice. "I think she just got the wind knocked out of her."

Potch looked up at Gracie with the most pitiful expression and said something that surprised her. "I never killed a man before." He paused, doing a mental tally. "Today... I've killed two." His eyes slowly rolled back and forth as if searching for the right words to express what he was feeling. "I never thought it would feel like this." He then bowed his head, as if in shame and added, "Even though they both had it comin', it just don't... feel right. I don't like it. I don't like it one bit." He started shaking and sobbing uncontrollably as he rocked back and forth holding Sugar Pie.

Gracie patted him on the shoulder again and said, "Consider that a blessing. You saved a good man's life, and probably mine too. Maybe that will help things sit a little better."

Sugar Pie was beginning to stir and made a motion to try and get back on her feet. Potch and Gracie helped the animal make it back up on all fours as Potch shouted, "Sugar Pie!" His relief and joy were unmistakable. He gave his mule a hug, wrapping both arms around her head. He kept repeating, "Thank you! Thank you!" to Gracie.

"Walk her around a little and give her some water in a few minutes, but not too much," was Gracie's advice as she patted Sugar Pie on the rump and then took off on a run to catch up with Jake and Doc Gibbons. Both men were navigating the steps up from the street and into the saloon when Gracie came up from behind, taking her position on the other side of Jake. "Need some help?"

Jake looked down at Gracie as she lifted his left arm and tucked her head underneath. "I would never refuse the assistance of a beautiful lady," said Jake, as he gave her a gentle but strong squeeze.

Gracie laughed. "Flattery won't get you into my bed, cowboy."

"Then what will?" answered Jake with a wink.

"Would you two lovebirds mind if I dug the bullets out of his body first, before you start with all the sparking?" scolded Doc Gibbons with a joyful laugh.

Jake never took his eyes off Gracie when he answered the doctor. "Better hurry, Doc. I'm not sure I can wait that long."

The three had made it up onto the porch and were just going through the bat-wing doors when the good doctor hit them both with a reality check on Jake's condition. Although the location of the wounds didn't immediately concern him, the amount of blood Jake was losing did. "I don't know how much you know about human anatomy, Jake, but if you keep losing blood like you're doing, you won't be doing any romancing for a long time, or ever again if I can't get the bleeding stopped." They stopped at the front of the bar, which had been covered with a clean bed sheet. The doctor's medical bag was sitting against the back of the bar, with his surgical tools spread out and cleaned, sitting in metal trays. Some tools, like probes, scissors and scalpels were sitting in jars of grain alcohol. Some of the volunteers had already boiled water and prepared clean bandages. "Think you can manage to get yourself up on my operating table, Jake?"

Jake looked around the room and then back at the bar/operating table. "I've been to a lot of saloons in my time, Doc, but I can honestly say I've never seen one set up for surgery before."

"There's a first time for everything, Jake." replied the doctor. "Now quit flappin' your gums and climb up here while you still got the strength. Gracie and I can't lift you up here all by ourselves."

During this entire exchange, Gracie had remained silent, not wanting to show her concern for Jake's condition. While it was true Jake's wounds didn't appear to be life-threatening, he was losing a lot of blood. The bullet that tore through his right shoulder appeared to be the one that was cause for greater concern. With the help of Gracie on the outside of the bar, and the doctor pulling Jake from behind the bar, all three managed to get him up and in a sitting position, with his legs straight out in front of him.

"Let's get that coat and vest off, Jake," demanded the doctor. When the coat and vest were pulled back, what was once a white shirt was now fully soaked in Jake's blood. The wound in his leg, though bleeding profusely, looked much worse than it really was. That bullet passed through the meat of Jake's thigh but missed the main artery. No bone damage either.

The doctor pulled a pair of surgical scissors from a beer mug filled with grain alcohol and began cutting away Jake's shirt. "Gracie, there's another pair of scissors in my bag there. I'm gonna need you to cut away Jake's pant leg so I can get to that wound as soon as I finish with his shoulder. But before I do that, I want you to apply a tourniquet to stop the bleeding. Can you do that?"

"I sure can, Doc," answered Gracie with a "can do" attitude that brought a smile to the old doctor's face. "It looks like the bullet passed clean through, Doc. I don't think it hit bone or an artery either. Just meat."

"That's good, Gracie. Real good. Don't keep the tourniquet on for more than ten minutes or so, then release it slowly for a few minutes and then tighten it down again."

"I know how to manage a tourniquet, Doc!" Gracie snapped

back at the doctor. She was beginning to show signs of fear and concern because she could see the color draining from Jake's face and it didn't look good.

"Clean it out with some of that alcohol in my bag," order the doctor. "It'll sting like the holy hell, but it needs to be done to clean out the hole." Then, he looked up at Jake's face, which was now pale and losing more color by the minute. "JAKE!" yelled the doctor. "Stay with me, boy! Stay awake. Fight it!"

Jake's eyes popped open at the shock of the doctor's loud voice booming in his ears. "I hear ya, Doc." His voice was a little groggy, but his focus was clear, and he was alert enough to attempt a joke. "No need to shout. I didn't get my ears shot off."

Hearing Jake make a joke brought a sigh of relief to both Gracie and the doctor. If a seriously injured patient can still find humor and show some awareness of his circumstance, it bodes well for his overall condition and chances of recovery.

"Lay back down now, Jake," ordered the doctor, who assisted Jake to recline onto the bar. "How's that tourniquet coming, Gracie?" The doctor was more concerned about the amount of blood Jake was losing than any real organ damage done by either bullet.

"Just fine, Doc!" snapped Gracie "Don't you worry about me. The bleeding has slowed considerably but hasn't stopped yet. How's things at your end?"

It was too soon to tell, so the doctor didn't answer. Jake's shirt had been cut away, exposing his chest and back. With his right hand, the doctor was holding a clean compress against the entry wound at the back of Jake's right shoulder. With his left hand, he reached around Jake's chest with his left. He was feeling for an exit wound, which would be a better outcome than his having to try and dig the slug out from either the back or cut in through the front to retrieve it. Either way, the bullet could not stay, as it would contribute to infection. The problem was that he could not immediately tell just where the bullet was and where it had settled. It appeared as though the bullet had struck Jake at an angle, entering the right side of his shoulder from the back and crossed through into his chest. His fingers were delicately probing what he supposed would be the bullet's path until he felt a lump just under the skin, below the clavicle. This was good news, as it didn't appear the bullet had struck his collarbone or any part of the shoulder joint. Cutting the bullet out shouldn't be too difficult, since it was already so close to the surface. The doctor looked at Jake to see if he was still conscious. He was, although just barely.

"Jake!" the doctor yelled. "Wake up, boy! I'm gonna need you to take a healthy swallow of this laudanum so you'll sleep." Jake's eyes were beginning to glaze over.

"Won't it be better if he just passes out, Doc?" asked Gracie

"Not if he wakes up while I'm cuttin' into him," answered the doctor. "I need to know he's out before I start digging into his chest near his heart."

"Is that where the bullet is, Doc?" Gracie was obviously scared now but tried not to give it away.

"It's close enough that I don't need him screaming and jumping around while I look for it." The doctor turned his attention back to Jake who was still barely conscious. The doctor tipped Jake's head back and held up a bottle of laudanum to his lips. "Here you go, boy. Drink this down."

Jake managed to swallow enough laudanum to do the trick. As his eyes rolled back, he sputtered a few words neither the doctor nor Gracie could understand and fell into a deep sleep.

"Atta boy, Jake," encouraged the doctor. "You take a nice

rest while Gracie and I get to work."

Once the doctor was confident Jake was sufficiently unconscious and would not move if cut into, he had Gracie come around and hold both of Jake's shoulders steady. The lump the doctor had felt earlier was, indeed, the bullet. It had come to rest just behind the sternum, a mere fraction away from tearing into the pericardial sack of the heart. The bullet wasn't deep but would have certainly been fatal had it gone in another inch. The doctor was relieved to see it clearly enough to not have to probe around looking for it. With as delicate a touch as his old fingers had ever managed, the doctor snagged the slug with his surgical tweezers and gently withdrew it without further damage. He held the bullet up for Gracie to see and said, "Got it!" and dropped it into a shot glass. If Jake didn't die of blood loss or infection, he stood an excellent chance of a full recovery.

After about an hour of trying to delicately balance further wound compression, Jake's blood loss was finally under control. Applying compression to both the entry and now the exit wounds greatly aided in slowing and ultimately stopping the blood loss from his chest wound. Gracie's attention to the tourniquet on Jake's leg wound proved masterful and the blood loss there was successfully contained.

It was difficult to determine just how much blood Jake had lost. Although Doc Gibbons was familiar with the early attempts at blood transfusions, he was dubious as to their success, given that many of the patients died or had severe adverse reactions. The accepted theory was that everyone's blood was not necessarily compatible with everyone else's. Blood typing was not fully understood and was still more than a decade away from acceptance in the medical community. Regardless, the doctor had only read about some of the theories and early attempts at blood transfusion. He had never performed one, nor did he have the equipment necessary if he did. Jake would just have to be strong enough to make it on his own.

When the doctor took a moment to rest and assess Jake's condition, he was surprised to see that the bar room had slowly filled with the townspeople, some seated, many standing waiting for word if their new-found friend and savior was going to live. Doc Gibbons stood up straight and arched his tired back and smiled at his friends. "He's got a good chance, folks. He's tough and the damage wasn't as bad as it may have looked. He's a strong young fella, and I give him better than a fifty-fifty chance."

Preacher Lee stepped forward. "My friends, I don't know if Mr. Benteen would be of a mind for some prayer, but I think it might do the rest of us some good to say a few words on his behalf. He may well have saved this town, but he for certain helped us all come together as a community. As a family. And that is something we should take to heart. So… may I ask that we all bow our heads and take a moment to give thanks in whatever way you feel comfortable." No one hesitated to honor the preacher's suggestion, with many of the women admonishing their respective husbands and neighbors to remove their hats. Everyone bowed their heads and took a private moment to give thanks to the man many had initially distrusted and more than a few even despised. Now, they were asking the powers that be to save his life. If Jake had been conscious, it is doubtful he would have objected.

Chapter Twenty-Three

The room was a blur of hazy images that were hard to distinguish. The muffled sounds made words unintelligible. Jake felt like he was in a bad dream he couldn't shake. It didn't feel like a nightmare, exactly, just unsettling and confusing. As he turned his head slightly to his left, he saw, through a cloud of mist, what looked like two figures sitting in chairs against a wall. The figures were talking about... something. He thought he heard a name, his name, mentioned a few times but wasn't sure. As the mental and verbal fog began to lift, he distinctly heard a female voice ask a question of the other blurry figure.

"What if he doesn't wake up, Doc?" the woman asked in a voice that was also oddly familiar.

"He may not, Gracie, and that's the hard fact of it," answered the other voice, also oddly familiar. "Jake lost a lot of blood. We were lucky we got it under control when we did. There's no telling what damage was done though. Maybe a lot, maybe only a little, maybe nothing. Losing that much blood can rob the brain of oxygen and bring on organ failure too. We won't know the full extent of the damage until he wakes up. If he even does. We'll just have to wait it out and see."

Hearing the last part of the conversation sent a shot of adrenaline through Jake's body that was enough to snap him out of his semi-conscious state. He knew who those voices and blurry images belonged to and had a pretty good idea what they were talking about. They were saying he was knocking on Death's front door.

"Now hold on there, Doc," mumbled Jake. His throat was dry, and his vocal protest made more of a croaking sound than anything resembling his normal, clear and strong delivery. He coughed to clear his throat before he continued. "I'm a long way from dying, so don't go throwing dirt over me just yet."

Gracie let out a scream that Jake thought sounded like his name, which it was. "JAKE!" She bolted out of her chair and over to the bed where some of the town's people had carried Jake's body. The bed was in the recovery room that was up in Doc Gibbon's office. It was oddly fitting that it was the same bed Doc had allowed Juneann to rest and recover in after the ordeal she had suffered; the one that started this entire sad adventure.

Doc Gibbons had taken his time to make his way over to Jake's bedside, allowing Gracie to have her moment alone with him. She was on her knees next to Jake, holding his hand. The foot of the bed was set against the wall so the doctor could get easy access to both sides of his patient. Doc hovered over Jake's head at first, looking down at him, then crossed over to the other side and raised Jake's right hand by the wrist to check his pulse. "I gotta say, you had me mighty worried there, Jake." Doc pulled his pocket watch out to count the beats of his patient's heart. "Your pulse is still a bit thready, but it's a damn sight stronger than I was expecting. Think you could handle a cup of chicken soup or some vegetable broth?"

"I'd rather have a cup of black coffee and a shot of whiskey, Doc," Jake answered, with a wink to Gracie, "But I doubt my nurse here would approve."

"You're damn straight I wouldn't," she replied, with her voice cracking and holding back tears. She even gave her man a playful slap on his shoulder, the one that didn't have a bullet hole in it.

Doc laughed and placed Jakes right hand back down and said, "I'll go rustle up something appropriate. I think I'll hold off on the coffee and whiskey for a bit though." With a wink of his own to Gracie, he turned and left his recovery room. Gracie raised up on her knees and leaned over the bed to give Jake a kiss on his forehead. Before she made it to her intended destination, however, Jake reached over with his left hand and pulled her head down to his face and kissed her hard on the lips, or at least as hard as his weakened condition could handle. It didn't matter, because it was enough for Gracie, who matched his passion with her own. It was a long kiss, not so much filled with lust, although there was certainly some of that, but it was more a kiss of love and relief. The kisses of love, mixed with passion, would come soon enough.

"How long have I been out?" asked Jake, whose mind was beginning to clear more and more with each kiss.

"Going on three days," said Gracie "You were hurt bad, Jake. I thought you were going to break your promise about getting out of this alive and coming back to me."

"That thought never even entered my mind," said Jake. "Besides, I always keep my promises."

Gracie settled her head as gently as she could, against Jake's chest. A knock at the door to the recovery room startled her as she popped her head up. "Who is it?"

"It's Pete Adams, Gracie," came the reply from behind the closed door. "I just passed Doc Gibbons on the stairs. He's heading over to the hotel for some stew for Jake. He said he was awake and that maybe I could talk to him."

Gracie looked at Jake to assess his reaction and to gauge her own. She didn't like being interrupted, especially now, after three days of wondering if the man she had fallen for was even going to make it. "You up for some conversation with our newspaperman, Jake? I'm sure he's got a few questions for you, but I can send him away if you'd rather not talk to him now. It can wait."

Jake hesitated, rolling his eyes at the thought, but relented with a feeble reply. "I'd rather spend my time with just you but... I might as well get it over with. Besides, I've got a few questions of my own he may be able to answer." He raised Gracie's hand and kissed it, then said, "Send him in."

Gracie could see the logic to getting it over with but resented the intrusion just the same. Reluctantly, she called out, "Come on in, Mr. Adams."

The door opened slowly, with Pete Adams poking his head around the edge. "Sorry to bother you, Jake. I just wanted to let you know that... well, first, we're all so very grateful for what you did and that you're not going to, I mean, that you're going to... make it."

"I'm pretty pleased about it myself," Jake said, with some very obvious sarcasm. "What's on your mind? You want some sort of story for your newspaper, I suppose."

Pete Adams stepped cautiously into the room. "No, no, nothing like that. I'm not here as a reporter. The people of the town asked me to... well, you know, to thank you for everything you did, of course, but also to tell you that we took a wagon out toward Tres Mesa to recover Sheriff Avery's body. It looks like those Tres Mesa boys wrapped him up in a blanket to keep the buzzards off him. I gotta say, that surprised us all to see that. Don't know why they would have done something like that for him, but it was mighty thoughtful. Didn't take those men as the considerate type. They even tied his horse up to scrub tree."

291

Jake looked at Gracie with a sadness that was hard to mistake, but easy to understand. The reality that his friend was dead had faded away briefly. Being reminded of it hit him hard. "Honor among thieves, I guess you could say," he said as he squeezed Gracie's hand tightly.

"Yeah, I guess," replied the newspaperman. "Anyway, we brought the sheriff's body back here for a proper burial so the town could pay its respects. We've got him packed in ice now, 'cuz we were hoping you'd... well, you know, assuming you made it, that you'd be able to come to his funeral and say a few words over him."

Jake muffled a sardonic laugh. "I would be honored to pay my respects to Val. He was a good man. Just give me a few more days to get my strength back and I'll be there. Assuming you've got enough ice to keep Val from turning more sour than he already was."

Pete Adams wasn't sure exactly how to interpret Jake's gallows humor but took it as one old friend chiding another. The newspaperman just smiled and then stepped fully into the room and said, "Well, Mr. Benteen, I mean Jake, we're all sure glad you pulled through. The townsfolk will be pleased to hear that. You take your time to get your strength back. We'll make sure the sheriff is well taken care of until then." He started to leave, stepping back into the doorway, even beginning to pull the door closed behind him, when he suddenly stopped and turned around, stepping back into the room. "Oh... sorry, Jake, Gracie, but I was supposed to ask you something else. Something real important."

Jake turned his eyes to Gracie and offered her a Cheshire Cat grin as if to indicate he was expecting what Pete Adams was about to say. He noticed that whatever it was the town's messenger wanted to ask him made him nervous because he was

292

shuffling his feet from side to side. "Well, don't just stand there shuffling your feet. Ask."

The newspaperman looked down at his shuffling feet and laughed at himself. "Sorry. If I didn't know better, I'd say I was dancing. I do that when I get nervous." He laughed again. "Anyway, the people in town asked me to... you know... to ask if... um... well, if you might consider taking over the sheriff's job?"

He knew this was a lot to ask, especially under current circumstances, but it was also imperative the town have someone to step into the position of town sheriff as soon as possible. The town's leaders didn't want word to get out that they were without any form of law and order. Just because the outlaws backed down the last time didn't mean one or more of them wouldn't reconsider making another attempt.

"Word has already gotten out about what happened here and that we're without a sheriff. Once we got the telegraph back up, the lines are burning up over Jake Benteen taking on Wolf's gang single-handed." He exaggerated the last few words as if he were reading a newspaper headline, which did not sit well with Jake.

The gunfighter lifted his head in protest at the reporter's description. "You are a newspaperman, Mr. Adams, and I trust an honest and truthful one. So, I hope you set the record straight on what really happened," countered Jake. "This town stood together as a community. *They* deserve the credit, not me. You also need to let folks know what Sheriff Val Avery did and how he died, and *who* he died for. I for damn sure don't want or need any more dime-novel nonsense written about me."

"Oh, you don't have to worry about that, Jake," assured the newspaperman. "Believe you me, I intend to tell the truth, the whole truth and nothing but the truth, just like I was sworn to in

293

a court of law."

"I'm glad to hear that, Mr. Adams. Glad indeed. Thank you." Jake dropped his head back on his pillow with obvious relief.

"We are damn proud of what we did here, believe me, and we want the world to know it. But that don't change the fact that we still need a sheriff." Pete Adams stepped back into the room and closer to Jake's bedside. He had more to say. "The men of Delgado Station have been taking shifts, patrolling the streets and showing a strong presence to anyone who comes through town," he continued. "And we've been getting a lot of curious riders coming in, I can tell you that."

"That's bound to happen, sir," answered Jake. "That will fade away soon enough. Just keep up the street patrols with a strong, united, visible presence and you'll be fine."

"The men are proud to do it, Jake, don't get me wrong. But the truth is, these men have farms, ranches and businesses to run. We're just not cut out for taking on the responsibilities of law and order too. We need a man like you."

Gracie pushed herself up from Jake's bedside to stand and face Pete Adams. "I thought you got a hold of the Federal Marshals and even the military once you got the telegraph lines back up. Aren't they coming to wipe out the rest of Wolf's gang?"

"That's the word we've gotten, Gracie, but they won't be here at full strength for another few months at least," answered the newspaperman. "We've heard rumors that a bunch of Wolf's men had already struck out across the border hoping they can avoid the Federales. A few more got gunned down fighting among themselves. I guess without their leader they can't seem to agree on things."

"Well, men like that don't last long without a strong leader, or a crazy one." Jake sounded relieved and took Gracie's hand again. "It was bound to happen." A forgotten figure in this whole affair suddenly popped into Jake's head. "Hey, whatever happened to that little man? Potch, I think his name was. After Teacher came bolting out of the barn and knocked that fella down, I kind of lost track of things," he said as he reached for Gracie and stroked her hair. "I remember the explosion, but not much else after that."

Gracie looked at the newspaperman with something of a sheepish grin and said to Jake, "It was Potch that shot the man that shot you."

"Really?" Jake was trying to replay the events of that day, but his memory was still too shaky and unclear. "I thought he dropped his scattergun back up the street?"

"He did," answered Pete Adams. "But he picked up your Winchester after you dropped it and hit the stick of dynamite the man was holding. It was one ugly mess I can tell you. They're still finding parts of him. The fact is the little man saved your life and probably a few others too."

Gracie felt the need to offer an explanation. "Jake, I know you made some deal with him, Potch, I mean, that he would be on the next stage out of town, but... well, after what he did, a bunch of us said he could stay on here as long as he got himself a job and stayed out of trouble."

Jake looked to both Gracie and Pete Adams and could tell there was more to the story. "And are you telling me he got himself a job somewhere?"

Gracie knelt back down next to Jake and said, "It turns out he is pretty good with horses and does a damn fine job of cleaning out my barn. He cleaned up Teacher's stall better than I ever did, too. And Teacher seemed to take to him easy enough. So..."

"And it turns out I could use an extra hand now and then back at the newspaper too, so we thought why not give him a chance?" Pete Adams shuffled his feet back and forth again, and added, "He's sure is a strange little fellow though. When I offered him the job, he just sat down and cried, like he was happy enough to burst. I think once we all get to know him, he'll fit right in. If that's all right with you, that is."

Jake just smiled. "I guess it's the least the town could do, eh?"

"Well, we're a growing town, Jake," continued the newspaperman. "And what happened here made us stronger. But we need a strong image of law and order to continue to grow. I think you know we stand together with our sheriff too. So… we'd be honored if our sheriff… was you."

Gracie was a mixture of emotions she couldn't contain. She looked back and forth from Jake to Pete Adams and then back to Jake. "Jake?" Speaking Jake's name as a question was loaded with multiple meanings.

"It's all right if you say, no, Jake. Really," assured Pete Adams. "We'd understand, given how many of us first treated you when you brought Juneann in. Oh, and by the way, she has come a long, long way in the past few days. Hearing that the man who saved her life was hurt bad made her sit up and take notice. Doc says she started healing herself when she knew you were ailing too. She's a strong young woman, Jake. She and her mother even asked me to ask you if it would be all right if they came by here to say thank you. Juneann said she wants to say so to you personally. Doc thinks it would be good for her too."

Jake pressed his head against the pillow and stared straight up at the ceiling as tears rolled down the sides of his cheeks. "Mr. Adams, you tell that young lady that I would be honored and proud to see her. The Doc may think her coming here would be good medicine for her but I could sure use some medicine like that myself."

Pete Adams had a few tears of his own to try and wipe aside. "Truth is, Jake, we've grown rather fond of you too, if you don't mind my saying. So, even if you say no to taking the sheriff's job, many of us hope you'll decide to stay on here anyway and maybe settle down." The newspaperman turned his eyes to Gracie and added with a wink, "It looks to me like someone else might want you to stay on as well."

Gracie gently settled her head back down on Jake's chest. Knowing he was overstaying his welcome, the newspaperman shuffled his feet again and turned to leave. "So, you think on it and let us know," he said, then smiled and stepped backward, out of the room, pulling the door closed behind him.

Jake turned his eyes to Gracie who was still staring at the door Mr. Adams had just left through. It was obvious she was thinking about what the question proposed by the town and was also wondering what Jake's answer might be.

Jake strained to get a look at Gracie's face, who had turned away, hiding her eyes. "Well?" he said.

She turned her head slowly back to Jake and said, "Well, what?"

"What do you mean, *what?*" Jake was perplexed by Gracie's stoic reaction and deadpan question. "You know damn well what. Do *you* want me to stay?"

She paused and looked back at the door, then back to Jake again. "I don't know, Jake," she said. "Part of me says, yes, the other part says, no."

"Which part is speaking the loudest, Gracie?" Jake's voice was clear and strong now. "I need to know. If you can't say yes…

then I will leave as soon as Teacher and I can get ourselves together."

Gracie turned again to look Jake square in the face. "Like hell you will!" Her eyes were on fire and her face flushed with emotion.

"Then answer me! Do you want me to stay?"

Gracie pushed herself to her feet again and paced around in a tight circle and stopped, looking away from him. "My heart and my gut says stay." She turned to face Jake. "I want you to stay." She crossed back to Jake's side and knelt down again. "I haven't felt this way about a man in a long, long time, Jake. Not like I do for you. Truth be told, I was beginning to give up hope I ever would." Her voice grew stronger. "But… damn it, Jake Benteen, you've done something to me. You've awakened the woman in me, and I like how that feels! I don't want to lose it. I don't want to lose you." But now she paused and bowed her head, unable to make eye contact with the man she had just poured her heart and soul out to. Finally, she raised her head and looked Jake in the eyes again and said, "But I'm scared, Jake. I'm not sure I can handle you being sheriff. You carry a lot of baggage, a lot of history that follows you wherever you go. I'm afraid it will follow you here, especially after what happened. The thought that, someday, on any given night, they could be bringing your body home on a kitchen door, shot full of holes… well, I just don't think I could handle it, the constant worry." Gracie began to cry. She had given up trying to hold her emotions in any longer.

Jake reached out with his one strong arm and signaled Gracie to come to him. She stepped to his bedside and knelt down next to him and laid her head against his chest. As he stroked her hair he said, "It's true I've lived a hard life, Gracie. A life that most men don't survive at for very long. I guess I've done better than most. But for the first time in my life, I honestly feel like I've found something, *someone*, to make me want to stop running. But I'm not going to lie to you or myself and tell you that there won't ever be trouble. My reputation will follow me wherever I go, just like you said. So, running from it won't do either of us any good. Running is no way to live. I know that now."

Gracie raised her head and looked at Jake. Her eyes were filled with tears, but her voice was clear. "Does that mean you'll stay?"

Jake gently ran his fingers under Gracie's chin and said, "It for damn sure means I'll stay. What I'll do to earn my keep is another question. The plain truth of it is that being sheriff is the only thing I'm really cut out for and is what this town needs."

"So does that mean you'll take the sheriff's job?"

"The only way I'll take the sheriff's job is if *you'll* take me."

Gracie sat up straight on her knees looking down at Jake. His eyes were wide and serious. "Take you?" she said. She swallowed hard, trying to comprehend what she thinks Jake just asked. "Are you… are you… asking me to…"

He cut her off. "To marry me! Yes! Gracie McCall… will you marry me?" Jake asked, proud and strong. Gracie cupped both hands over her mouth. She was unable to speak. "I know that's asking a lot, and everything you say is true. That horrible night may well come. But if I get one night, one week, a month, a year or the next thirty years with you, it will be worth it. So, what I'm saying is… I'm willing to take that chance if you are. So, the question you have still not answered is, will you marry me? Yes or no?"

Gracie raised herself up on her knees again and reached across the bed to caress Jake's head in her hands. "Yes, damn you! Of course, I will marry you, Jake Benteen! But you damn well better not die on me for at least the next thirty years! We've got a life to share and a family to raise!"

Their lips met again, but this kiss was filled with more love, devotion and passion than either of them had ever known or dreamed was possible. They knew that whatever amount of time they had together, their love story was going to be epic.